Bitter Echo of Memory

Book 4: Tales of Tasimu
by Celu Amberstone

Bitter Echo of Memory

Tales of Tasimu, Volume 4

Celu Amberstone

Published by Kashallan Press, 2024.

BITTER ECHO OF MEMORY

First edition. September 2, 2024.

ISBN: 978-1990581236

Written by Celu Amberstone.

Dedication

This book is dedicated to all the refugees and displaced indigenous peoples around the world. It is also dedicated to my children and grandchildren. Not being a woman of material wealth, my writing is my legacy to both them, and all the children who are our cherished future. Also in dedication, I offer my eternal gratitude for the traditional teachings of my grandparents, aunties, and the other Elders I've met over the years who have taken the time to teach me. The wisdom and strength of my Elders has always been, and will continue to be, an inspiration in my life.

Acknowledgements

I would like to thank for their support, my four sons, my daughter, and those of my friends who were there when I needed them. Paula, Lila, your friendship and help with proof reading, book covers, and other important book related things, was greatly appreciated.

I would also like to thank the folks at Kegedonce Press for their dedication, hard work, their vision, and their fearless determination to encourage Aboriginal writers of all types.

Note to the Reader:

Bitter Echo of Memory is a work of fiction. I hope you'll read and enjoy it as such. Though I've drawn material in the abstract from places I've lived and from my own mixed race background, any resemblance to people, places, languages and cultures, Indigenous or other, in our world is purely coincidental.

A Further Note:

This book not only contains graphic scenes of violence, like in the earlier books in this series; book 4 also contains depictions of sexual violence that may be triggering for some readers.

A Brief Summary of the Earlier Books

In book One, *Taste of Memory,* Tasimu is a youth with special gifts he has inherited from his mysterious father dwelling in another world that has a portal at the bottom of Big Ice Lake. Tasimu is forced with his family to move away from their ancestral home when the invaders discover gold in their northern mountains. Tribal members who converted to the invaders' religion signed a treaty in which all the northern peoples were forced to relocate to a newly created Tribal Preserve in a southern desert, a wasteland the invaders didn't want.

During their traumatic journey to this new Tribal Preserve, Tasimu finds a man who knows of his unique heritage, and can teach him how to use his magical gifts, if he will agree to help with his own quest for revenge against the converts whom he blames for giving away tribal lands.

Fearing that he also has unwittingly been the cause of his baby cousin's illness and death, Tasimu agrees to end his studies with a man of questionable ethics. Book one ends with Tasimu morning the loss of family members and fearing what will await them in this new southern land.

IN BOOK TWO, *When Memory Dies,* Tasimu and his people finally arrive on the barren, water-starved land they have been allotted only to discover that they have been lied to by the invaders who took their northern homeland. The treaty goods they were promised are slow to arrive or never show up at all. They will endure another winter of starvation, illness and despair.

Conflicts between different factions grow and fester, ending in violence, and a massacre of innocent women and children. In retaliation for their agent's thievery a faction of warriors who see the converts to the invaders' religion as traitors attack the agency, burn down their temple, then leave the Preserve to raid enemy settlements nearby for cattle and horses to feed their starving relatives.

Caught in the middle between two warring factions Tasimu endures beatings and scorn by both sides, but he also is defended by a girl cousin who chafes at the confines allotted to women in the new order.

Spending a great deal of his time hunting in the desert to avoid trouble in the convert settlement, Tasimu is able to connect with the spirit guardians of his new home, so when he is contacted by the outlaws who need a person with power to help them with their raids on ranches for food and horses, he agrees, and so Tasimu and his unhappy cousin run away to join the outlaws.

Tasimu agrees to use his Gift and help one of the desert tribe's war leaders on a daring raid into the enemy's territory to bring back food beasts for their starving peoples. The raid is successful, but while returning to the Preserve with their plunder Tasimu is contacted by one of his spirit helpers, warning of a danger to his mother and grandfather.

The desert war leader, who is starting to see Tasimu like a son, agrees to help Tasimu and his uncle rescue the pair who are being held for trial at the agency, but during the attempt the war leader is badly wounded and he and Tasimu barely escape with their lives.

IN BOOK THREE, *Abandoning Memory,* Tasimu's rescued grandfather tells the war leader that he should go to the summer ceremonies the Prophet is holding to receive a healing of his injuries. Meeting up with another band of warriors off to go raiding, two of the men are appointed to escort them to the Prophet's camp.

Unfortunately the man and his son chosen to accompany Tasimu, his mother, and the wounded war leader have a different agenda in mind. The warriors are surly and uncooperative, in spite of the horses they are promised, and there is a long-standing feud between the two families.

In an act of revenge against the war leader Tasimu discovers the father trying to rape his mother when she was washing clothes away from camp. Inhabiting the body of an eagle Tasimu's spirit manages to wound the man severely, but the man and his son escape, taking with them the war leaders favourite horse.

In the Prophet's camp the war leader does receive healing and he and Tasimu's mother marry and Tas will have a baby sister before spring. While living among the Kukiya off the Preserve the Kukiya war chief Golannah is summoned by the fort commander to a peace negotiation at the fort. The war chief includes Tas in the delegation so he can use his skills if needed.

Once at the meeting they discover the soldiers and government men plan to jail the delegates to prevent more violence and force other delegates to sign a new treaty, giving up more land.

By invoking his Gift, Tas and the Kukiya delegation are able to escape the soldiers trap and ambush in the desert, but by his use of power another man, a malicer and old enemy of the war chief is alerted and seeks revenge that will set into motion events that will end in a massacre of innocent women and children and the hanging of Tasimu's beloved adopted father. Tas is captured and sentenced to be sent to a live-away school, which he names a prison for children.

BOOK 4, *Bitter Echoes of Memory*, is the story of what happens to Tasimu and the other youths captured and sent to the live-away school.

A Tribal History of Long Ago, Rushton Archives: fourth interview with Indigenous Zacatik subject 297

THE CHAMUQWANI SOLDIERS and priests took children as young as six years away from loving families. They kept us in their live-away schools where devil priests and their mercy women—who had no mercy—beat and tortured us for the crime of being born a zaunk.

They said they were beating the heathen savage out of us, so we wouldn't burn in their god's fiery pit like our older relatives after we died. They said what they did was for our own good.

In such a place you learn to hide your feelings, rarely smile, never laugh, cringe when touched, always afraid of a blow. When I was sentenced to their prison for children I often tried to make my heart a stone so I could feel nothing. The problem with stone is that it grows heavy and is hard to carry around.

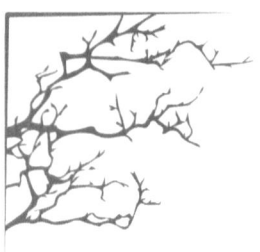

Part One
Chapter One

THEY CAME FOR US TWO days after the hangings, four big, muscular men and a grim-faced priest who stank of bitterness and rage. After the morning meal the guards at the jail brought us out to the open space in front of the big stone building once more wearing chains. Attorney Ricosen was there as well as a few other black-robed men from the court.

One of the men held up a paper from which he read, and then we were marched to wagons and our ankle chains were removed so we could climb in to take our places next to and atop sacks of supplies for the school. When Attorney Ricosen protested our still being bound he was told that the chains around our wrists would remain till we reached Saint Yon's Live-away School to insure we would cause no trouble, or try to escape along the way.

During our journey no one explained where we were going or how long it would take. They only growled their orders at us. And the priest made us kneel and bow our heads while he prayed over us in the morning before we were loaded back into the wagons and again at night when we were herded into a barn or sturdy shack and locked in for the night.

Still lost in my grief I cared little what they did to me. Numb inside after losing so many I loved, I endured their harsh treatment, did what the men ordered with no complaint, and spoke little.

For the rest of that day and the two that followed we headed west and south, following the bank of the muddy river I had sensed from within Train's cart while on our way to the jail. Many Chamuqwani lived in that settled land. We rode through several small villages where people came out to stare. Later the dwellings grew farther apart replaced by more isolated red and white houses surrounded by wide fields of growing food plants I couldn't recognize.

Behind many of the houses with their painted barns, spotted milk cai dotted fields thick with fenced in grass. But no wild spirits sang to me from the small clumps of trees we passed through. Only the soft sounds of ancient ghosts whispered of their loss on the sighing breeze.

It was a beautiful land in its way, though so different from my northern home and the desert land to the west I had grown to love. Though the land we traveled through was warm and green, alive with sweet smells and beauty I paid little attention to its loveliness. The spirits who called out to me, were talking mostly about their own great sorrows, though to be fair, they sometimes tried to comfort me in my own sadness. But I was too far gone into my own misery to care or appreciate their kindness.

As we had left Town several soldiers on horseback fell into step with the wagons. They had joined us to protect the men and their cargo for the journey, Inishkim told us later. But all afternoon when no Chamuqwani was near enough to hear Cohasi had been joking about us being such a dangerous enemy that the priest and the men from the school had to send along soldiers for fear of us.

After the priest had prayed over us again and we were once more left alone in the dark, locked in someone's barn for the night, he'd started up again with the same tiresome joking. Matoqwa laughed, but then Inishkim explained, "I would like to think that is true, brother, but after listening to their talk all day I think the real reason is that the soldiers are guarding the wagons, because there are outlaws in this land who make trouble for them and might try to attack the wagons and steal the goods if the soldiers weren't here—not because they are worried we might escape."

Matoqwa snorted in disgust. "Stupid Chamuqwani, none of our warriors are left to travel this far east to rescue us, no matter how tempting the plunder."

"Sad but probably true," he agreed, "but this far to the east they are worried about Chamuqwani outlaws, not our people, as best I can tell from the little I know of their language."

Atuusca, the Kukiya youth with the symbol of an eagle tattoo on his cheek chuckled. "Fighting and stealing from their own people... You are right, brother, to call them crazy."

Without knowing I was going to speak I found myself suddenly saying, "I think there are many kinds of Chamuqwani in the Father Emperor's land. Because of their many wars many people are starving and homeless, even in the empire. Some are just trying to feed their families, like we were doing. While others, like the fat agent on the Preserve are greedy and will take from others if they think they can get away with it."

Because I had spoken so little in the past few days everyone had turned to stare at me by the time I'd finished.

"Why do you say that, Tas?" Cohasi asked when the silence had dragged on too long.

I shrugged. "That's what the Wind says to me when I pay attention."

Matoqwa snorted and pushed up some of the musty straw behind his shoulders to form a backrest. "And what else does the Wind tell you? Anything useful, Siyatli boy, like how to get away from the soldiers."

I shrugged and returned my attention to the grass in my lap that I was plaiting into a tiny golden braid. If Kitahtla was here I could make a pretty headband and put some purple and golden flowers in the band... gold to match her yellow Cougar eyes...

Lost in my own musings again I ignored him and his questions, reliving my time with my baby sister, only dimly aware he was still speaking to me. Matoqwa growled and then he punched me—hard. "Pay attention, stupid Siyatli," he grumbled and repeated his last question. "What else have the Spirits been telling you? Have they told you a way for us to escape?"

"Escape...Yeah, Tas, I have no wish to spend the next six years in their rotten prison for children," Cohasi said. "I want to go home."

Home... And where was that, I wondered, up north among the miners at Big Ice Lake? Where, if we even managed to get back there we would surely be captured and made slaves to work for them. We wouldn't be free trappers and hunters, but just slaves to dig from the earth, disturbing the graves that held our ancestor's bones, hoping to find the gold the Chamuqwani craved above all things?

Or should we run back to the Preserve where we could starve with the rest of our relatives. The Tribal Preserve, it was closer. But it was a place with many dangers. We could try to find our outlaw kin. But if we couldn't find them, we might die in the desert. Or we could just try to hide among relatives where we would be talked about and probably be caught by the agent's soldiers—and killed. Or if not found by the agent's men we might be betrayed by well-meaning but deluded relatives and sent to another live-away school. Where was my home anymore in the land the Chamuqwani had stolen from us?

When I didn't answer fast enough to suit him Matoqwa punched my arm and growled his question again for the third time. And as he hit me the foretelling came on me, and I gasped dropping the half-finished straw braid to the dirty floor. I shuddered, gulping for air caught up in the terrifying images sent to me in the darkness behind my closed eyes.

Suddenly I heard children screaming, and smelled the smoke of a large building on fire. Inishkim and a slim brown-skinned girl each had a smaller child in their arms as they hurried out a doorway collapsing in flames behind them. I saw Matoqwa's face bloody and bruised surrounded by flames and then someone hit me again and the visions dissolved, leaving me curled up on my side, puking into the straw.

Still gasping for breath I flopped backwards when I finished, keeping my eyes closed till I was sure the sending had passed and I wasn't going to see anything more. While I lay there willing my breath to become slow and even, I heard someone whisper, "What's wrong with him?"

Another answered in a low voice, "I don't know. Maybe the Qwani'Ya dog humper hit him too hard."

Then, I heard Inishkim grumbled to Matoqwa in a louder voice, "You shouldn't have hit him, stupid dog turd. He is a powerful Puhani. The Unseen Ones may become angry with us if he isn't treated with respect—"

"Oh shut up," Matoqwa snapped. "Tas is fine—I've seen him do this puking stuff before—several times—and I didn't hit him that hard. He's fine—or will be in a moment."

In spite of myself I had to smile. Matoqwa was right, I would be fine, but my arm did hurt. He'd hit me hard enough to bruise, but I was grateful he had broken the Sending's power nonetheless. I had no wish to see any more terrible things.

When I at last sat up Atuusca asked in a solemn voice, "What happened to you, Puhani?"

"Yeah, Siyatli dog turd, what did you see? Tell us before I hit you, too," Cohasi grumbled.

Ignoring his idle threat, I turned to Matoqwa and said, "You will not have to spend six years at the live-away school. There will come a time when fire and water will free you—all of you. Those who survive that terrible time will travel east, not back to the Preserve." Looking directly at Matoqwa I looked him in the eye. "When you are an old man you will go back to the Preserve."

As a broken man you will go back to die of heart ache and drink, I could have added, but I had no desire to be cruel. It was times like that when I hated my Gift.

BARNER'S CROSSING TURNED out to be a Chamuqwani village on the bank of the big muddy river that we'd been sort of following as Road wound its way through rolling forested hills and grassy open meadows that once might have been villages or farms.

At the farther end of the settlement a long bridge had been built where two muddy streams blended into the larger river that wound its way further south-east towards the big lake of water Collin had called Ocean. He also said that Ocean tasted of salt. I hadn't wanted to believe him, but then I remembered that Sargent Ma'leubwey had told my Aunt Tula that his home was on an island in that salty water, so I guessed it was true.

Sun was making his way towards his western home when the soldiers and the wagons clattered across the bridge and into the village. Brightly painted stores with pointed roofs were lined up, nearly on top of one another, along the stone-paved road that led through the village and continued to wind around a steep hill.

Unlike other settlements we had traveled through to reach the school these Chamuqwani paid us little attention as we were carried through their settlement. I even saw pity in the eyes of some, when they noticed our chains. When we passed by a big trading store I realized why, though we were far to the east of the Preserve, surrounded only by Chamuqwani, with the school so near they were probably used to seeing the occasional zaunk in their village.

Then to prove my thought, coming out of the store I saw a gray-robed priest and a group of brown-skinned youths dressed in Chamuqwani clothing. Each boy had a heavy sack across one shoulder and the priest was directing the youths to load a wagon similar to our own. When they saw us the boys stared wide-eyed at us until the priest shouted at them to keep loading the wagon.

"Greetings, Praiser Simms," the priest atop our wagon said.

Studying us with hard eyes as he approached, the new priest gave the intercessor atop the wagon a grim smile. "Administrator Rizdale, I see that you have made good time on your return journey. The Director will be pleased to get the expected supplies," he paused, spat on the ground, giving us another thoughtful appraisal, "but perhaps not so pleased with the good Intercessor Raymonel's other 'gift'. These savages look like trouble—too old to be easily managed."

The sour intercessor snorted. "If they cause trouble after we remove their chains then you and Doff will have to discipline them until they learn the error of their ways and behave, hmm?"

Praiser Simms laughed, then noticing his own charges were finished with the loading and just standing around staring, he climbed onto the wagon. He waved a hand in farewell and shouted for the boys to climb atop the wagon's load as he gathered up the horses' reins.

When the wagon was only a dust cloud ahead the Intercessor motioned for his driver to continue on through the village, ignoring the few people who paused to greet him. We continued up Road and turned onto a narrower path that wandered off through the aspens.

Saint Yon's Live-away School was located on a wide meadow overlooking the muddy river I learned later was called the Waymon River. The Chamuqwani named the Water after one of their famous soldiers, a cruel but mighty war leader who killed most of the original people who lived on that land. I never learned the river's true name. It was forgotten when the land's original caretakers were all killed a couple of generations before the school and the village were built.

As we approached I could see that the live-away school was made up of several buildings with fields of food plants and pastures for cai and horses, spreading out around it. In the center of the cluster the school itself was a large white building with a red roof, consisting of four levels, or floors as I was told to call them. On either side I noticed two smaller dwellings. The one on the right I recognized as a temple to, Djoven the Thunderer, because it had the symbol of a lightning bolt on the peak of its roof. I shivered to see it, but in truth the symbol was little more than a painted piece of carved wood. No stone monsters hung from its roof to torment me.

To the left of the big building there was another painted house which I realized next day was where many of the priests and teachers lived. Continuing on past these buildings the wagons halted in a muddy yard near a big red barn that smelled of animals and dung. As the priest climbed down from the wagon the driver shouted and several workmen, who wore regular Chamuqwani clothing, and older boys hurried out of the barn's interior to help with the horses and unloading the wagons.

Forgotten for the moment in the chaos we just sat in the wagon, with blank expressions, only our eyes moving now and then to watch the activity. Huddling closer to Matoqwa and Cohasi I heard the boy named Qwatola from a village down river back home whisper to the brothers in our language, "Do you think they will keep us chained in the barn with the animals?"

"Hope so. I'd rather live in a barn with the animals than share space with any of those convert turds over there," Matoqwa growled. As if they had heard him and could understand our language a couple of the bigger boys unloading a nearby wagon curled their lips and glared.

Not looking away or backing down Matoqwa stared right back, showing lots of predatory teeth and had the satisfaction of seeing them drop their eyes and turn back to unloading the wagon.

Watching them go Cohasi snorted a laugh, but I also saw his eyes darting here and there around the yard, watching for trouble. "Who knows what these crazy people will want us to do next," he muttered and patted Qwatola's hand when he thought no one was looking.

Feeling a cold shiver of warning slide down my spine I ignored the whispered talk around me, my eyes searching for the source of the threat. In all the confusion of people and animals it took me a while to locate the source of my unease, but when I did, I knew with the certainty of another sending that the stern-faced, dried up priest with iron gray hair and eyes, picking his way across the mud of the stable yard was far more threatening to me and my brothers than any stone monster sent to torment me by the Chamuqwani's alien god.

As he drew near his cold eyes met mine, sending another chill of fear cascading down my back. I dropped my eyes and sunk lower into the wagon, hastily throwing up an inner shield of protection, though I feared it might be too late. Though I had been proud of my tattoos since I was gifted with them, if this newcomer or anyone else at the school had Spirit Power they would see and recognize what my dragon glyph meant—and I would suffer for it.

<<Have no fear, Young Siyatli,>> the crystal being said into my mind. <<Though you are right; there is evil here, there is no malicer among these sniveling priests. Several are cruel and capable of many terrible deeds, but none have Qwakaiva enough to cause you harm within the Dream. I will help you shield and I will translate for you when it is important. You will survive this time if you are clever.>>

<<Thank you, that does ease my mind somewhat,>> I told it.

Knowing there was little time to offer a warning I turned my face away from the approaching priest, and murmured in the Kukiya language, "Beware, brothers, trouble is near. Be strong; the enemy comes." Though not everyone had heard my words, they instinctively understood my warning. Everyone in the wagon sat up a little straighter determined not to show fear.

When the newcomer was nearly up to the wagon where we waited, the priests who were supervising the unloading and talking among themselves finally noticed his approach. Placing their hands together as if in prayer Administrator Rizdale and the two other men bowed to the newcomer. "Director Harriscot, I hope we haven't disturbed you with our late arrival," with crystal's help I heard Rizdale say.

Answering only with a nod Director Harriscot returned his attention to us, still sitting in our chains in the back of the unloaded wagon. Without turning away from us he said, "They are older than I was led to believe when his Divine Holiness contacted me. The Intercessor must have a persuasive tongue."

Administrator Rizdale nodded a sympathetic agreement. "He does. I had a post with him when a young man. Intercessor Raymonel was a self-righteous holy prick with a golden tongue even back then. His family has money and influence at court. He probably knows the Divine personally."

"Mm, that would explain a lot," the director mused. "The question now is what to do with them."

Praiser Simms finally said, "As you said, Director, they do look too old for scholarly tasks, but most are big and look strong enough to do some of the hard farm work needed to make the school land profitable. And I hear most of the western savages are good with horses and other beasts.

"Give them to me, or at least that one and that one." He pointed to Matoqwa, Cohasi and three of the taller Kukiya, including Inishkim. "I can beat any rebellion out of them if they try to cause trouble. As for the others," he shrugged. "I'm sure we can find something for them to do."

"Very well, praiser, we will sort it out and officially enroll them in the morning. It grows late."

Then the director narrowed his eyes and his mouth twisted with his contempt. "These heathen savages are filthy and probably riddled with lice and other disgusting vermin. Get them cleaned up before you bring them into the temple for the evening prayers. I'll tell cook we are having more 'guests' for the meal. And send one of your lads to tell Celibress Vomica to find beds and bedding for them in the older boys dorm."

Celibress Vomica was here? She was the mercy woman that hated me on our march south. The thought of her recognizing me, made my gut twist in a knot.

<<There may not be a malicer at the school,>> I told my inner guide and helper, <<but it won't be easy for me either with so many people who hate me living here.>>

Did I detect amusement in the beings sending as I was ordered down from the wagon? <<When you chose to walk this path you created this weave in the pattern of your life. Like your Chamuqwani friend you are being tested. As the Great One and I have told you, if you are clever and fearless you will survive.>>

Ah, but did I want to?

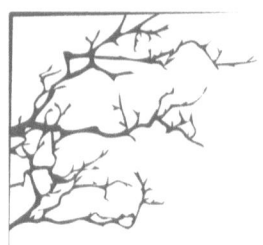

Chapter Two

When the director had walked away we were marched to another building I hadn't seen upon our arrival. It was a long low structure made of wooden planks with a large open door somewhat like a barn. As we paused by the open doorway I could see inside two rows of big metal basins, leading into its shadowy darkness.

One of the muscular workmen had been ordered to make a large fire to one side of the open door. Several boys were carrying armfuls of chopped wood to feed it, while others walked back and forth from the well to the shadowy room inside, carrying buckets of water. Passing us with heads down they refused to speak to us under the watchful eyes of the workmen and priests.

"What do you think they are going to do with us?" I heard Qwatola murmur to Cohasi.

Answering his question Matoqwa snorted. "Nothing good."

Qwatola was slightly younger than the rest of us. He was a kind thoughtful boy with luminous dark eyes, full lips and a slender half-starved body just beginning to mature into manhood. He was another whose Qwani'Ya mother had left an unpleasant marriage and had chosen to live with a Kukiya man related to Talulsit.

I didn't know much of him because his family hadn't wintered with us, but his Kukiya father had adopted him and he wore the tattoos of his new clan on his cheeks as did I. he was no warrior and had never ridden on a raid into the Chamuqwani settled lands. It was only because he'd snatched up a dead man's weapon, trying to protect and help his mother and younger brother flee the soldiers during the massacre that he'd been captured at all.

Looking us over Praiser Simms pointed to Qwatola and the Kukiya boy, named Iwaz, who were smaller than the rest of us and motioned for them to come forward and sit on the chairs placed near the fire. "Pay attention," he snarled. "Your turn will come."

While still keeping them chained, so they couldn't run, their long and matted hair was cut off. The hair was then thrown into the fire, creating a terrible stink. I could see portions of their bleeding bare scalp through the stubble that was left when the priest finished.

Qwatola looked like he wanted to cry his dark eyes moist with unshed tears, but then he looked at Cohasi's grim face and swallowed his fear.

When the hair cutting was done the boys were ordered to strip off all their clothing, which also went into the flames. Next their chains were removed and they were ordered, frightened and shivering into the dark building, where I learned when it was my turn, a white smelly powder was rubbed into their heads and places where hair grew around a youth's twig.

The nasty stuff stung the eyes and burned the scalp where the hair cutting had broken the skin, I also learned. Then after what seemed like endless torture we were ordered to stand in one of the big basins called tubs and boys with taunting smiles poured bucket after bucket of cold water over our heads until all the white powder disappeared down the hole in the bottom of the tub.

After watching what was being done to the first two I glanced around at my brothers waiting their turns, and I knew when I saw Matoqwa and a Kukiya youth named Komonti exchanging glances that they were going to start something.

Matoqwa had that grim look on his face that over the years growing up with him, I'd learned meant somebody was going to get hurt. And, I also knew if he started anything Cohasi would be right there, as his shadow, to back him up—and probably the one who would suffer the most in whatever they were thinking of doing.

Stepping closer to him I murmured, hoping none of the priests were watching, "Don't be stupid, dog turd. You will only get yourself and more of us hurt if you try to fight them right now.

"There's no point—wait. There will be a better time—later. And besides after being in the filthy Chamuqwani jail, you do need a bath," I added, trying to joke him out of whatever foolishness was circling around in his ptarmigan brain.

The Bear in his Spirit Fire lifted its lip in a silent snarl, and Matoqwa himself glared and said a Chamuqwani bad word, which did catch the attention of one of the workmen who told us to shut up.

And then, it was mine and Cohasi's turn. I gave the men no trouble when they motioned me to the chair for the hair cutting. I sat with what I hoped was a mask of indifference on my face. I was a warrior of the Real People. I wouldn't give my enemy the satisfaction of seeing my fear. My hair, my clothes—what did it matter anymore? I had lost so much already; this was just another part of the enemy's attempt to break me—crush me.

I shivered as I walked naked and bleeding into the dark room behind Cohasi. <<Oh, Kunai, I pray I am strong enough to endure all that you have envisioned for me.>>

Matoqwa and Komonti did try resisting the hair cutting and stripping when it was their turn, but it did them little good. The one in charge, Praiser Simms, was ready for them and merely called for more men to help him.

My war-brothers did manage to get in a few good punches, however.

Simms had a long cut oozing blood on one cheek and one of the workmen had a bloody nose, and another man now had a black eye when it was over. But as I'd warned him, their defiance only made the Chamuqwani all the madder, and the two fools suffered for it. When they arrived in the bathhouse they were more bruised and bloody than the rest of us, but just as shorn and naked.

After the "bathing" that first evening we were given clean but patched Chamuqwani clothes similar to what I'd seen the other boys at the school wearing. Since most of us were older than all but the oldest of the students the clothes given us didn't fit well. The shirts were a little tight, the trousers too short and there were no moccasins or Chamuqwani boots for our feet.

Praiser Simms finally pronounced us suitably cleaned and dressed, and then we were marched to the temple for the evening session of prayers and sermons. Herded by the priest and his men we were the last to arrive at the temple and the singing had already begun. We were ordered by gesture to be quiet and take our seats in the last row of wooden benches on the right.

Looking around the temple when none of our guards were watching I realized with some surprise that there were girls here at the school, too.

Their long hair had also been cut short, though not to the extreme that was inflicted upon us boys.

A few of the bravest of the children glanced back at us but most remained facing forward, at least pretending to be listening to the thunderous sermon the director was giving about what would happen to bad little zaunks who broke the god's laws and wouldn't behave.

When it was finally over the two stern-faced mercy women dressed in green robes and white veils covering their hair and lower faces that had stood on each side of the room near the front, clapped their hands once, and the children in the first row of benches stood up, and silently marched down the left and right isles out of the temple. When they were well on their way to the door the women clapped twice and the second row of students followed the first.

As they passed us many more who hadn't been aware of our arrival earlier now stared wide-eyed at the wild, heathen savages among them. Like the convert boys I'd known before a lot of the older boys and some of the girls looked down their noses at us and curled their lips with contempt.

But what distressed me the most was the fear I saw in the eyes of some of the younger ones. I wasn't sure at that time if the fear was directed at us, or if it was directed at the cruel men and women who had stolen them away from their families and placed them in this terrible place. I would learn in the next few days it was a bit of both.

When it was our turn to leave we followed Praiser Sims into the main building then we were ordered into a large chamber with long tables in rows down each side of the room. At the far end away from the door where we entered was another table with large metal pots set a top it and people going back and forth through another door that probably led into a kitchen.

Once inside we were split up. As an added humiliation, for the brave warriors among us, Matoqwa and Komonti were marched to a table near the back and forcibly pushed into chairs to join several younger students with an older girl in charge of serving the food.

To the priest's surprise the two endured their humiliation in a grim silence. But their expressions also promised retaliations later to any child who dared to snicker at them when the priests and mercy women weren't looking their way.

When he at last realized the two weren't going to make more trouble for him Praiser Simms continued assigning us to our places. He sent Cohasi and Atuusca to another table. Inishkim, Qwatola and I went to a third. The other two, Kuweya and Iwaz, left standing in the doorway were led to another table near the door.

Sitting in the hard wooden chair, the mercy woman in charge of this part of the hall told me with gestures and a loud voice, so I would be sure to understand, "This is your place—your chair. Every meal time you sit here." She thumped the back of the chair hard with her hand. "You sit here—nowhere else, understand?"

I understood her. I knew enough Chamuqwani by that time in my life that I understood most of the basics in that language, but I also didn't want to give her the satisfaction of letting her know that. I was determined to cling onto my language as long as possible, since they had taken everything else away from me. So, I just stared at her blankly until she gave up and turned away, mumbling about stupid heathen zaunks.

When everyone was finally settled Administrator Rizdale stood up, clapped and immediately the room fell silent. "We have some new students who have joined us today, as you can see. I doubt if they speak a civilized tongue, so it will be up to all of us to teach them the rules and how to behave like proper good citizens of the Empire. Now let us pray and give thanks to all mighty Djoven for the food we are about to receive."

As before in the temple everyone put their hands together and bowed their heads and the priest droned out another long-winded prayer. At the end of it everyone relaxed, and the older boy named Ronalton at the head of our table took a bowl from a stack beside him and ladled out a portion of soup. Then the bowls were passed around to each person sitting at the table. A tasteless lump of some kind of bread was also passed around and a bowl of thick white grease called lard to spread upon the bread.

My portion when a bowl finally made its way around the table to me was a thin soup of boiled white beans with a piece of fatty bacon floating in its center. I sighed and ate the tasteless stuff, because I was hungry, but it would seem that the school's prisoners weren't going to be fed any better than the rations we had been given back on the Preserve.

Everyone in the hall ate their meager meal in silence. Besides the three of us newcomers there were nine other children seated at our table, five along each side and one at each end to make twelve in all. Not counting us, Ronalton seemed to be the oldest. He was as tall as Matoqwa and Komonti and nearly as muscular. From his behavior he seemed to be in charge of the younger ones. He was a hard-eyed brown-skinned youth with bad teeth. His Second, Yohan, sitting at the other end of the table was a mixed-blood boy with a ragged scar just below his hair line on his forehead and was nearly as large.

Noticing Qwatola and my tattoos he started in that night and every meal afterwards, making fun of the heathen savages with whispered nasty comments whenever he thought he could get away without being caught. He whispered to the younger boys that we might kill them in their sleep and maybe eat them, if they were bad and peed their beds.

At first I thought the older boy in charge would put a stop to the teasing, but he didn't. I finally realized he was subtly encouraging the ridicule. Like Matoqwa and Cohasi, this Yohan was Ronalton's shadow. And as his shadow, he was willing to help carry out any meanness the two could dream up. Idly I wondered if they were also related, or had just found each other once they were confined in this place.

Living in a convert encampment back on the Preserve I had heard it all before, and so, like water running off a seal's oily fur I ignored the jibes.

Qwatola was not so lucky, however, I could tell he knew enough of the Chamuqwani language to be hurt.

I leaned over when I passed my bowl to the boy collecting them, and said to Qwatola in a low voice, "Ignore the smelly fish guts. You are the adopted son of a proud Kukiya warrior and have a fine Qwani'Ya woman for a mother. His words are nothing."

I thought I'd been careful, but evidently not careful enough, because the next thing I knew I was being whacked hard on the head with a wooden rod and Celibress Vomica was standing by me, yelling, "Do not speak that heathen tongue here or I will wash your mouth out with lye soap, you nasty heathen savage. This is your only warning, understand?"

Well, it hadn't taken me long to get myself into trouble, I thought, and with this woman in particular, who might become a true danger to me.

I hunched over and murmured something I hoped she would take as an apology. Fortunately for me I had changed so much in the past few years that she hadn't recognized me—yet and I hoped I could keep it that way. With my shaved head, tattooed face and somewhat taller, I thought I must look quite different from the boy she'd known on the march to the Preserve that she had accused of being a witch.

After the meal was finished Brother Simms collected us again. We were shown the indoor privy and then we were led up to the fourth floor where two long rooms lay on either side of the staircase. Here we were once more split up five going into a room on the left and four into the room on the right.

I was shown into the room on the left, along with Iwaz, Matoqwa, Atuusca and Kuweya. Cohasi, Inishkim, Komonti, and Qwatola were herded into the room on the right. I could see the flicker of desperation in Cohasi's eyes as he followed Inishkim into the other room. Those two brothers were rarely apart, and I hoped neither of them was going to start more trouble over the separation.

Our room was cold and stank of pee. It had two rows of narrow beds along each side and a sloping roof that ended in a low wall about the height of a youth sitting up on his bed. Here and there along each side glass windows had been placed, which were closed and shuddered to block some of the night's chill.

An older mercy woman directed a servant girl to give us each two big pieces of white cloth and then show us how to make our beds with them. We were also given a scratchy wool blanket to go on top.

"Every morning you must do this," she instructed us. "If you don't, Intercessor Fredderoth, who is in charge up here, or the Director will give you a whipping as a punishment." When she turned away Matoqwa curled his lip in a silent snarl.

There weren't five empty beds together so once again we were split up. I chose a bed near the far wall under a window, so I could see some tree branches and a sliver of sky. But once the weather turned colder I regretted my impulsive choice.

The beds near the room's only source of heat, a crusty wood stove, were already being claimed by Ronalton and his friends. Matoqwa claimed the bed next to mine and Kuweya chose one across the aisle but two beds down.

Atuusca and Iwaz, who I knew were cousins, chose beds together further down that same row.

When our beds were made to the Mercy women's satisfaction we were told to remove the clothes we'd just been given and place them in the wooden boxes we found under our beds. Then we were told to take out the long white garment that resembled a woman's dress. Looking around I saw that all the other boys were already wearing similar clothing they called a nightshirt.

I put on my night shirt as instructed, but Matoqwa and Atuusca, in an unspoken agreement, remained dressed in our day clothes. When it was clear they weren't going to obey the Mercy woman's order she stomped out of the room. As the door slammed Ronalton and two of his friends, boys nearly as big as Matoqwa, rose as one, and headed in our direction.

"Put on your nightshirt, you stupid savage." Ronalton demanded in the Chamuqwani language.

Matoqwa's eyes flicked to assess the two others coming to stand beside Ronalton then returned his attention to the head boy. Out of the corner of my eye I could see both Atuusca and Kuweya readying themselves to back him up if it came to a real fight.

Matoqwa glanced down his nose at the skinny bare legs of the tall youth, now quivering with rage at his defiance and curled his lip with contempt. "Why you dress like womans when sleep? Want me fuck you like woman, eh?" Ronalton's face turned purple with rage and his friends muttered angry curses and raised their fists.

As Matoqwa was speaking the Kukiya had left their beds and were slowly coming up to stand by him. I said a bad Chamuqwani word and was getting to my feet as well, hoping to stop this before someone got killed when the room door was flung open. And Praiser Simms and his men rushed back in.

Matoqwa and Atuusca, the only ones still in day clothes were quickly bound and dragged out of the dorm bleeding and cursing. A smile of satisfaction curving his thin lips Ronalton ordered everyone back to their beds as his two friends moved around the room extinguishing the lamps.

I sighed. Stupid dog turd, I hoped Matoqwa was all right. When he passed by me sitting on my bed, I gathered my courage and asked in my best Chamuqwani, "Where priest take?' I now motioned with my lips to the closed door behind which we could still hear thumps and faint shouting.

His face widening into a broad smile, he said, "After they finish with him, they will leave him at the gateway to the Abyss, the 'Perdition Box'. And, have a care, or you'll be next, savage, if you don't obey orders."

He expected me to cringe and drop my eyes in fear, like I'd seen others doing when Ronalton glanced their way, but I surprised him. I looked him straight in the eye and gave him my own version of a predatory smile. "Maybe, but maybe me send you first, eh? You can tell devil friends me come—later—kick ass."

And thus ended my first day at the Chamuqwani prison for children, Saint Yon's Live-away school.

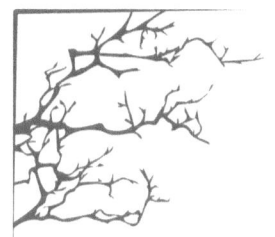

Chapter Three

Just as the sky was turning pink with the new day we were jerked awake by the sound of our door being banged open and the blue-robed priest Intercessor Fredderoth came in shouting for us to get up.

Still hungry, frightened and confused it had taken me sometime to fall asleep the night before. I had laid there on the lumpy bed in the cold room, listening to the unfamiliar sounds in the dark around me. Boys snored while others cried out tormented by their dreams, and the acrid smell of fresh piss stung my nostrils as it spread its scent throughout the room. I shivered and pulled my blanket over my head and willed myself to relax.

When sleep finally came my dreams were sweet. Amima's spirit enfolded me in warm loving arms and I felt content. So content that I had trouble waking up to face the uncertainties of what the new day might bring. Trying to cling to the sense of well-being conjured in my sleep, I rose, washed in the cold water poured into a metal basin and dressed back in the day clothes I took from the box under my bed.

Ignoring the hard eyes of the priest focused on my war-brothers and me as he walked down the center aisle inspecting our efforts, I continued to dress and make my bed as I'd been shown. Evidently I was too slow to suit my new tormenter, because when I bent over to tuck in a corner of the blanket the intercessor was suddenly standing behind me, and then whacked my bum with a peeled willow branch he'd been holding and slapping into the palm of his other hand.

Startled, I jerked up and spun around, fists clenched, a curse forming on my lips. Thinking it was the head boy I was getting ready to fight, but stopped myself just in time. Intercessor Fredderoth, the priest in charge of the boys on the fourth floor was the one who had hit me, not Ronalton.

A balding man with mocking brown eyes and a purple birthmark on his neck, when he saw me touch my body where the wand had stung me, he smirked. "Hurry up, tattooed savage or you'll be sent to work without your breakfast." He watched me a moment longer then continued his inspection.

As I hurried to catch up with Iwaz and Kuweya I heard a young boy's hysterical crying begin behind me.

"I warned you what would happen if you soiled your bedding again, you filthy, nasty, little zaunk!" the intercessor roared over the frightened boy's screaming. Then his outburst was followed by several whacks of his willow wand upon the child's legs and bum.

I had just felt the sting of that wand and knew its power to hurt. I needed no imagination to understand the cruelty inflicted upon the boy. I had turned, thinking in some stupid way to protest such brutal treatment to one so young, but Kuweya walking behind me put a hand on my arm, shook his head and pushed me forward.

Though I hated to leave the defenseless boy to endure such a harsh punishment, I heeded Kuweya's warning and followed the other boys down the stairs. As I kept trying to tell Matoqwa this wasn't the time for war, so maybe I should listen to my own self, eh?

<<Yes, you should, young Siyatli, your perception of another's suffering and your courage to combat the Evil One's creatures often pleases your Benefactor, but direct confrontation is not always the way to achieve the results you and the Great One desire. One of your tasks while at this prison is to learn more subtle ways to win a victory,>> the Crystal Being lodged near my heart said into my mind. <<Like your Seal father you favor impulsive action over careful planning. You must learn balance and restraint.>>

Like back in the convert settlement on the preserve there would be no food before prayers and god talk, so we were formed into two lines, girls in one, boys in the other, and marched to the temple like we'd done the night before.

Once inside the temple I looked for Matoqwa and Atuusca, hoping that whatever the priests had done to punish them they would be let go to join us for the prayers. But no they were still missing and that twisted the knot of worry in my gut a little tighter.

Ever sensitive to one another, Cohasi had noticed his brother's absence as well, and was glancing around frantically searching for him. Kuweya had observed Cohasi's growing panic, too, and mouthed as he opened a gap in the line between him and Cohasi for me to slip into, "Can you help him, Puhani?"

"Don't even think about doing anything stupid," I murmured next to Cohasi's ear as I slid unnoticed into the opening. When we were sitting on the wooden bench in the back row again, he snarled, "Where is he?"

"Calm down…" I whispered as I pressed my hands together, covering my mouth. "Don't know, but I will find him for you with my Gift as soon as I can, if he doesn't show up soon. So don't worry."

"Atuusca is not here, either, what happened?"

I snorted a mirthless laugh. "What do you think happened? The stupid dog turd started another fight—a fight he knew he couldn't possibly win."

At last Director Harriscot walked to the front of the room where several candles burned at the feet of a carved statue of Djoven, the Thunderer. A resinous smoky incents already thick in the air he tossed more on the glowing coals and raised his hands to begin the prayer.

It wasn't a surprise to me that when he got around to his thundering sermon Matoqwa and the rest of us heathen savages were the subject of his rant. Shouting and red-faced he went into great detail describing to all the children the eternal torment awaiting anyone who defied the god and persisted in their heathen ways.

By the time he finished many of the children were trembling and quietly sobbing. Knowing my mouth was set in a thin hard line, I dropped my eyes and bowed my head, trying to hide the simmering anger churning inside me. Frightening people—especially children into obedience with threats of everlasting pain and suffering, this was a cruel and unnecessary way to make them behave. Truly the Chamuqwani and their thunder god were a destructive force in our land.

Feeling suddenly defiant and rebellious I prayed Iyantsha and his followers could gather enough Qwakaiva soon with their songs and dances to make these unnatural people disappear.

When we arrived in the "dining hall," as I was told to call the place where we ate, most of the children were already seated with hands folded, silently waiting for the morning prayers to begin. I took my assigned place and waited with the rest for more prayers and the lumpy burned mush I learned was our usual morning meal.

After the meal was over the priests and mercy women organized all the children into work details to clean the kitchen, the classrooms, the indoor privies and all the rooms shared by everyone at the school. Being new and not assigned any work yet my war-brothers and I remained in our assigned seats unsure what to do next.

We didn't have to wait long. When everyone was about their assigned work for the morning Director Harriscot and Administrator Rizdale came to collect us. Before we could be assigned to a work crew we evidently needed to be officially registered into the school. So they could get paid by the Father Emperor's men for imprisoning us, I learned later.

And, just like when we arrived on the Preserve the director brought out a big book in which he wrote our official Chamuqwani names. But for convenience and everyday usage we were also assigned a number and given a small disc to wear around our necks displaying it. I became number 297. For the rest of the time I spent in that terrible place all the teachers and priests referred to us only by our number not by either our Chamuqwani assigned name or our real tribal name.

Attorney Ricosen had said nothing about being given numbers, but he had warned us that at the school we would have to use the Chamuqwani names we were given on the Preserve. If we didn't have one, or couldn't remember it, we should choose one, or risk being given one not to our liking by the priests at the school.

I had no wish to continue any association with my maternal uncle, Royston Fishspear, so I became Tassele Cougarson instead. Collin helped me choose the name Tassele in his language before he left with his friend Lord Bronworthy. I wasn't sure of the names meaning, nor was he, but it was close to my own name, Tasimu, and Collin said that a famed ancestor in his lineage also had that name, so I felt honored when he gifted it to me.

For my second and new family name I chose my adopted father's name of Cougarson. I wanted to honor his memory and remind myself of his bravery, service to the People and his love.

Cohasi, Inishkim and a couple others had family back on the Preserve that they were still close to, so when the director asked they gave him their assigned names to write in his big book. After that was finished. Praiser Simms and a workman name Doff showed up and we were led away to finish out the morning working around the barn feeding and cleaning the animals' stalls.

They watched us closely at first, but the tasks weren't much different than what we'd been doing when we traveled with our people on the Preserve and the desert, so we knew what was required of us in spite of the language barrier. No one argued or wanted to fight or try and escape. It was better out here with the animals, rather than being stuck indoors under the hostile eyes of the mercy women and priests.

We weren't alone, so I had no time to talk with the others. Boys from the school shoveled and raked piles of dung into large mounds right alongside us, and Praiser Simms and his Chamuqwani workmen from the village at Barner's Crossing were always there to supervise and occasionally lend a hand.

As I worked I kept searching for a piece of stray rope, or an old leather thong I could hide away to later use to make another magical cord for myself. With it I could weave the patterns I needed to find our missing brothers. I was skilled enough by that time that I could go into the Dream and search for them, of course, but I was reluctant to do so. Azogi and other enemies might be looking for me there as well.

I finally found a ragged piece of muddy rope hanging on a nail inside a stall I'd been assigned to rake out. I quickly pulled it off the nail and tied it around my waist, as if I needed it to keep my trousers up. Hopefully later I would be able to find the quiet time to clean it and reweave it into the magical tool I needed.

Glancing at Cohasi from time to time I saw that he and Iwaz were growing more and more worried when neither of their relatives made an appearance by the time Doff called a halt and told us to line up and wash before returning to the dining hall for the midday meal. Falling in behind Cohasi I touched his back and allowed a touch of my power to calm his worry, then I murmured, "Keep strong, I will find him for you."

When we arrived a bruised and disheveled Atuusca was slumped in his chair waiting for us, but Matoqwa was nowhere in sight. His absence twisted the knot of fear in my gut a little tighter. Cohasi caught my eye and gave me a pleading look. I touched the rope around my waist, hoping to reassure him. As the director came in to offer up the midday prayer, I saw Cohasi lean over and try to speak to Atuusca, but I doubt if he got anything useful for an answer, because one of the priests came over, whacked Cohasi on the head and snarled at them both to keep quiet.

I would have liked to speak to Atuusca myself when we returned to the barn, but that wasn't going to happen. After the meal of bean soup and bread we were assigned other chores. Most of the convert boys were marched up to the second floor to the classrooms where they spent the rest of the afternoon studying their lessons.

The girls were not so lucky. Some were assigned cooking and sewing tasks while others followed an aging servant and a young mercy woman back into the yard to do laundry. Qwatola, Iwaz, and I were ordered to go with them to do some of the heavier work, like chopping wood for the fires lit under the big wash tubs and hauling endless buckets of water from the well to fill them.

As we passed Ronalton and his friends I heard him make a comment about the new cloocha-girls better not leave any itchy soap in his sheets this time. Qwatola glanced at me and rolled his eyes.

"That one is lucky I no longer have my hunting knife," Iwaz mutter to me as we followed the girls out into the sunlight.

My lip twitched, but the mercy woman was watching us so I dared not openly smile. "Ignore him; there will come a time of reckoning. The dog turd's not worth the trouble it would cause if you gutted him now," I said to Iwaz as I passed him and stepped out into the sun.

Unlike most of the Chamuqwani at the school Celibress Dinana was young with pretty green eyes that reminded me of Nachoga's. But there was no cougar in her Spirit Fire, or any other spirit guide that I could see. if she had been born with a guide and protector the fierce god to which she had dedicated her life must have scared it away.

I could easily tell she was curious about us, I'd caught her staring at my and Qwatola's tattoos on several occasions. But I was wary of her interest and tried to avoid her if I could. Compared to the others I'd encountered at the school she seemed a kind person. Maybe because of her youth, she wasn't cruel or hardened by her surroundings yet. As we worked she talked to the girls, lent a hand from time-to-time and even joked with them on occasion.

She seemed a little nervous of me and my war-brothers at first, as did most of the girls, but when we carried out the tasks she assigned us without complaint she relaxed and even tried to include us in her talk.

Iwaz was ordered to chop wood while Qwatola and I were assigned to haul buckets of water from the well to fill the big tubs filled with dirty bedding and clothes.

The poor boy, number 241, who had peed his bed that morning, had been assigned as a further punishment to wash his sheets. When he arrived snot and tears drying on his cheeks, the mercy woman sighed. "Oh I am so disappointed in you, 241," she said as she motioned for him to dump his bundle into the steaming tub a girl with a long wooden paddle was stirring.

The boy I knew only as 241, because he died not long after our arrival, hung his head and mumbled an apology and said he would be good in future.

Celibress Dinana nodded and patted his shoulder, and then told him, "You will just have to pray harder and the Mighty Djoven will take this terrible affliction away, I'm sure of it."

As I continued to haul water and fill the tubs I kept my eye on the boy. His legs below his short trousers were dark with bruises and he was limping and seemed to be having trouble lifting the heavy cloth out of the steaming tubs. When I studied him with my Gift I could see the muddy colors of fear and sickness swirling about in his Spirit Fire.

He was big enough to do the work asked of him, but the illness, whatever it was, was probably at the root of his trouble. Unfortunately I didn't have Grandfather's healing gift, nor would the boy himself or the priests let me work on him, even if I did have that kind of Qwakaiva.

Later as I emptied my bucket of clear cold water into the rinse tub I saw 241 struggling to lift and hang one of his wet sheets on the rope strung up to hold the newly washed bedding and clothes while they dried.

As he struggled, almost dropping the heavy cloth into the mud I hurried over and held it up for him. When he saw who it was trying to help him his eyes grew wide and he almost dropped his end so great was his fear of me.

"No be 'fraid. Me no eat, like stupid Ronalton say. Him dog turd." I pointed to my eyes and continued as I clipped the little wooden pins over the rope to keep the sheet from falling. "Me see. Boy sick. Me just want help, eh?" his eyes went wide when he heard me call the head boy in our room a bad name, finally he mumbled his thanks as I picked up my buckets and headed back to the well near the barn.

I thought I hadn't been noticed helping the sick boy, but evidently I had. When I returned Celibress Dinana was waiting for me. "That was a very kind thing you did for that boy. You are new here so you probably didn't know that he is being punished. No one is supposed to help him. If Intercessor Fredderoth had seen you…"

She left the rest of her thought unvoiced, but I understood well enough what she meant. I shrugged and told her, "Is Qwani'Ya way take care children—old people." I shrugged again. "Boy not bad, sick not strong now, so me help."

Her eyes widened when I mentioned 241's illness. "How did you…"

"Everybody can see. Why you no take to…" I opened my mouth but stopped myself before I spoke a word in my language. I shrugged in a hopeless gesture. I didn't know the Chamuqwani word for a Qwakaihi like Grandfather.

She seemed to understand me anyway. "Doctor," she supplied. "A doctor is a person who takes care of sick people."

"Doctor," I repeated and she smiled.

"Yes, that's right, doctor. And you may also be right that 241 should go to the infirmary and see the doctor."

She studied me for a moment then said, "I won't report you—this time—because you are new. When someone is being punished, don't help them in future." Then with her lips threatening to curve into a smile, she added, "Or, if you do, be more careful."

"Me be careful," I promised, gave her a sly smile of my own and returned to hauling water.

Remembering the taunt the head boy had said last night on my next trip to fill a tub, I decided to ask my new friend a question that had been troubling me all day. As I poured the water where he was working, I murmured, "What is perdi-shon box where Brother Simms take relative?"

241 shuddered and when back to scrubbing his other sheet. When I didn't move away he corrected in a voice barely above a whisper, "Perdition Box. It's the place bad children are put to punish them." He shivered again and went back to scrubbing, refusing to look at me.

"Intercessor put you in box?" he nodded slightly and continued working. Looking around to see if we were being watched I finished pouring the water, trying to see a building that looked like a box. I saw none. "Where Perdition Box?"

"Inside priests' house—down in the ground." He shuddered again and I quickly moved away from him as I saw the old servant start to walk in our direction. Some of the converts back on the preserve dug big pits in the ground where it was cool, in which they could store extra meat and fish to keep from spoiling.

I didn't know what it was called in the priests' language but there must be such a place under the earth in their house. I sighed. And, of course, that would have to be the very place where they were keeping that stupid dog turd Matoqwa.

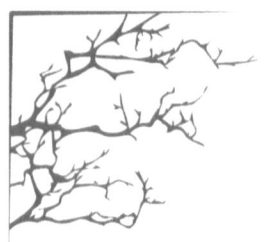

Chapter Four

Just as we were emptying the last of the tubs for the day, one of the cook's helpers came out with a request from cook for more clean towels if any were ready. Fortunately, there was a stack of small cloths they called dishcloths that one of the older girls was just finishing folding. Since I was the only one nearby that was free the older servant directed me to pick up the folded towels and take the basket to the kitchen.

My empty stomach growled at the good smells of roasting meat and onions that wafted out to greet me as I stepped into the room with my burden. My expression must have reflected my longing because the boy who had been my guide gave me a mocking laugh.

"That food is for the priests and the teachers, not you. You'll be eating beans like the rest of us, savage." Then he stepped past me and closed the door in my face.

From the floor above I could hear a teacher asking questions and the sounds of children reciting their lessons. Confused by the many doors and twisting halls, I was trying to retrace my steps back to the laundry area outside, when my crystal sent me a warning and I hastily shrank back into the darkness under the stairs. Throwing up an illusion of being invisible, this time a bat in a cave, I waited, breathing as silently as I could. From the floor above I could hear two men talking in low voices as they headed down the stairs. As they drew nearer I recognized the voices of Praiser Simms and the director passing overhead.

"I noticed one of the new boys was missing at the noon meal. What happened?" the director was saying as they came near.

Praiser Sims let out a nasty chuckle. "The inevitable. The big one with the broken nose is trouble. I could see that right away, Director. He is probably a leader among them of some kind. He needed to be taught a good lesson, that's all. The sooner he's broken to the harness the better it will be for everyone."

"Where is he now, in the infirmary?"

"No, that didn't seem appropriate. Doctor Tomkins was on duty last night; he would have made too much of a fuss after the recent deaths of 156 and 173. I put him in the Box after we finished with him. I'll check on him later tonight if you like. But it would probably be better if we just leave him down there until we need to bury his corpse."

"Hmm... Maybe..."

They continued on in silence for a few more steps, then, "He isn't officially registered with us at this point. If he were to die we could always say he just ran away," Simms offered, hoping to influence his decision.

Director Harriscot stopped abruptly and slammed a hand against the stair rail, making me almost cry out and give myself away. "Don't be a fool, Praiser!" he snarled. "These particular savages have powerful friends both within the temple and at court. I recognize your need to maintain order and discipline among our unruly charges, but in future control your murderous impulses, or we will all suffer for your bungling.

"Later, in a few months, a year, if the zaunk is still causing you problems then we will consider 'other measures,' but not now. It's too dangerous."

When they disappeared down the hall I crept out of my hiding place and hurried back outside. The servant was scowling when I returned. "What took you so long?"

"Sorry get lost me." She frowned as if she wasn't sure she believed me, but decided to let it pass. The bell had rung and children were starting to line up for the evening prayers.

I HAD MANAGED TO WASH off my muddy rope in one of the wash tubs while emptying it, without attracting unwanted notice. That night with evening chores done I sat on my bed in my nightshirt, unraveled its strands and began reworking it into something more suitable for my purposes.

When Intercessor Fredderoth came in to pray with us for the last time that night he noticed me sitting atop my bed, and headed in my direction to see what I was doing. I continued weaving, not wanting him to become suspicious if I tried to hide it or appear nervous.

"What are you doing 297?" he said as he stopped by my bed.

I looked up and held up the half-finished weave to show him. "Me make..." I wasn't sure of the proper word, so I pointed to my waist and made a surrounding motion. "Trousers big. Fall down maybe. So me make."

He took the half-finished cord, examining it carefully. The rope fibers were still stained with dirt in places. It was very obvious I hadn't cut it off a usable coil, but all the same I trembled inside for fear he would take it away from me out of meanness, if for no other reason and I would have to risk going into the Dream to find Matoqwa anyway.

"Did you steal this rope to make a belt?" he demanded.

Well, maybe I did, if he wanted to call taking a piece of cord that was too small and frayed to be used for anything, left hanging abandoned in a dirty stall, stealing, but I wasn't going to be stupid enough to admit it. Instead I shook my head vigorously. "Me work in barn today. Me find in muck when..." I made the motions of shoveling the horse turds onto the dung pile.

He inspected my working a moment longer then handed it back. "That is good work, but time for prayers now. Tomorrow ask one of the servants or Celibress Vomica for a proper belt if you need one."

I breathed a sigh of relief when I took it back, but I wasn't going to ask Celibress Vomica for anything if I could help it, but I might ask Celibress Dinana—if I found her.

After the lamps were snuffed out I sat up and by the firelight coming through the stove I hastily finished the cord, and then looped the cord over my hands. With the other boys asleep around me I conjured an image of Matoqwa in my mind, and formed the pattern of the Seer's Pool in the center diamond.

As still as death itself he was lying in a puddle of his own blood and urine. Only darkness surrounded him, so it was hard for me to tell exactly where the priests were keeping him. I only knew I had to find him—and soon, because I could also see Death's Raven waiting in the shadows.

I let the pattern fall and lay back under my blanket to think. 241 had said Perdition's Box was dark, cold, and inside the priests' house. So it would have to be somewhere secret away from the rooms where everyone stayed when not on duty at the school.

Hmm, cold and dark... probably underground then... Putting my hand over my chest, under which I knew crystal being lay, I formed the question in my mind, conveying the image I had conjured with my string. <<I need to rescue my war-brother, Shining One, before Death's Raven can claim him. Can you help me?>>

There was only silence for a time while I continued to listen to the snoring and whimpering of the boys asleep around me. It had been a long and tiring day for me and I would have liked nothing better than to join them. But if I did, I was afraid, my relative, my friend, might not survive the night. What would I tell Cohasi if that happened? And maybe just as important, what would he do in revenge? He was counting on me—they all were in a way. I would try very hard to protect them—if I could.

As the troublesome brothers had reminded me several times during my own period of grief and despair, *"Us boys from Big Ice Lake gotta stick together."*

Finally my inner companion answered, <<Yes, I will help you. Kunai is in agreement with you about this. He is needed if the Pattern of the Future is to play out in a favorable way for you. Get up, put on your trousers and put your blanket around your shoulders. There isn't much time.>>

Once again projecting an image of a black bat hanging upside down in a dark cave I crept past the sleepers, the on-duty praiser's room, and down the hall stairs. All was quiet in the yard outside, safe for the occasional noises from the animals in the barn, and a far off dog barking down by the village. I breathed in several breaths of cool night air smelling of cut grass, and river mud. I centered myself, and focused on the work I must do.

With my blanket to conceal my white nightshirt I stayed close to the wall and the bushes as I crept out into the yard and at last came to the door of the priests' house. It was unlocked, like the school and I had no trouble entering, but once inside in the dark hallway I was uncertain where to go next. All seemed quiet in the house, but it was an unfamiliar place and I dared not make a light.

<<Shining One, where now?>>

<<Come.>>

The Shining One lending me the night vision of mighty Owl, I moved silently down the hall. To my left was a large room decorated with a fine braided wool rug and several comfortable chairs, and small tables standing beside them. On the far wall away from the curtained window was a large fireplace, Fire's embers faintly glowing as it dozed ready to sleep.

The room reminded me of the sanctuary Collin had created for himself within the Dream. I would have liked to go in, sit on one of the soft chairs, but I dared not stray from my purpose.

Across from the big room were a series of three closed doors. Not hearing any noise coming from inside I eased each one open and peered in. each contained a large wooden table Collin had called a desk, as well as shelves along the walls stacked high with books and other items the priests used in their work.

Opposite these, were rooms that must be bedrooms, because I could hear snoring coming from inside them. Those I left unopened. My guide would have let me know if what I sought was inside one of them. In the hall, past the second set of stairs leading to the upper floor and just outside the kitchen I found a locked wooden door.

The wood felt cold and rough when I placed my bare hand upon it. I shivered and hesitated, not wanting to open the door for fear of loosing its caged malice. I could hear ghosts crying, and feel the dark evil inside wanting to come out.

<<Open it, Siyatli Boy. As the Great One commands; I am shielding you. Have no fear.>>

Taking a deep breath I focused my Qwakaiva on the inner workings of the lock and soon had it open. The blackness that confronted me when I flung the door wide was terrifying and thick as river mud with an unknown malevolence. The abyss waiting to swallow me whole stank of pain and despair. In its shadowy depths I could hear the echoes of children screaming.

As I closed the door behind me the being lodged in my chest began to glow with a white radiance through my skin that pushed back the shadows. Carefully I made my way down the dusty stairs. At the bottom there was a flat open area of pounded dirt and a row of wooden shelves opposite me that once probably contained food stores. Now, however, only a few dusty bottles of waskyja were left in one corner.

On either side of the bottom step were sturdy posts on which hung a couple unlit lanterns. On the side walls of the small chamber were two more narrow locked doors. I sighed. Then I risked calling out in a low voice, "Matoqwa, where are you brother? I've come to help."

I called out twice more, but received no answer—not even a groan from inside either of the locked enclosures. A ghostly fear rose up to taunt me and I shuddered. Was I too late? Moving quickly forward I placed a trembling hand on the door nearest me.

When I got the door unlocked the tiny box-like cell it revealed was empty, though a ragged blanket stained with brown patches that were probably dried blood lay in a crumpled heap in the middle of a mound of musty straw. In the shadows farthest from the door the ghost of a young girl, surely no older than my fourteen years, cradled a tiny baby in her arms. The baby was still covered in its birthing blood. She stared fearfully at me and asked me not to hurt her any more.

Wondering which one of those filthy priests was its father, red spears of anger burned in my gut when I realized what had been done to her. I wanted to help her—release her from this evil place, but I was also aware that my time here was limited—if I didn't want to join her in this ghostly prison.<<I'm sorry but I can't stop to help you right now. If I am able I will come back—later.>>

She gave me a sad smile. <<It's all right, Puhani. I know the other needs you more than me.>> She held up the baby to show me. <<I have my little one to keep me company.>>

Swallowing hard to clear the lump in my throat I hurried to the other cell and opened it.

Matoqwa was lying much as I'd seen him in the Seer's Pool. Tossed carelessly atop a bed of rotting straw, he was breathing with difficulty through his broken nose and bloodied mouth. When I spoke to him he gave no indication that he was aware of my presence in his cell. Trying not to burst into tears at the sight of him lying so battered and unmoving, I took off my blanket, covered him and then sank to the straw beside him, cradling his head on my lap.

"Oh you crazy bear, what have those evil men done to you?" I said, choking on a sob.

Since I had learned to use my Gift I had, on many occasions drawn up Qwakaiva from a source deep within the earth and shared it with another needing my help. But always before the one receiving the Gift I offered had Qwakaiva, too. Matoqwa didn't have any special powers. He had only the Qwakaiva that all living things born into my world shared. I wasn't sure if I could help him. Truly he needed someone like Grandfather right now, not a stupid, half-trained Qwakaihi like me.

<<Stop feeling sorry for yourself,>> Crystal Being growled in my mind.<<There is no time for your self-pity. Place your hands on each side of his head and allow me to flow through you. Watch and learn,>> it commanded.

Sucking up my tears I placed my hands as the Shining One instructed and allowed my guide and protector to begin Matoqwa's healing unhindered by my blubbering. "Stay with me, Bear, we need you," I murmured as I closed my eyes.

Time slowed for me then, as I forgot about the fear, and the darkness surrounding us in this terrible place. My attention was focused only on my war-brother's dying body and what needed to be done to keep his spirit in our world.

Unaware of passing time, I at last sensed a change and knew Matoqwa's spirit was once more safely within the confines of his physical body. Death's Raven had left us. The Shining one retreated to its nest within my chest and the blackness returned. Exhausted and shivering I crawled under the blanket with him and held him gently to share my warmth.

Maybe I slept a bit, but at some point I became aware of his body tensing up and knew he was finally awake. Fearing he might cry out or start fighting me and undo the healing work the Shining One had begun I whispered next to his ear, "Lay still, you stupid dog turd, it's only me. You're safe—for the moment anyway."

"Tas?"

"Yes, it's me. Lie still now, I'm not Grandfather so the healing process has only begun," I told him.

"Hurts," he slurred through his broken teeth.

"I know—I'm sorry. I don't have Grandfather's gift to take the pain away. I have to go soon, but I need you to focus—listen to me before I go."

"W-where are we? Aiya, it hurts!"

"We are in something they call Perdition's Box. It's in a room dug into the earth below the priests' house," when he began muttering to himself I snapped, "Matoqwa, pay attention, Dog Turd, this is important!"

"All right, what?"

"My Spirit helper says I must go now or be caught, but don't worry I will come back if they don't come for you by tonight."

He started muttering about what he was going to do to that dog humper of a priest, Praiser Simms when he came back.

Growling a curse of my own, I slapped his face, just hard enough to get his attention. "You're in no condition to kill anybody. Don't undo all my hard work saving you from Death's Raven and be stupid. There will be another time—when you're strong and healed."

I slipped out from under the blanket and stood, crossing to the door. "Yesterday I overheard the director become angry with Praiser Simms because of the beatings. He's afraid Lord Bronworthy or his attorney friend will come and check on us. When they come for you pretend to be unconscious if you can. They may be rough when they take you to the Chamuqwani healing place, but I doubt if the priest will dare kill you—unless you provoke him—so don't, dog turd, don't. Think of Cohasi, eh? What's he gonna do but get himself beat up or killed if you be stupid."

I chuckled. Trying to leave him with a joke, I said, "Besides who's going to punch me and call me stupid siyatli boy if not you, eh?"

He did try to laugh, then swore at me for making his ribs hurt. As I stepped out of the box he called to me one last time. "Is Atuusca down here, too? Is he all right?"

"No, he's not down here. He's beat up, but not like you. He's back in his bed tonight. You have only the ghost down here for company. But don't listen to her; she will only want you to come join her."

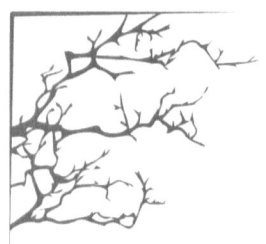

Chapter Five

I had made my way up the stairs and out into the hall when I heard them coming for him. Quickly I ran to the nearby stairs and flattened myself in its concealing shadows.

Intent on their task, Praiser Simms and Doff passed my hiding place without looking my way and stopped by the door to the room below. Closing my eyes to mere slits I watched and waited for them to descend, but they didn't.

Holding up the lantern Doff said in a low voice, "Look, Praiser, the door's unlocked."

Muttering a curse the priest hurried forward and inspected the door. "You're right."

"Who could have been here?" Doff said, a note of fear coming into his whispered voice. "If those damned reformers have discovered... Has director Harriscot seen—"

"No, you fool, and keep your voice down." yanking the door wide he hurried down the stairs, not waiting for Doff's light.

"If there's another commissioner's agent, poking around like before..."

"Shut up, you fool. Nothing to worry about, hurry up with the light, damn you. The director will find and deal with the snooping filth if there is another spy among us."

I didn't stay to hear Doff's reply. My guardian goading me to hurry I raced for the front door as soon as they had disappeared into the abyss. It was only when I was inside the school and creeping up the stairs to my bed that I remembered I'd left my blanket with Matoqwa. They were sure to discover it, and worry about who else knew about their cruelties, but it was too late to go back for it now.

Dawn was a faint gray line on the eastern horizon when I slipped into my dorm and crept down the aisle to my bed. Sitting down on the tangled sheets to take off my trousers and catch my breath, I wondered how I was going to explain my missing blanket.

They probably wouldn't consider me as the late-night visitor to their nasty little torture box—not at first anyway, but I would be in a lot of trouble with Intercessor Fredderoth if I couldn't think of something. Crystal Being wasn't going to help me out of this one, so I didn't even bother to ask. It was up to me to figure it out for myself.

Then glancing at the empty bed beside mine—Matoqwa's bed, I hastily took off his blanket and put it on mine. The sheets and pillowcase I also removed and stuffed them in Matoqwa's box. I hoped that whoever came to check on us would think that one of the servants had stripped the bed when its occupant didn't come back, assuming the boy had been moved elsewhere.

There was no time to even consider falling asleep; the intercessor or his assistant Praiser Tom, would have us up for the day and making our beds soon, so I just laid back and closed my eyes, wishing I could sleep. Time seemed to slow to a turtle's crawl as I lay listening to the snores and trying to control the trembling taking over my body. This always happened after I was used by the Unseen One's power. I just hoped I wouldn't start puking, before I could make it to the privy...

I swallowed hard. No, I wasn't going to make it.

At last I heard Yohan put some wood in the stove and Ronalton began shouting for everyone to get dressed, complete their morning tasks and get in line. Before he'd finished his first call I jumped up. As soon as I was properly dressed and my bed made I hurried for the open door.

Then someone grabbed me from behind, jerking me back. "Where do you think you are going, 297?"

Swallowing and trying hard not to spew, I met the gaze of a fuming and red-faced head boy, and choked out, "Me sick need go privy—now."

"Ronalton snorted. "No, you're not going anywhere. Get back in line and wait until it's your turn."

"No can wait. Me be sick—now!"

"Get back in line," he growled. "Stupid savage, we have to wait for the intercessor or Praiser Tom to come inspect."

He might have to wait but my body wasn't listening. When he shoved me to make his point I nearly lost my balance. As I flung my arms wide to keep from falling and then swayed back upright the contents of my stomach roared up in a disgusting gray flood that splattered to the floor at the head boy's feet.

With a startled cry Ronalton leapt backwards crashing into the wash table and setting the water jar atop it to shaking and nearly falling. Then with a roar of outrage he lunged for me.

"Here now, what's going on in here?" a new voice shouted from the doorway halting his fist in midair as he was about to pound me.

Trembling in outrage the head boy faced the man who had just entered, opening and closing his mouth several times, but the words couldn't find their way past the burning anger clogging his throat. At last he just pointed to me, and the fresh puddle of slimy vomit lying on the floor.

Sensing the presence of a war-brother at my back I straightened up. I wiped my arm across my mouth, breathing raggedly. Kuweya put a hand on my back to steady me and chuckled.

In the confusion, he murmured next to my ear, "Matoqwa was right about your puking when you use your power, eh? I saw you leave last night. Is the Bear all right, Puhani?"

"He'll live—for now. He should be where they take the sick and injured around here. Tell his brother if I can't." and then there was no more time for talking as the praiser was staring right at us.

I'd learned since coming to the school that a Praiser being of a lower rank in the God's temple than the Intercessors and the Grand-Intercessors, Praisers did a lot of the menial chores with the children that those of a higher rank didn't want to do. I learned over time that normally Praiser Tom was a cheerful but lazy man who laughed a lot, looked the other way when rules were broken, and brought the boys treats whenever he could.

He was a short round man with pale skin that turned red easily when he was joking and when he was angry—like now. "Don't make me repeat myself again. What is going on in here?"

In the silence that continued it was Kuweya who finally spoke, "Boy say him sick want go privy. Head boy say no. Say get in line." Kuweya pointed to the stinking mess on the floor. "Him sick anyway."

The praiser frowned and then came over to touch my forehead. "Hmm, your forehead is a little warm." Lifting my chin so he could look me in the eye, he asked, "How do you feel now, 297?"

I shivered, finding it hard to stare into his pale gray eyes. Like the others I'd met at the live-away school so far he had no Qwakaiva, but there was something about the man nonetheless that made me feel uneasy when I was forced to be around him.

Nervous at his continued study of me, I finally said in a weak voice that was only half a lie, "Still sick me."

"Hmm," he repeated as he thought about the matter. Finally he pointed to the dirty clothes basket in the corner. "Get something out of the basket and clean up the mess on the floor, then go sit on your bed for now and I'll take you to the infirmary after I lead the boys to morning prayers."

When everyone was gone I quickly pulled the sheets out of Matoqwa's box, used them to clean up the vomit, and then buried them in the laundry basket for a servant to take away.

THE INFIRMARY WAS A series of three narrow rooms with open doorways that connected one to the next without a person needing to go back into the main hall. There was one room for the boys another for the girls and a smaller third room in which the doctor and his mercy women helpers examined and treated the sick and injured. The two rooms for sick children contained a row of beds similar to those in the dorm rooms upstairs.

Praiser Tom led me through the doctor's examining room. When we entered the boys sick room I was surprised to see that several of the beds were already occupied. In the bed farthest from the door we had entered a tall thin man with bushy eyebrows in a white priest's robe was bending over someone, next to him stood a mercy woman with a white apron over her green robe. She held a metal basin in which the white robed priest was rinsing a bloody cloth and muttering angry words to himself.

"Hey, Doc, gotta 'nother one for ya," the praiser called as he directed me to sit on the side of an unoccupied bed.

The one called doc stiffened and turned to face us, scowling. "Is he really sick or just beaten up by Praiser Simms and his thugs like this one?" returning his attention to the youth he was treating, probably Matoqwa, Doc told the mercy woman to empty her basin and bring him more clean water.

"No, he's just sick," Praiser said, "This boy here woke up this morning and threw up all over the dorm room floor." Letting out a hearty laugh, he added, "And he hadn't even eaten any of Cooks burnt mush today, so he must be truly sick."

Taking a good look at me as he walked over, Doc frowned when he caught sight of my tribal tattoos. "He's one of the new ones the director has been grumbling about, isn't he?" he motioned to my face. "Why would anyone disfigure a child's face like that? The western barbarians are a truly disgusting race. The world will be a lot better when they are all dead."

"Mm, that's what the director and Intercessor Fredderoth think, too," the praiser agreed.

"How many more of them are scarred like this one?"

"One or two others, I don't remember exactly," he pointed to Kunai's mark on my jaw, "but he is the worst of the lot." Praiser Tom chuckled. Including Doc in his humor, he added still laughing, "His parents must have really hated him to burden him with a face like that."

No, my parents loved me very much dog turd of a Chamuqwani. I belong to the Qwani'Ya and Kukiya peoples and I am proud to wear my loyalties plain for all to see, I thought to myself and allowed their ignorant hateful words to flow away, like water off a seal's oily fur.

"Hope these barbaric heathens haven't brought a new plague of the spotted fever with them," Doc muttered as if talking to himself.

"Oh, he's probably not that bad. Just a bit nervous about being here in a new place got his stomach all unsettled," Praiser Tom offered.

Doc grunted and motioned for me to open my mouth. "Does he speak a civilized tongue?"

The praiser shrugged. "Not well, but he gets by. He's one of the quieter ones among our new charges. He shouldn't give you any trouble." The praiser said and patted my shoulder.

Doc gave me a quick exam, poking and prodding many places on my belly and chest. Then he gave me a chalky white liquid to swallow that tasted terrible, and then told me to get under the blanket, lie down and try to rest.

I needed no more persuasion than that. I was hungry and exhausted and welcomed the prospect of sleep and escape into my dreams.

During the rest of that day people came and went in the room around me, but I paid them little attention. Someone in a bed further down the row had a bad cough that woke me up now and then, and I heard 241 asking a mercy woman for a drink, but mostly I slept. I only woke enough to use the piss bucket and drink a cup of broth when a mercy woman offered it to me and then I went right back to sleep.

Once or twice a priest I didn't know came in to pray over us, but his words became just distorted fragments of a troubling dream.

DURING THE NIGHT I awoke clear headed and rested, my empty stomach growling in protest. With eyes nearly closed I pretended to sleep while I decided if it would be safe for me to check on Matoqwa and then hunt for food. Most of the room lay in shadow with light coming in from a lamp burning in the hall outside the sick room. Beside me there were three other occupied beds illuminated by the dim light.

None of the priests or mercy women were here, but in the girls' dorm next to us I could hear a young girl whimpering and coughing and a mercy woman trying to make her drink some bad tasting medicine. Finally the sick girl settled and the woman on duty for the night retreated, taking her light with her.

I waited a bit longer until I was sure she wasn't coming back anytime soon, then rose and crept to Matoqwa's bed. His Guardian Bear watched my approach with a wary attention unsure whether to snarl. In the dim light I could make out little but pale bandages covering much of his head and face. Studying him with my Gift I saw the pain lines still radiating outward in his Spirit Fire. Perhaps the Bear had warned him, because he was awake and staring at me when I crouched beside the bed and took his hand, allowing some of crystal's Qwakaiva to flow into him to aid his recovery.

"Tas, is that you? What are you doing here?" he mumbled, his voice slurred by some medicine Doc or the mercy women had given him.

"Yes, it's just me," I murmured. "Just wanted to check on you."

"How did you get in here?"

I snorted a soft laugh. "I've been here all day, lying in a bed over there. I puked on that dog turd Ronalton's feet yesterday morning and the praiser decided I was sick and brought me here to see Doc."

Knowing I really wasn't sick, only recovering from the use of my Gift, Matoqwa snorted then chuckled at the images my words made in his mind. "I would have liked to see that."

"Yes it was pretty funny," I agreed.

Noticing a nearly full bowl of cold mush on the little table beside his bed my stomach rumbled. He saw me eyeing it and said, "Go ahead eat it if you want."

I hesitated, then asked, "I can help you if you want me to feed you."

"No, dog turd, I don't want you to feed me. I'm no baby and I'm not that bad off. Eat the disgusting shit if you want it."

Well, he was that bad off, actually. One arm was broken, two of his ribs were cracked, he'd lost a couple teeth, and there'd been bleeding inside his skull that my crystal helper had had to heal. I could sense he still had a bad headache and his nose was broken again, but he was on the mend.

I needed no other urging, took the bowl and wolfed down the gluey mess. When I'd finished I picked up the pitcher and poured some water into the cup. "Want a drink then?"

He licked his dry lips and weakly nodded. I poured him a cup and helped him to sit up while he drank it. When he'd had all he wanted I drained the last of the pitcher into the cup for myself.

"In the morning Doc will probably send me back to our dorm so I won't be here to check on you, so behave. I'll let Cohasi know you are healing, so don't worry about him. I will sneak back to check on you, if, and when, I can."

He grunted, and I could see his eyes starting to close, so I rose and stepped away, leaving him to rest.

As I was creeping back to my own bed I heard someone whisper my name. "T-Tas, is that really you?"

I froze. That voice had come from one of the other occupied beds in the room. But it wasn't 241, because whoever it was had spoken to me in my own language, not Chamuqwani.

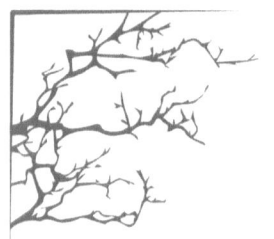

Chapter Six

There was a cough then the speaker repeated himself, "Tas?"

Retracing my steps I stopped by a bed nearly across from the now sleeping Matoqwa. A boy about my own age with short dark hair and pale skin was raised up on an elbow and staring at me. Studying him with my Gift I could see that there was something familiar about him, but in the dim light I couldn't see his features clear enough to recognize who it was.

He started to say my name again, coughed, and groped for a cup on the little table beside him. He missed the cup, and nearly knocked it to the floor instead. I hurried to catch it then handed it to him. As he took it from me and drank I got a better look at him.

"Kutima? Is that you?"

"Kutima... It feels so good to hear my true name again. Yes, it's me, but don't call me that where others can hear you. My Chamuqwani name is Keveneth Jobonnington. You can call me Keveneth, or use my number 168. I don't want you to get into trouble by saying my Qwani'Ya name."

I held up my disk for him to see. "I will try and remember. My number is 297, but you can also still call me Tas." When he widened his eyes, I explained, "Yes, it's true. The Chamuqwani name written in the director's big book is Tassele Cougarson—Tas."

He let out a phlegmy laugh and sipped the liquid. "I thought I was dreaming of home when I heard your voice speaking our language, but when I opened my eyes I wasn't sure if it was you or just a part of the dream. You look very different than what I remember."

In a way his words were a relief; maybe the Celibress wouldn't recognize me—either—if I was careful. Back home at Big Ice Lake Kutima's father had been the head Chamuqwani trader at the post where we traded our fish and furs, before miners from the empire found gold on our land and we had to leave.

I laughed softly. "Well, I'm taller for certain." I pointed to the Tattoos on my cheeks and jaw. "Amima married a Kukiya war leader on the Preserve and he adopted me as his son."

"Oh, Tas, I'm so glad for you and her. How is your family doing? Did they send you to Saint Yon's for your education?"

How was my family? I had to swallow hard before I could continue. "They didn't send me to this school. Mother and my new father are both dead now, as is my Grandfather and so many others from Big Ice Lake who marched south to the Tribal Preserve." Not wanting to open the scars of my grief any further I decided to change the subject.

I needed to get back to my bed before we were discovered. We could find a quiet place to talk more later. "But what about you; why are you in the sick room?"

Kutima shrugged. "It's just a bit of a cough. It comes and goes. Been that way—ever since I came here."

"And, what are you doing in this Chamuqwani prison for children anyway? "

"Prison for children," he snorted, "I never thought of Saint Yon's in that way, but I think you have the right of it, Tas, my old friend."

"So why are you here? I thought—"

"My mother died the winter after the People left Big Ice Lake and father... All the miners—it was terrible there when the People left. Father didn't want to stay when mother was gone. His boss, Lord Hyrum, transferred him to another post—and he couldn't take me with him." Kutima shrugged. "Saint Yon's has a good reputation, so he sent me here."

"I'm sorry to hear about your mother. She was always kind to us boys." Kutima just nodded and I could sense the sadness welling up at the mention of her. "How long have you been here?"

"Too long," he said bitterly.

"What about Jombonni? Does your father come visit you at least?"

Kutima hesitated then admitted, "No, he's too far away to visit, and he can't leave his new wife and my baby brother to come so far. But he writes to me and asks how I'm doing. When I finish school he will likely have me come work with him."

I heard the desperate longing in his voice, but I doubted if his wish would come true. I patted his arm as I rose. My crystal was warning me I had to go. "Someone is coming; I need to get back to my bed. Keep strong and get well soon. You're not alone here now. And as Cohasi keeps reminding me us boys from Big Ice Lake gotta stick together."

"Cohasi is here with you? What about Samiqwas—who else?"

"Samiqwas is still running free with Uncle Tli and the rest of the outlaws as far as I know." I pointed with my lips to the bed across the aisle. "Matoqwa is right over there, you probably didn't recognize him either."

"No I didn't. I heard Doc muttering about Praiser Simms harsh disciplines, but I didn't realize it was someone I knew."

"Simms... that one will be lucky if he lives through the winter." Kutima's eyes widened at that. I quickly shut my mouth. I doubted if the other sick children in these rooms heard or understood me, but I had no wish to take a chance of someone figuring out that my war-brothers and I would find a way to take vengeance on the cruel man.

"Matoqwa's pretty beat up so he will be in here for a while, but they will send me back to my dorm tomorrow I suspect. Keep a watch on him for me will you. I'll try to come visit both of you when I can."

NEXT MORNING I WAS correct that the doctor wasn't going to allow me to laze around in one of his beds for another day. After Doc's hasty exam one of the mercy women had me up and dressed once more in my day clothes. Out in the hall I was just in time to join the line of boys heading to the temple for the morning prayers.

As we took our places in the back row Cohasi managed to slip into the space next to me. I met his troubled eyes and then bowed my head. Placing my hands together as if in prayer, so our guards couldn't see my lips move, I murmured in a voice barely above a whisper, "Don't worry he will be all right if he doesn't do anything else stupid. He is badly wounded and in a lot of pain, but he will heal."

Copying my gesture, he asked, "Where are the dog humpers keeping him? The head convert piece of shit in my dorm room has been taunting me, telling me my brother is buried in some kind of box in the earth."

"Perdition Box," I corrected, "and he *was* there. In the priests' house there is an underground jail where they sometimes put the children. I found him wounded in a cell last night when I searched with my Gift, but he isn't there anymore. Now he is in a place for sick children the priests call infirmary. That's where the praiser took me when I puked on the head boy's feet after using my Qwakaiva to help the Bear.

"When I left infirmary this morning I saw the Chamuqwani healer give him a tea for the pain and he was sleeping, so be at peace in your heart."

He would have liked to ask me more questions, but I turned away and refused to answer. We were beginning to attract the attention of Intercessor Fredderoth and I had no wish to be put in the box myself for breaking the rules by talking during prayers.

After the morning meal I was sent back to the barn to help with the animals and I was able to find a quiet moment to give him and the others more information about our wounded brother.

MATOQWA REMAINED IN the place for sick children for almost a moon. I checked on him nearly every day with my string and I visited him late at night whenever I could to share with him stolen food and my power. His broken bones were healing well enough, but the blows inflicted on his head were slower to mend. He still suffered from terrible headaches and that troubled me most of all.

Sometimes he reluctantly admitted that he would fall when the dizziness overcame him unexpectedly while on his way to or from the privy.

I wished, not for the first time, that I had Grandfather's gift. With my Qwakaiva I could help him only so much. I prayed it would be enough. While working around the barn or out in the fields helping with the harvest I looked for plants I'd seen Grandfather collect. Maybe when he got out of the sick room I could steal a big can from the dump and collect them for a healing tea.

Cohasi was worried about his long absence, of course, in spite of my constant reassurances. He begged me to take him with me on one of my night visits, but I refused. He had no Qwakaiva to conceal himself and might get us sent to that evil perdition box if we were discovered.

I did, however, manage to talk to Celibress Dinana when next I was ordered to help with laundry. Fortunately, Cohasi too was assigned to help by chopping wood for us that day.

When I emptied my last bucket into a full washtub I saw that Celibress Dinana was standing alone, drinking a cup of tea and watching two older girls hang clothes on the ropes strung out between the school and the bath house. I walked over to her and in my halting Chamuqwani I managed to explain. "Brother of that boy," using my hand in the Chamuqwani way I pointed to Cohasi, chopping wood nearby, "him bad hurt. Him stay infirm-a-ry long-long time. 305 him worried 'bout brother. Him worry, want see brother. You take see maybe?"

"What? As of this morning there is only one sick boy in the infirmary. He has been here a long time—and his brother is only a baby. There are no new boys sick that I've heard of."

Interesting. Was the director keeping Matoqwa's beating a secret even from the workers here? Hmm...

"Him no sick," I insisted. "Him beat up—bad."

She frowned in thought. "Who is this boy?"

"Don't know him number. Him name Petrous Blueshirt."

I don't recall any new student with that name. Are you sure, 297?"

I pointed to Cohasi again. "That one Thonny Blueshirt. Boy beat up him brother, him worried."

Lowering my voice I stepped closer. "First day we come Petrous angry. Praiser Simms and Doff angry, too. Praiser beat up. Boy bad hurt." I pointed to my head, then pointed to arm and ribs and repeated, "Bad hurt. Him no sick."

When I mentioned Praiser Simms, for just a moment I saw the fear come into her eyes, quickly masked by an expression of suspicion.

"How do you know this? What's really going on? Are you trying to get you and your friend out of work today?"

I shook my head vigorously. "No. Want work me. 305 want work—no lazy zaunk him. Him just worry. Me worry too." I shrugged and dropped my eyes. I feared I had gone too far and given myself away. Of course she was wondering how I knew about Matoqwa when no one who didn't work in the infirmary knew about the beating.

Her mouth was still a thin hard line, as she continued to study me. I felt the first tremor of fear twist in my gut. I wasn't sure she believed me. I should have kept my big mouth shut, even if I was worried sick that Cohasi would go off on his own and do something stupid—like his brother.

In the past I'd never considered myself a leader, but it was becoming clear to me ever since our capture that my war-brothers looked to me for protection and guidance—for the moment anyway. And I in turn felt responsible for them and valued their trust.

"How do you know about this boy?" the Celibress demanded, focusing me back on the present situation.

I shrugged. When she was still not satisfied I pointed to my eyes. "Me see fight with head boy in dorm room. Praiser and Doff come, beat on brother. Head boy say put in per-disi-on box. Boy no come back in..." I held up my hands with eight fingers extended.

"Me see hurt boy when sick—puke on dorm floor. Me see when go infirm-a-ry with Praiser Tom. Sick boys when come back dorm say boy still bad hurt." I shrugged, hoping my expression conveyed a mixture of innocence and pleading.

I was saved further questioning when Praiser Tom showed up and called to her. She gave me a last searching look and then walked away to speak to him.

I guessed the Celibress asked Praiser Tom or someone else about Matoqwa, because that evening Praiser Tom took Cohasi to the infirmary for a short visit with his brother. Next morning as we were mucking out the horses stalls Cohasi told me about the visit, and then he surprised me by thanking me.

Later that day I got another surprise when Kutima showed up in our dorm room just before the nightly prayers. It seems his regular bed at the school was next to Kuweya in the row across from me. Hoping not to attract attention to himself he had quietly slipped in while everyone was doing their evening chores and getting ready for bed.

When he showed up with a bundle of fresh sheets in his arms I smiled and offered a greeting, but he dropped his eyes and didn't acknowledge me, just continued to tuck in his sheets and spread his blanket. I must admit I was a bit hurt and maybe a little angry, but soon enough I understood why, using my Gift I saw the swirling colors in his Spirit Fire that spoke of both dread and hopeless suffering.

Wanting to understand his strange behavior I continued to observe him out of the corner of my eye as I dressed for bed. My old friend was nervous, constantly glancing over his shoulder at the group surrounding the head boy gathered by the woodstove, talking loudly and warming themselves before climbing into their cold beds.

Finally someone at the edge of the group must have noticed the newcomer in our midst and told Ronalton. After a whispered conversation the head boy and his friends left the warmth of the fire and headed in Kutima's direction.

I had finished my preparations for bed and was sitting on my blanket, ignoring everyone. Pretending just to be waiting for one of the priests to come in and lead us in our nightly prayers I idly played with my string. I'd formed the pattern of the Aseutl's Gift, planning to check on Uncle Tli and the outlaws, but I changed my mind when I saw them heading in Kutima's direction.

Out of the corner of my eye I saw Ronalton and his pack of scavenging dogs surround my old friend. Suddenly the sense of terror was so strong in the air I could almost taste it.

Kutima glanced up as Ronalton dropped a heavy bag on his bed barely missing the hand he was using to tuck in the last corner of his blanket. When Kutima stood, saw his tormentors and shrank away from them, Ronalton smirked. "Hello, Drudge, have a nice holiday, hmm?"

"It w-wasn't a holiday. I-I was sick." He coughed to emphasize his point. "I was sick," he repeated. "Doc Tomkins said so."

Yohan snorted a laugh and some of the others joined in. "Sure you were. Lazy zaunk! You were probably just trying to get out of work, that's all," he scoffed.

"N-no I was sick."

"Well, you're not sick now—so don't try to lie—Doc sent you back to the dorms." Ronalton pointed to the bag lying on Kutima's blanket. "Here's my last three homework assignments. Get to work."

"I can't. Praiser Tom or the intercessor will be here any minute for prayers. He will catch me and I can't go back to the Box. I'm still recovering—"

The rest of his protests were cut off as Ronalton drew back his fist and punched him. With a strangled cry Kutima doubled over clutching at his stomach. He pointed to the window behind Kutima's bed that had been closed for the night. "Open the window after the prayers. There's plenty of moonlight to see by to finish my assignments."

"Please, n-no," Kutima stammered. "I can't; it's too cold at night this time of year. I might get sick again—or the little ones," he pointed to the younger boys like 241 in the beds near his. "Please—maybe tomorrow."

"They're due tomorrow. I need them done tonight, you stupid drudge!" Ronalton shouted.

I'd seen and heard enough. Though not a war-brother exactly; he was a Qwani'Ya friend from home, and as Cohasi reminded me, "Us boys from Big Ice Lake gotta stick together."

Smiling to myself I plucked a string in my pattern.

In the woodstove a spark leapt out of the improperly closed lid and hopped onto the head boy's nearby bed. Hungry it burrowed deep, causing the wool to scorch and smoke, then burst into flames.

As Ronalton raised his hand for another strike one of the younger boys sitting on his own bed cried out and pointed. Leaving off his torment of Kutima Ronalton swore and raced for the water pitcher, just as Intercessor Fredderoth stepped into the room.

I wondered if the head boy enjoyed his paddling and his comfortable stay in the Perdition Box that followed the uproar that night.

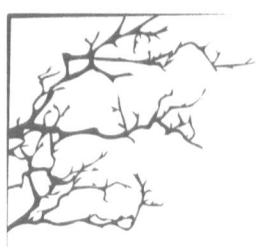

Chapter Seven

Next morning it was a snarling Yohan and Praiser Tom who got us up and ready for the day. Ronalton was still absent, either in the box or the infirmary. I didn't know—or care as long as he couldn't hurt anyone or cause more trouble.

Later in the afternoon when our chores were done and most of the children were either outside playing a ball game or quietly working on their school assignments, I was wandering through the school portion of the second floor, looking for a quiet place to hide when I happened to glance in an empty classroom and saw Kutima.

He was sitting alone at a table his head bent in concentration over a school book. I recognized the book bag as belonging to Ronalton and that annoyed me, which is why I chose to go in and talk to him. In spite of all my efforts to avoid this, he was doing the dog turd's work for him anyway.

He never even noticed me until I placed a hand on his arm as I sat down beside him. At my touch he jumped as if a bee had stung him, his eyes growing wide with fear. When he saw it was only me he relaxed somewhat, his attention returning in the next moment to the book spread open before him. "Oh, hi, Tas. I can't talk now I have to finish—"

Returning my hand to the page, I said, "No you don't have to finish. Let the smelly fish guts do his own work."

Before I stopped speaking Kutima was shaking his head again, the fear coming back into his eyes. "You're new here, so maybe you don't understand. I do have to do this, because if I don't he will—"

"No, my friend, I think maybe it's you who doesn't understand. I'm not going to let Ronalton and his mangy dogs hurt you—or the others anymore."

Kutima let out a mirthless laugh and removed my hand from the book. "You can't stop them—no one can—I've tried."

There was such a note of hopeless resignation in his voice that it tore at my heart and made me say something dangerous. "Kutima, look at me—really look at me." When he met my eye, I pointed to the dragon glyph on my jaw, and said, "Can't stop them, are you sure about that?"

I let my words sink in for a long moment, before I continued, "I think back home when you listened to all the rumours going around the village about me, you probably knew more about my origins than I did myself." I tapped the glyph again. "Well, that's not true now. I have met my Qwa'Nayhi Seal father and pledged my service to the Great Kunai. So, when I tell you that Ronalton won't bother you anymore, I mean just that."

I saw the realization come into his eyes as he figured out what that meant, followed almost immediately by a return of his fear. Trying to ease his mind with a joke I smiled. "Besides, didn't I tell you back in the sick room that all us boys from Big Ice Lake got to stick together, hmm?"

My attempt at a joke must have fallen short; he still seemed agitated as he interrupted, "Yes but there's only you and maybe Cohasi. Matoqwa is still too ill to beat anybody up—and those brothers never liked me much anyway. They won't help me—"

"Are you sure about that?" I repeated. I looked him rudely in the eye till he lowered his gaze back to the page in front of him. "You are wrong about the brothers. Back home they picked on everybody—me most of all—if you recall. But things are different now.

"And, you are also wrong that there are only two of us; there are actually nine young warriors imprisoned here with you now."

"Nine? I haven't seen nine Qwani'Ya—"

"Not all from Big Ice Lake or down the Socanna River, true enough, but my Kukiya war-brothers will stand at my back—if I ask them—and I will. You aren't alone here anymore—I promise you that."

He opened his mouth to answer me when a cool voice from the doorway made both of us freeze in place. Glancing over my shoulder I saw Celibress Dinana standing there, a scowl on her lips, her green eyes giving me a stern glare. No longer having Rattlesnake to alert me of danger I mentally kicked myself for my lapse of attention to my surroundings.

"When I passed by just now I thought I heard someone speaking a heathen tongue. What are you doing in here, bothering this boy, 297? He is studying."

"He wasn't bothering me, Celibress, Tas is from my home," Kutima hastily said. "He just wanted—"

Groping for Kutima's Chamuqwani name I suddenly heard myself saying, "Me see Keveneth, Me want learn read in book. Me ask him teach."

I had surprised her so much that she'd forgotten for the moment about hearing us speak in our language. Well, I had surprised myself, too, and formed a question to the shining one I carried within for the answer.

<<Learning to read the enemy's script will be a useful weapon for you in the future,>> the crystal being replied.

"Hmm…" she studied me carefully judging the sincerity of my proposal. At last she said, "The proper way to say that is, 'I want to learn to read. Will you please teach me.' Say it right this time."

I repeated the words after her until she was satisfied with my efforts. "I will speak to Director Harriscot tomorrow on your behalf. If you or any of the new boys want to learn to read, we should be encouraging that. And, I think it's very noble of you, 168, to want to help your friend."

As she reached over to pat his shoulder she happened to notice the notebook of problems Kutima had been working on. Snatching up the book she ignored his half-hearted protests and studied the writing, then laid the book back down on the table with a slap. "This isn't your assignment, 168, what are you doing with this?"

"I-I was just trying to help the head boy in our dorm," Kutima stammered, "so he won't fall behind—"

"Yes, I heard about 47's punishment, and you know better than to try and help him. You have been warned before—"

"Head boy say him beat up 168 if no do work." I interrupted and pointed to the work in question. I couldn't help the mischievous smile that wanted to curve the corners of my lips. Under the table Kutima gave me a hard kick. I had just wanted to help, but I saw his hands shake before he put them out of sight in his lap. He was terrified and to my surprise, didn't welcome my interference.

Turning back to my friend she demanded, "Is this true?"

Kutima dropped his eyes and swallowed hard, but under her continued glare he finally admitted, "Yes—sometimes, but I really don't mind helping him—not really."

"Why didn't you tell me, or one of the intercessors if you were being bullied or threatened?"

Still with his head down, unable to meet her eyes he said, "I told Intercessor Fredderoth. He said he would look into it."

"And, what happened?"

Kutima shrugged. "The head boy said I was lying and the intercessor believed him." Unconsciously Kutima began to stroke the bent little finger on his right hand that I hadn't noticed before.

Celibress Dinana noticed the gesture and her mouth hardened into a thin line. "I see. Well, it seems I will have more than one topic to speak to the director about in the morning."

She was a nice person—though seemingly ignorant of the undercurrents of evil churning in the dark recesses of this place. A part of me wanted to warn her, but I chose to keep my mouth shut this time. I was too new here, and maybe Kutima was right; maybe I didn't understand. So, until I swam the waters of the school and discovered the hidden snags waiting below the surface to entrap the unwary myself, I would tread water and observe—or so I promised myself.

And then we were all saved any further comment when the temple bell chimed for everyone to line up for the evening prayers. Ignoring Kutima's reproachful glare, I patted his shoulder, and murmured. "Don't worry. It will be all right. You are one of us now." Still shaking his head with disbelief, Kutima moved away from me.

When we arrived at the temple, he ignored me and took his place on the bench near the front set aside for the good students. I let him go, but when I took my seat next to my war-brothers I touched Kuweya's hand and when I had his attention I pointed with my lips to Kutima just sitting down several rows ahead of us.

"That breed-boy is friend from back home. Tell the others he is a brother now, too, and under my protection so we watch out for him, eh?"

Next morning when Kutima was washing up Ronalton and his gang surrounded him. The head boy demanded his finished homework and Kutima got a better idea of how things had changed overnight in our dorm.

"I c-couldn't finish it. Celibress Dinana took—"

As Ronalton raised his hand to hit him he suddenly froze. Ensnared in a loop of my power I watched his eyes grow wide as he tried to struggle free, but remained as frozen as a block of ice in the lake. Yohan stared at him curiously, but I had stuffed his mouth as well, so he was unable to speak. Only his frightened eyes betrayed his distress.

Before he got too frightened I let him go. He took a deep breath and glared at Kutima, but my friend seemed as wide eyed and scared as the head boy was himself. Yohan asked him a question, which he ignored and stomped away without answering. And then Praiser Tom was in the doorway and no more was said about the incident.

<<Watch yourself,>> my inner companion warned. <<It is in your nature to help those who are weak and vulnerable, but if you are discovered you may still burn for the witch they will believe you are.>>

TRUE TO HER WORD CELIBRESS Dinana did speak to the director on our behalf about learning to read. After the noon meal that day a sour-faced Praiser Simms told us to report to the classrooms on the second floor to begin our reading lessons.

"This doesn't mean you'll get out of work if you agree to do this," he growled. "I will expect you to complete your tasks in the barns and the fields just as before so don't think you are getting away with something."

I'm not sure if it was through ignorance or by design, but the classroom we were shown to, was the one set aside for the youngest students in the school. For some among us this was a heavy blow to their budding warriors' pride. I knew they weren't going to last long here, and so when we were all working in the fields later that afternoon I managed to speak to everyone to try and convince them to stick it out for a while.

"I know it's insulting, but my spirit helpers say it is a good thing, so please try. Learning the enemy's magic of reading and writing is just another weapon we can use against them in the future," I argued.

There was a lot of grumbling about it, but even the angriest, like Komonti agreed to try it for a while—if for no other reason than to annoy Praiser Simms.

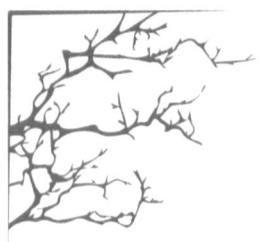

Chapter Eight

When Moon was nearing her fullness, Matoqwa was sent back to us. With a splinted arm and bandages wrapped around his head, he still looked a bit shaky on his feet, though he growled that he was fine if anyone but me or Cohasi dared to ask. Next day when he came to check on his patient, I happen to hear Doc warning Praiser Simms to go easy on the Bear, because he still had a lot of healing to do. A suggestion Simms ignored as soon as the doctor returned to the infirmary.

I'm not sure what was wrong with the man, but over the coming days he seemed to take a special delight in tormenting the Bear with tasks he knew would be nearly impossible to manage with his injuries, and then teasing him mercilessly when he was unable to complete the assignment without help.

In spite of the director's warnings maybe Simms was hoping Matoqwa would explode and lash out so he would have an excuse to beat on him again, and this time make the Bear's stay underground permanent.

I warned my war-brother several times that this was the dog fart's game, and I know he listened—tried to hold his temper, but it was hard; it was so against his nature. On more than one occasion I used my Gift to glue his mouth closed when he looked like he couldn't hold himself back any longer.

Unfortunately on the day everything exploded I wasn't near enough to prevent trouble. I was in the orchard with a work crew made up of older children from the school and a few Chamuqwani from the town to supervise our efforts. We were singing together as we collected the last of summer's juicy apples. As I picked I moved further away from the group to a place deeper among the trees that hadn't been harvested yet.

Inishkim, who was with me that day saw me edging away from the others and slowly began harvesting in my direction, maybe thinking I had a great escape plan in mind I needed quiet to talk to him about. But in truth I was only looking for a safe hide-away where I could put a few nice fat apples that I could later retrieve to share with my war-brothers and some of the sick ones.

Then one of the older girls, who I thought liked my war-brother, ran over to tell Inishkim and me about Praiser Sims attack on Matoqwa.

"There's trouble," she said in a breathless whisper, pointing towards the big barn across the hay field. "The workmen from the village helping pick the apples are saying that it's one of your brothers being 'disciplined' again."

Now that she'd brought it to my attention I could hear the shouting coming from the barn area that hadn't surfaced into my awareness until that moment. Inishkim and I exchanged a troubled look. Matoqwa, Cohasi and Komonti had been assigned to clean out horse stalls in the barn this morning. One or more of them must be in trouble—and I guessed Matoqwa would be right in the middle of it.

The girl, 187, was watching Inishkim with sparkling dark eyes, her expression both adoring and expectant, and probably wondering what he planned to do next. With full lips and skin a warm honey brown she was pretty, tall and slim, her breasts just starting to show the bloom of her maturing woman's body under the loose ugly clothes all the girls were made to wear. I knew my war-brother liked her, too. He had whispered to me of wanting to run away with her and make a life for them back in the desert among our outlaw relatives.

Ignoring her Inishkim glanced at me and I saw the fear in his eyes—and shared it. "Go," I murmured and touched the braided cord I'd taken to wearing around my neck under my shirt. He knew what I meant. I would see what I could do to help with my Gift. I had no need to risk going over there. "Do what you can to help, but be careful."

Inishkim gave me a slight nod and took the girl's arm. As he led her away she turned and asked, "Aren't you coming, 297? He's your brother, too isn't he?"

Cousin actually, but who's quibbling. I merely made a shoeing motion and smiled. "Me stay pick apples. Praiser be angry everybody go. No want go box me." She gave me a disgusted glare and allowed Inishkim to hurry her across the orchard.

When they were gone I took off my pack-basket, set it by the tree, and then moved away into the taller grass growing at the edge of the hay field.

Within the grasses concealment I sat and bent my head and arms over my lap so I couldn't be seen. To my surprise a little brown spider hopped onto my hand and began crawling up my arm.

<<Hello, little sister, will you watch for me while I use my Gift to try and help my war-brother?>>

<<I will watch if you hunt some fat beetles for me and my eggs,>> she bargained.

<<Gladly, when I finish here.>> Taking off my string, I hastily formed the pattern of the Aseutl's gift and peered into the center diamond, searching for Matoqwa and my war-brothers.

As I focused my intent it didn't take long for the images to form in the center. While I had been occupied picking fruit this morning two wagons loaded with winter firewood had unexpectedly arrived early at the school. My three war-brothers as well as Yohan and two more of Ronalton's mangy dogs were the crew assigned to help in the barn that morning, so when the wagon arrived the praiser or Doff must have ordered everyone to stop other chores and help the Chamuqwani unload the wood, and then restack it under the roofed area just off the school kitchen.

Some of this I learned later because all I could see at first was a shouting group of men and boys clustered about someone on the ground near the back of the first wagon. Praiser Simms stood over the figure with a raised whip in hand.

I didn't need to see the one huddled on the ground, trying to protect his bloody face to know it was Matoqwa. Quickly scanning the scene for Cohasi I saw Atuusca holding him over by the kitchen wood pile. Doff, his own whip in hand, was glaring at the tall youth nearby, as if warning Komonti to stay out of it, or he would join his war-brother in the mud.

Atop the wagon just behind Praiser Simms a burly workman stood frozen in place with a heavy round of wood cradled in his arms. He was staring with an open mouth, astounded by the violence he was witnessing.

Through the Qwakaiva swirling in the center diamond I felt the whip's next blow as if it had lashed across my own flesh. I wasn't sure what the Bear had done—if anything—to provoke Simms's rage, but I knew instinctively that I had to stop this or Matoqwa would die.

"The lad's arm is broke, Praiser. He couldn't help it that he dropped that big piece—it was too heavy to lift with just one working hand. Stop it, damn ya, STOP!" I heard him cry in disgust as Simms continued with his bloody work.

When I touched his mind ensnared within the pattern I sensed that this workman hated to see such cruelties, remembering similar whippings done to him by angry relatives in his youth. The Chamuqwani's arms holding the big chunk of wood were getting tired. To my surprise he gave me his silent agreement to help with my plan when I asked....

And so, as Simms raised the whip the next time, I plucked a loop in the pattern surrounding the inner diamond. A large red whelp blossomed on the workman's arm as if he had just been stung by a horsefly or a wasp. Insects of this nature were always flying around the animals and it wasn't cold enough that day for them to be sleeping in their nests. My ploy was beyond suspicion and believable.

I made the bite painful enough to cause the man to jerk back in surprise. I planned only a distraction, something to stop Simms from his murderous purpose, but I got much more than that. I wasn't unhappy with the results of my meddling, though it could have cost me dearly if a quick-thinking Inishkim hadn't been there.

As the man let out a startled cry, lost his balance and fell to his knees, the large round he'd been holding was suddenly hurled onto the remaining wood. The unbalance pile trembled as the log struck, and with another nudge from me the entire load started to roll to the edge of the open wagon and fall off onto the ground.

And, Praiser Simms was right in the path of the descending avalanche. The first of the cascading rounds caught him behind the legs, dropping him to his knees. The rest of the heavy load bounded out of the wagon bed, many of the pieces flattening him to the mud and then burying him under their weight.

Not understanding all the consequences that my meddling with the pattern might have, I suddenly realized that Matoqwa, too, was in the path of that lethal torrent. Fortunately, for both of us, Inishkim and his girlfriend were and the group watching by then, and had the quick wits to pull Matoqwa away from the worst of it.

Simms wasn't so lucky, however. Nearly buried under the wood he was alive, but unconscious. While still watching from within the Pool I made the decision to meddle one last time. Like when I used my Gift to pick open a locked room I focused my Qwakaiva and sank my awareness into the core of his injured spine and pulled. There was a distinct crack that I heard in my mind and the cord holding his bones together severed.

He might live, if his god favored him, but he would never use a whip to punish a child, or even walk again. I hoped his life would become the living hell into which he had condemned so many others over the years.

Allowing my string to slide off my hands as a wave of dizziness overtook me, I thanked the little brown spider for her watchfulness. When the feeling passed I caught her several fat beetles for her trouble before I left the hayfield.

I knew I deserved more than a cramped stomach in future for my bungling of this day's work, that so easily could have become a tragedy if it wasn't for another's quick thinking.

Berating myself for not foreseeing all possible outcomes before changing the Pattern with my Qwakaiva I retrieved my apple basket and headed out of the orchard. I wasn't worried about being punished for abandoning my harvesting by then. Most everyone had left, drawn to the chaos by the barn like moths to a flame.

When I arrived I emptied my apples into the big bin waiting there. But with everyone's attention focused elsewhere I was able to conceal nearly half the basket's contents in a hollow I'd dug into the far side of the bath house where the dirt had been mounded up to protect the wooden wall from the rot caused by the drains.

Before I went to stack my now empty basket with the others, I used my Gift like a sent marker to keep the mice or other animals from bothering my cache. The apples would stay safe for a while that way. Though I hoped I could retrieve them soon. I would cut one up for Matoqwa and both Kutima and 241 were coughing again....

Dusting off my hands when I finished I quietly took my place among my war-brothers. Each time the school doors opened a new influx of onlookers joined the milling throng gathering around the wagons. Children were frightened and crying and many of the mercy women and priests were praying to their god to save the praiser.

The ones crowded around Praiser Simms' body, still covered over with wood, were loudly arguing what to do with him. Some wanted to remove the wood and carry him into the infirmary, while others claimed he should stay where he was until the messenger sent to the village to bring back Doc, had time to return.

No one in charge was paying any attention to the bleeding and also injured Matoqwa. Fortunately Inishkim and Cohasi managed to drag the injured bear away from the Chaos. He was sitting propped up on a mound of straw against the barn wall when I came up to them.

187 had dampened a part of her shawl and was wiping the blood on his face as she cooed to him like he was an injured younger sibling. And wonder of wonders, he was not growling, but letting her do it—enjoying her attentions maybe.

Crouching beside him, I took his hand. When he felt my crystal's Qwakaiva flowing into his wounds, he turned to look at me. "I'm all right, Siyatli Dog Turd—or I will be, if that damned Chamuqwani dog humper will ever leave me alone."

I chuckled and continued to pour the crystal being's gift into his injuries. "He won't be taking the whip to anyone—for a long time—if ever, once they have him out from under the wood."

I pointed with my lips to the arguing people surrounding the wounded man. The director and Administrator Rizdale had come out of their offices and were now joining in the argument.

"Of course that doesn't mean that in future we won't have to worry about Doff, or the one sent to replace Praiser Simms. So you will need to be wary, my grumpy old bear. I may not be able to rescue you next time."

He snorted and turned back to the anxious young woman fussing over him. 187, whose name was actually Jamiya, glowered at me for disturbing her patient. I just smiled and continued to hold the Bear's hand.

When I felt I'd helped enough I looked around and saw Atuusca heading towards us with a bunch of plants clutched in one hand. I recognized the flat gray-green leaves as one of the plants I'd seen Grandfather and the Prophet use for treating wounds like the ones Matoqwa now had.

Releasing Matoqwa's hand I stood. "We need to move him over by the bath house so we can wash his wounds clean of mud and horse dung," I told them. Then turning to Jamiya I asked, "Sister, do you know where is clean cloth for—" I made a wrapping motion like I was putting on a bandage. I didn't know the word in the Chamuqwani language and I figured we had all been breaking enough of the school rules to risk being overheard speaking our own "savage" tongue now, and put in the Box as a punishment.

Still scowling at me she knew what I meant and hurried off to get what I needed. By the time she returned we had stripped the Bear of his shirt and had rinsed off the worst of the blood and mud. While Cohasi finished cleaning the wounds Atuusca handed me some of the leaves he'd brought. Jamiya must have thought we were crazy when she returned with the bandages, and saw the green goo dribbling from our mouths and us chomping away like cai beasts.

She became even more alarmed when we started plastering the medicine onto Matoqwa's open wounds. "What are you doing, stop! Don't hurt him more with that disgusting heathen—mess."

Spitting out the last of the plant onto one of the bleeding cuts I wiped my mouth on my sleeve and faced her. Using a bit of my gift to emphasize my words, I said, "We aren't hurting him, and a part of you knows that. My Kukiya brothers and I have used this plant before when someone was wounded on the war trail." I pointed to the wound which had already stopped bleeding.

"See, the cut has stopped leaking blood and starting to heal. This plant doesn't harm him; it is a simple plant medicine nothing more. Though you are from a different tribe, I'm sure your ancestors too called upon plant spirits to help them heal just as we do. He will be all right."

Now that we were away from the Chamuqwani I had been speaking to her in the Kukiya language for my war-brothers sake, and with the Shining One's help, she was hearing my words in the language she could best understand.

"But Doc says—"

I gave her a mirthless laugh. "I can guess what Doc will say about our 'heathen' ways, but that is of no matter. If—or when, Doc gets around to examining my brother he will see that the wounds are healing well. And that is all that is important."

In the continued confusion we managed to sneak Matoqwa up the back stairs and into his bed in the dorm. When we had him settled I realized Kutima had followed us. Bringing up some hot water from the kitchen he shyly offered the steaming pot to me, before I could ask someone to get some. I thanked him and rummaged in a hidden corner under my bed near the wall where I'd been collecting some herbs. I tossed some bark shavings into the pot, and when it cooled I gave the Bear some willow tea to drink. He was soon asleep.

Leaving Cohasi to watch over him as the temple bell began ringing for a prayer service, I ushered the rest of my war-brothers downstairs and lined up with the others outside the temple. We would be missed if so many of us didn't attend the coming service.

Doc arrived not long after we returned to the yard. So our devotions were delayed for a time while Praiser Simms was placed on a wooden litter and driven into town, never to return to the school again.

LATER THAT NIGHT WHEN all was quiet, I lay in my bed unable to sleep. I was troubled by the part I'd played in the day's events. Evil was all about me and it had become so easy to call upon my Qwakaiva to solve the problems of my life. Maybe too easy, I thought...

I had been gifted power by my unique lineage, being half human and half Qwa'Nayhi Seal. I could commune with the Dead, walk within the Dream, foresee the future—sometimes, and change the pattern that would affect reality in my world. But along with my special Qwakaiva came a great responsibility to use my Gifts wisely.

Because of love I had become entangled in a net of Kukiya family obligations and a feud with deep roots in the past—a past I knew little about. Maybe Grandfather was right, in part, to warn against our involvement in Kukiya tribal matters. I loved Nachoga, Amima and my sweet baby sister so I'd promised. Even if I couldn't be with Kitahtla I wanted her, Samiqwas, Xyilaha and Uncle Tli and his family to keep safe.

And so in an attempt to protect them, I'd burdened myself with another oath of vengeance, a promise which I didn't know how to accomplish without causing even more harm. Already since leaving my northern home I'd tempted discovery time and time again. In spite of the danger to me personally I wanted to help my People, fight injustice and do only good in my world. But did I always know what good meant? I wasn't sure anymore... And with those troubling thoughts swirling about in my mind I slipped into the Dream.

Feeling lost and miserable, I found myself listlessly floating in the inky channels under the Earth, which is where Star Swimmer eventually found me. In his glowing seal form he was suddenly there beside me. Together we swam to the pool where I often met my Benefactor. As I surfaced in the water beside him he glided to the rocky beach and assumed his human form. Climbing onto a rock ledge he smiled when he saw the shining being nesting in my chest next to his shell token and motioned for me to join him.

When I, too, was once more human he put an arm about my shoulders and drew me closer. <<I can taste your pain on the currents of the Dream, my son. Tell me what has happened to cause you such torment.>>

And so I did. I told him about Amima's death, and how a pair of greedy traders had betrayed Nachoga and his brother to the soldiers for money and gold. I spoke of how I had sacrificed Rattlesnake to take my vengeance for that treachery. I told him about the massacre and my capture. How I'd been saved from hanging, but now found myself in a live-away school with my war-brothers counting on me to plan our escape and save them.

And I admitted to him that I had bound myself once again with a promise to Nachoga to keep my sister safe by ending forever the threat Azogi was to her future.

When I finished he was silent for a long time, but at last he said,

<<I am sad to hear about your mother. Qwadalah had a fierce, shining spirit. I would have liked to go back to your village and live as her husband and your father for a time. But if I had done so, the Evil from another world that was trailing me would have destroyed your village, so I could not. But I am glad she found companionship and love with the Cougar. He was a good man. I wished you and them well.>>

My spirit shuddered when I recalled those fearsome alien creatures I had seen when, at Chumco's urging, I spied on my mother's dream. He was right if they had followed a wounded Seal man and Amima back to our home they could have destroyed us. As hard as it was for me personally to grow up without a father, I knew in my heart he had done the right thing.

<<You are still quite young, Tasimu—too young maybe for all the hardships that your destiny has given you to bear,>> Star Swimmer continued. <<I wish it could have been otherwise. But you have also gained much wisdom and understanding along with the pain and sorrow you have suffered.

<<And, from what you have just told me I can also see that now you are starting to realize that you lacked the wisdom and the skill of our dragon benefactor to know the future and understand all the possible consequences of your impulsive actions. And that, though it may not seem so right now, that lesson will be of great importance to you in the future.>>

<<Do you think our Benefactor is angry with me and disapproves of how I have used the Qwakaiva he has gifted me to help my people?>>

<<He neither approves, nor disapproves. It is up to you to use the Qwakaiva gift you as you wish, but also bear in mind that any use of power has consequences. Someday you may be discovered and if that happens then you and many others will suffer. So be careful in future how you use your Gift. Explore other trails first if you have a choice to achieve what you want.>>

True enough his words were of little comfort to me at that moment. Looking up into his enigmatic deep violet eyes, so like my own, I begged, <<Father, please take me away from this terrible place. Everyone is looking to me, as their Qwakaihi, to solve their problems for them. But if I use my power to help them the Thunderer's priests may learn of me and want to burn me as a witch. I don't know what to do. It's too much—too hard here. I can't—>>

Star Swimmer shook his head and rose to his feet. <<I'm sorry, my son, but I can't do that at this time. Our Benefactor has told me that now that you have chosen to swim this channel there are lessons you must learn that are hidden in its treacherous currents.>>

At his words my heart sank. How could he do this to me? How could Kunai do this to me? <<Does the Great One want me to die in this terrible place? Please take me with you.>>

Star Swimmer chuckled as he slipped back into the water. <<Be easy, my son, and no childish whining. I can't and won't go against Kunai's wishes in this, but I will do something to ease your mind in part, Tasimu. I will assume your oath of vengeance. I will see that this Azogi and his apprentices never harm your sister or the rest of your family who shelter her.

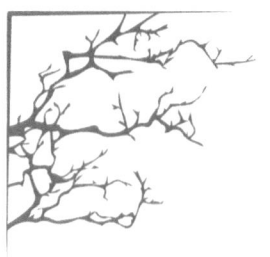

Part Two
Chapter One

<<WAKE UP, END IT. WAKE up!>> I commanded myself, but iron bands of fear were constricting my chest; I wanted to scream, but I couldn't. I'd forgotten how. My body—my mind was no longer under my control. I was hopelessly ensnared within the dream of another.

Together we stood in the shadowed hallway of the boy's dormitory late at night. It was cold. My/his scarred hands twisted the folds of our ragged night shirt in agitation. I knew instinctively that I/we had to get away—find somewhere safe before something bad happened—again.

Urging my/his trembling legs to go forward we continued down the corridor. Like a blind man, we ran a hand along rough walls until our fingers brushed against a doorknob. The icy metal was so cold it burned our hand like fire. <<Have to get away—hide,>> he pleaded with me.>>

Dread lending him strength, we gritted our teeth against the pain and yanked the door open. The room beyond was silent. No light spilled out to welcome us, but we stumbled through anyway and the door closed. We leaned against its heavy wood. Our heart was pounding, our breath coming in ragged gasps.

When my/his breathing slowed and he looked around, I discovered that we had entered the outdoor bathhouse at our own live-away school. Damp towels hung in neat rows along a wall stained with mildew. In a corner, steam burbled from the neck of a wide-bottomed kettle atop a sooty wood stove. Two sinister rows of copper tubs were lined up like soldiers along either side of the center aisle.

Unlike the real bathhouse outside the school dorm where I slept, however, in this dream there was a door on the other side of the perilous room. Behind it I heard people singing and light spilled onto the bathhouse floor. The golden sanctuary beckoned. The yearning to open that door was like the bittersweet taste of red berries half fermented on the vine by the autumn sun. At my urging we started down the aisle between the tubs. I was suddenly sure that healing and freedom from pain lay beyond. If I/we could only reach out and open it, then like the Prophet's predictions all would be well in our lives and our land again...

<<Unclean-n-n.>>

<<No! Not true,>> I snarled.

I/we forced ourselves to keep moving, ignoring the whispers in the shadows, not daring to look into the tubs, but their accusing malice echoed in our wake. Raising our fist I/we whirled round. <<Stay back,>> I/we warn the monsters that lurked in their depths.

I/we tried to make our voice sound manly and fierce. The words echoing back to us from the bathhouse walls, however, sounded more like a bird's peeping than a warrior's challenge, but we were content. For now the tubs were keeping their secrets; their submerged horrors were quiescent.

But while we'd turned our back on the sanctuary to challenge the tubs behind us, steam from the mean-spirited tubs we'd yet to pass boiled up to veil the door. Panicked, the dreamer shouted, <<No, come back—please—don't leave me here!>>

Dry, rasping laughter answered him from the gloom. <<Behind that door lies the honor of warriors,>> the shadows whispered. <<Only the Pure can enter there.>>

<<Pure?>> I asked the dreamer. <<What are they talking about?>>

Tears blurred the dreamer's eyes, but he doesn't answer. A torrent of emotion welling up in our throat, I/we sank to our knees and covered our face with our hands.

<<Dirty Zaunk, filthy savage! Unclean-n.>>

The words began as malignant whispers in the depths of the copper tubs, but they grew in volume, echoing off the walls, growing louder with each reverberation. <<Unclean-n.>> They brushed our unprotected skin like nettle switches, leaving behind trails of stinging fire.

The dreamer writhed, but we were powerless to stop the accusations. The shame seemed too much to bear.

<<Uncle-ean-n.>>

Wake up, stupid Siyatli Boy, I commanded myself.

Then as I felt the control over my burden of fear and guilt threatening to shatter my own spirit, I screamed to the dreamer, <<Release me—stop!>> Unable to hear or answer me, I remained ensnared in his net. <<Who are you? Please tell me so I can help you!>> I begged.

Still ignoring me the dreamer grabbed onto the rim of the nearest tub and pulled us up. The pitted metal slid along our torso like a reptile's skin. Peering down into the black water with him, I gazed through the wisps of steam, hoping to find more answers hidden in its obsidian depths.

But only the blurred unrecognizable image of a sallow-skinned youth with a shaven head looked back at me. His high cheek-boned face was gaunt from repeated starvation, all sad dark eyes and sharp angles. The watcher that was me wanted to take this lonely, betrayed child in my arms, but even if the dream would permit it, I sensed that he wouldn't allow it.

<<See the nice pudding and sweet almond cake I have for you? Are you hungry, boy?>> a wheedling voice in the shadows coaxed.

<<Not safe—never safe,>> the dreamer muttered.

The simpering voice can't stop our dream-body's shudder, but I/we will not look in that direction. That much defiance is still ours to command.

<<See, it's a nice, sweet almond cake and it's all for you. Come here, my sweet boy, and taste it. You know you want it, hmm?>>

<<No, no I don't want your treats! I don't want,>> the dreamer's words end with a sob.

Mocking laughter...<<Nasty little Zaunk. Tempter of the Mighty Djoven's righteous. I know your tricks. Filthy savage you do want it—all of it. COME HERE!>>

For both of us, I wanted to resist, scream out our defiance, our rage, but no sound could escape the spell of protection his terror has laid upon us. <<The pain and humiliation hurts less if we don't fight it, and just go away. Turn to stone inside like me,>> he advised me.

<<No!>> Cruel laughter mocked me, growing louder as we struggled.

Within his/our dream the fire in my/his groin and buttocks became a flaming agony, as we were bent over the tub. Then our face was beneath the dark water and I was choking. Pleasure, pain, white-hot spasms spew a molten river down our thighs, as fiery heat explodes in our chest. I can't move; I can't breathe—

<<Young Siyatli, cleanse yourself of this evil or you will die,>> the voice of my crystal guardian commanded.

<<Yes, wake up; we have to wake up. Damn you, do it,>> I screamed to both the dreamer and myself. <<Wake up!>>

I heard a noise like a pop and then I'm awake, shuddering, and gasping for breath, the coppery taste of fresh blood in my mouth. I've torn myself away from the dreamer's nightmare at last, but my bedding is coated in icy sweat, the blankets in a snarled heap around my legs.

Swallowing down my unease I glanced around with my spirit sight, trying to determine the dreamer's identity in the Waking World. There was no other gasping boy nearby to attract my attention. Must be in the other dorm room, I reasoned, but who?

The room about me was quiet, a monochrome setting of indigo and silver. No demons were lingering in its shadows. What had just happened to me? Whose dream had I unwittingly become a part of? Both were good questions, ones to which I had no answers.

Had the vivid images I had just witnessed been a foretelling of the future, or only a cruel manifestation of a child's fear. It had been several moons since I had felt a sending of such force. All was quiet save for a few snores. The dreamer's whereabouts eluded me now that I had surfaced from sleep, but perhaps I could find out more by contacting my inner companion.

Placing my left hand atop my chest I summoned the powerful being my Benefactor Kunai gifted me, as a sign of his favor. The being now magically lodged within my body, instead of around my neck on a cord, was there to guide and protect me when needed. <<Shining One, can you help me understand the dream I witnessed?>>

<<No, I cannot; Kunai doesn't wish it. Its meaning will twist your future into a path that will be dangerous for you to swim.>>

<<But someone I care about is in trouble—or will be. I have to help him. I am his Puhani—>>

<<No, you do not. You aren't mature enough in your power to combat the forces massing to destroy our plans for you.>>

<<But as a Puhani it is my duty to protect my war brothers, care for them—I've sworn it,>> I argued.

<<A foolish oath, perhaps. You have been warned not to use your Qwakaiva or you will attract too much attention from your enemies. The dreamer must solve his own problem or wait until it is time for all to escape.>>

<<And when will that be,>> I grumped. <<We have already been at this live-away school over two years and my brothers and I grow impatient. When?>>

<<Discipline, young Siyatli. The Great Dragon who flies high and guides the fates of many worlds sees the entire vision and directs us accordingly. You and your warband aren't the only concerns on his mind. Careful how you test your favor with him, don't disobey and meddle in the dreamer's affairs or he might abandon you to the malice of the Evil Ones who are his/our enemies. Patience and learn the lessons meant to guide you to your true purpose in the future.>>

No help from my companion or my Benefactor. Well, there was nothing new about that; I was often left to solve my own problems. With a sigh I lay back in my bed, staring at the ceiling; it was still dark outside, but I dared not go back to sleep in case the nightmare was lying in ambush to trap me again.

Was the dreamer thinking about escape? Too long, it had already been too long since my war brothers and I had been sentenced to live in this chamuqwani prison for children. My father, the Seal Man Star Swimmer, had promised me he would come for me when our benefactor, the Great Kunai told him it was time for our escape, but I was tired of waiting—like the rest of my warband. After being driven to this prison in chains, we had already been here too long.

But we'd had little choice it was the school or hanging. Most of us at first tried to stay out of trouble and blend in to our new surroundings, but as time passed it became harder to endure the hunger and beatings that were a part of the daily routine at Saint Yon's Live-away School.

Thinking about it now I could see how by separating us into different work groups, sleeping chambers and even tables for meals the bond of our warrior brotherhood that had kept us strong during our outlawry had broken down. We were becoming nothing more than isolated, vulnerable, and lonely youths no different than the other children in this cruel place.

New alliances were forming, even the strongest kinship ties, like the bond between brothers were affected. Some were good, like the connection that formed between Qwatola and Cohasi when his brother Matoqwa was assigned a different dorm room and table at meals. Cohasi now treated Qwatola like a younger brother, needing his protection, which had always been his role, before he and Matoqwa were separated.

Other bonds weren't so good, like the one formed between Komonti and the cousins Atuusca and Iwaz. They caused trouble by breaking things and stealing at every opportunity. Then, of course, they usually were caught and ended up punished in the cellar under the priest's house known as the "Perdition Box." In spite of my warnings and my efforts to counsel patience, they ignored me, hid in dark corners and plotted escape.

And as for me, my own loyalties had changed somewhat, too. As their "Puhani" I still worried about them, but I saw less of my war brothers than when we first arrived at the school, because I was spending less time outdoors doing farm work.

With the approval of Celibress Dinana and Praiser Tom much of my spare time now was spent studying with my old friend from home, Kutima, or should I say Keveneth, to use his Chamuqwani name. With a little nudge of my Gift to help keep him away from Head Boy Ronalton's torments, I got the Celibress to assign him to help me learn the magic of reading and writing the enemy language. Because of this, I was unaware of the trouble brewing until disaster was upon us and I chose to ignore my Benefactor's warnings.

It was summer when I had that fatal dream and later that morning I was harvesting peas from the vines near the kitchen garden fence. On the other side Qwatola and Cohasi were chopping and stacking wood outside the kitchen nearby. As best I could tell they seemed to be arguing about something when they passed one another. Curious I slowed my picking and listened. Then I heard Qwatola say quite clearly, "I can't wait, elder brother," and there was such a note of tearful desperation in his voice that it tore at my heart.

"I know, I know," Cohasi agreed. "I'm working on it—but I have to ask my brother—"

Can't wait? Feeling a sliver of ice slide down my back I straightened and peered over the fence, hoping to catch Cohasi's notice. Before I could ask him what they were talking about, however, Praiser Jonash, the priest who now supervised the farm work shouted at them to hurry with the wood, because he needed them to finish mucking out the rest of the horse stalls before the midday meal. After that both boys were too far away to speak to them without attracting attention to myself and risking a reprimand.

Before coming to the school I had thought the brothers' kinship bond unbreakable. My cousin Samiqwas and I used to call Cohasi, Ha'an, which means shadow in our Qwani'Ya language. Cohasi never did anything on his own, always following his brother Matoqwa's lead. All that changed when they were separated at the school, however.

Matoqwa was loyal, brave and a fierce warrior, but he was also reckless and impulsive, never considering the consequences of his deeds. He often got himself and his brother into serious trouble back home. And after their separation with Qwatola right there, needing the older Cohasi's love and protection, it was natural for the two to form a bond with Cohasi the wiser older brother this time.

The new relationship would be good for both of them I reasoned and encouraged it a bit with my Qwakaiva. But what did they need so urgently to talk to Matoqwa about? I picked up my basket and hastily finished my task. My curiosity would have to wait—and so would they.

Fortunately I had made Matoqwa go to the infirmary the night before because he was still suffering from the occasional fearsome headache as a result of several severe beatings he had received from Praiser Simms and his men, before I had used my Gift to take care of the problem Simms posed for all of us.

Qwatola was younger than the rest of us who were captured protecting our families when Chamuqwani miners and soldiers attacked and slaughtered our kindred. He was Qwani'Ya like me, Matoqwa and his brother Cohasi, but Qwatola was from a downriver village and I hadn't known him well before we were captured.

I had noticed at the time he'd been tossed into our jail cell that he was no warrior-trained youth, but a slim pretty boy with dark luminous eyes and full lips. And because of hunger and the poor food on the Preserve and now here, like me, he had yet to gain a man's height and muscles in spite of his age.

Qwatola like Cohasi had been assigned to a different dorm room, so other than Qwatola sitting at my table at meals I didn't see either of them much. And truth be told, I wasn't paying attention to the boys in that room, leaving their petty troubles up to the sensible Inishkim to sort out, unless they made a point of asking for my help.

Over the past year I had become very cautious about using my Qwakaiva unless there was no other recourse. I'd been warned by my Seal Man father when last he came to me in the Dream to be careful or I would attract the attention of enemy beings with evil intent from the Beyond, who also took an interest in my world. At least that was the justification I wanted to believe was the reason I hadn't foreseen the disaster approaching until it was too late.

And though I cursed myself for my blindness, in truth I had enough troubles of my own to occupy my thoughts without going hunting for more. I was still grieving the deaths of Mother and my adopted father Nachoga and I had my hands full keeping Cohasi's older brother Matoqwa and the other headstrong war brothers in my own room from doing something rash when the head boy, Ronalton, constantly provoked them.

And before my father's recent warning I'd spent many a restless night, when I should have been sleeping, awake and searching the center diamond of the Seer's Pool, fearing for the lives of my baby sister Kitahtla and the rest of my outlawed family still running free but hunted in the Kukiya desert basin west of the Preserve.

No I certainly hadn't been paying attention in the last few moons I realized. But now that I'd become aware of the danger, I could think of nothing else while doing the rest of my morning chores, earning several reprimands for my carelessness. At meal time I tried to find a quiet moment when Ronalton or his second Yohan weren't watching to have a word with Qwatola but he sat hunched over his bowl of beans with eyes cast down, ignoring everyone.

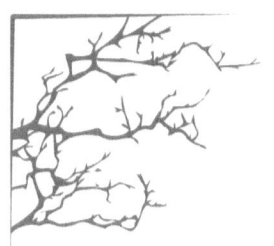

Chapter Two

Unfortunately for my peace of mind after the midday meal I had no time to seek out Qwatola or Cohasi because Praiser Tom assigned me and Kuweya to help move boxes filled with used clothes and other donations from the loft storage in the barn into a back room at the temple for Celibress Vomica and the servants to sort. The clothes suitable for a child to wear were collected to be washed and repacked while the rest were placed into a rag bin to be made into quilts or utilized for other dirty tasks.

When we finished it was nearly time for prayers and the sermon in temple. I was exhausted and covered in hay dust that clung to my sweaty neck and arms.

As we washed off at the pump Praiser Tom surprised us by walking over to us when Praiser Jonash wasn't looking. With a sly smile he slipped us each a half of apple. "You boys did good today," he murmured. "Let this be our little secret, hmm?"

Kuweya nodded, slipped his part of the apple in his shirt and hurried away to hide in the barn before enjoying his share. I was so hungry I just stood right there, chomped down my half, core and all, in several quick bites. Praiser Tom grinned and I grinned back. He patted me on the shoulder before he heard the other priest returning and moved away. At the same moment the temple bell rang and I hurried to take my place in line.

Praiser Tom was short and round with pale skin that turned red easily when he was joking or angry. He was a cheerful but lazy man who laughed a lot, often looked the other way when rules were broken, and brought his favorites among the boys treats whenever he could.

I stared at his retreating back puzzled. He had never singled out me or Kuweya for a treat before. I'd overheard him talking with some of the teachers and I knew he found my tribal tattoos ugly. Usually he didn't pay me much attention, so I couldn't help wondering why Kuweya and I were now included among the group of his "special" boys.

That night Matoqwa ate the evening meal in the dining hall with us. His place was across the hall from mine, but I saw his brother have a word with him as we filed off to wash before getting ready for bed.

Matoqwa's bed was next to mine, so when he crawled under his blanket and the lamps were blown out I lay flat on my bed and whispered just loud enough for him to hear, "Your headache gone?"

He snorted. "Gone enough that I have to go back to pitching horse turds tomorrow."

"What did Cohasi want to talk to you about?"

He was silent for a long time refusing to answer, even when I repeated my question. Finally he growled, "My head hurts. Shut up and go to sleep, dog turd."

I swore under my breath, turned on my side facing him, and growled back "Tell me; I want to help."

"It's nothing go to sleep."

"Tell me, dog fart! I feel like something bad is going to happen—and I don't know how to stop it. I just know that Qwatola and Cohasi are in the center of the trouble that's coming whatever it is."

He was quiet for a long moment, lying flat on his back, staring at the ceiling. He snored, trying to convince me that he'd drifted off to sleep.

I wanted to hit him, or at least throw my pillow at him but didn't dare. "I know you're not asleep; tell me..."

Turning to face me, he finally murmured, "Have you had a foretelling, Siyatli dog turd?"

"No," I reluctantly admitted. My crystal's warning still twisted a knot in my gut, but since helping me release myself from the dream the being had remained silent, leaving me to come to my own conclusions. As of yet I didn't know the cause of my unease or what I was going to do about it when I figured it out.

"This morning I was working in the kitchen garden and overheard your brother and Qwatola arguing about something as they chopped and stacked wood by the kitchen... I only heard a few words, but their talk worried me. Are they planning on doing something stupid, like trying to escape?"

"And what if they are thinking about it," he shot back. "You promised us that we wouldn't have to be here long, but I don't see you doing anything to further our plans, eh?"

"And, I've told you—and the others it isn't time yet. My Guardian will tell me when it will be safe for us—"

Matoqwa snorted his disgust. "Sure you will 'Puhani'."

"It will—I will."

"Well maybe I don't believe you. Maybe you like it here too much, and aren't listening so good. I think you don't want to escape this place. Maybe you like being the pretty celibress's pet and sitting in the study room with that half-breed dog turd from home while the rest of us work, eh?"

I was stunned and yes, hurt by his accusation. Was that how they all felt now? Yes, we had been here much longer than I had hoped we would, and maybe I wasn't paying attention, or helping someone with my Qwakaiva every time they asked, but I'd been warned. Damn, I did want to leave—I did.

"That's not fair, war brother. I hate this terrible place.... And when we go we will take Kutima with us. He hates it here as much as the rest of us."

In spite of talking just above a whisper he must have heard the hurt in my voice that I was unable to disguise, for he said, "My head hurts. Shut up and go to sleep."

Well that was about as close to an apology as I was going to get from the grumpy bear, so I turned my back on him and went to sleep.

AT BREAKFAST QWATOLA'S chair remained empty throughout the meal. With Yohan keeping an eye on me I managed to choke down the lumpy oat-mush I'd just been served, but it lay like a rock in the pit of my stomach. Was he sick—or as a punishment, was he lying hurt in the cellar room under the priests' house known as the "Perdition Box"?

A battered Cohasi was in his chair, but judging by the amount of blood and bruises on his face and arms, he had received a recent beating—for something. Knowing he and Qwatola were so close I guessed his "condition" had something to do with the missing boy.

Though he refused to look at me I could read the anger and worry radiating in piercing waves in his Spirit Fire. He was furious and afraid for our relative. Glancing around the hall I noticed that most of the children and staff behaved as usual, seemingly oblivious to the missing boy's absence.

That wasn't true of intercessor Fredderoth or Praiser Tom. They were probably the ones responsible for Cohasi's beating, and likely knew something about Qwatola's disappearance. The chaotic aura of the intercessor was smoldering with a murderous rage. He kept glancing at Cohasi and balling his fists like he would like to do him even more physical harm. The man was usually angry about something, but combined with the young brother's absence sent more icy chills slithering down my spine.

When I glanced at the normally cheerful Praiser Tom, however, he didn't seem angry, but petrified. He was trying to hide his worry, but looking with my Sight I could see that his aura was choked with a maelstrom of guilt and fear.

I would have liked to talk to the praiser, the more approachable of our supervising priests, to ask about our missing brother, but he and the intercessor were called away to the director's room just after the meal. And then I was assigned to help in the barn so I had no excuse to hang around the dining hall waiting for him.

But while mucking out dirty straw from the horse stalls I was able to catch a quiet moment with Inishkim, who slept in Qwatola's dorm, to ask, "I noticed our younger brother wasn't at the morning meal today. Do you know if he is sick and has gone to see the priest-doctor at infirmary?"

Inishkim shrugged and forked another mound of dirty straw onto the growing pile. "Maybe. He seemed all right yesterday—though more quiet than usual. I don't know where he is."

"He may be sick," Komonti said, overhearing us. "Late last night I thought I heard one of the priests talking to him, but it was too dark to see which one."

"What did the priest say to him?" I asked.

Komonti shook his head and picked up the handles of the cart filled with hay he'd been pulling. "Don't know. I went back to sleep."

Hmm... "What happened to Cohasi?" I asked next.

Inishkim leaned on his shovel and gave me a disgusted look. "The stupid dog turd was going to run away—so the head boy in our room and the intercessor say. Doff found him in the stable early this morning trying to throw a rope on one of the horses."

My mouth fell open at that revelation. Komonti passing by with another load of hay laughed when he noticed my expression. "Stupid Qwani'ya dog turd!" he growled. "If he'd asked me to come with him we wouldn't have got caught."

"This is crazy talk," I protested. "Cohasi loves Qwatola, true, but he would never try to run away without Matoqwa no matter what Qwatola wanted. Why would Cohasi do that? There has to be some other reason for him trying to run—if that was even what he was doing."

Komonti shrugged and walked off with his cart just as Doff hollered at us to keep working. Not wishing to feel the crack of his switch on my back or legs I went back to work as well. Still puzzling over the events of the morning as the bell rang for the midday meal I managed to take a quick peek into the infirmary before slipping into my seat in the dining hall. Qwatola was not in the sickroom and still absent from his seat at our table.

Later in the afternoon when it was my study time with Kutima I couldn't focus on my assignments. My mind whirling like a leaf caught in a devil wind I was distracted, my fear growing worse with every circle of the maelstrom.

When Kutima had asked me the same question three times without me answering he closed the book and stared at me. "Tas, what's bothering you today? This isn't like you."

I shrugged, but closed my own book. I didn't want to look at him; what could I say? When he repeated his question then just continued to watch me I finally blurted, "Qwatola, um 292, is missing. And the priests say Cohasi tried to run away, and was beaten for it—but he would never leave Matoqwa—so that can't be right."

I broke off, swallowed hard and met his eye, stupidly hoping for his assurance that the missing boy was all right and would turn up soon. When he didn't try to reassure me and just sat back, looking thoughtful, I finally blurted, "I overheard Qwatola tell Cohasi that he couldn't wait any longer. But I don't know what that means."

My friend's continued silence made me uneasy. Finally I touched his hand and when he glanced over I rudely stared into his eyes and begged, "I think you know something. Please, Kutima, tell me. I don't want to see anyone hurt—if I can help them."

"My name now is Keveneth, Tassele, please call me that," he said, using my own Chamuqwani name and removed his hand from mine.

"All right, all right, I'll use your chamuqwani name. Stop trying to evade me and answer my question, 'Keveneth,'" I said a note of impatience coming into my voice.

He sighed. "I'm surprised with all your Qwakaiva that you haven't figured it out yourself."

His rebuke hurt. No, I hadn't figured it out—whatever the problem was. My constant hunger was a goad to sharpen my survival skills for foraging food, but that focus combined with my grief for my lost family I suddenly realized had dulled my mind in other ways. Like everyone else I went about my daily work and tried to stay out of trouble as much as possible and that was a full-time task. "Figured out what?"

At first his silence was my only answer. When I gave him an impatient growl, he said, "In spite of his Kukiya tribal tattoos, like you yourself, student 292 is a—a good looking boy."

Me, good looking? I'd never thought of myself that way. Though I had started to finally grow I still was slimmer and shorter than the others in our little warband. But he was right about Qwatola; he was good looking in a way that made me wonder if he was a two-spirited child—though that wasn't the point at the moment.

At another growl from me he hastily added, "Some of the priests living here, some of the older boys, too—and one of the mercy women, like the pretty ones among us in—in unholy ways."

"Unholy ways? What do you mean?"

He took a deep breath and shuddered. "I mean ways that would ensure the mighty god's wrath. It would condemn anyone to Djoven's fiery pit if they were discovered doing…"

He broke off shaking his head, dropping his eyes and trembling. I leaned back in my chair frowning. I could tell I had upset him, but I still wasn't quite sure what he was trying to tell me with his talk of fiery pits and Djoven's wrath. Everything seemed to make the Chamuqwani god angry.

Then his hidden meaning struck me like one of the god's lightning bolts right between my eyes. "Ku—Keveneth, I saw the ghost of the girl and her baby when I snuck out to help Matoqwa when he was beaten and tossed into the Perdition Box, so I already know these men are guilty of great evil. But are you trying to tell me now that one of these foul priests humps boys, too?"

He grimaced at my use of a bad word. Still without looking at me in a voice barely above a whisper, he said, "I thought you of all people—with your Gift would know—I thought—"

Yeah I should have known—guessed. What kind of Puhani was I? I shook my head unable to speak. No I didn't know—or hadn't wanted to know, though now several unrelated facts like pieces of a puzzle fell into place in my mind. The friendly smiles, the pats on a child's back, and little treats secretly offered, and the quiet footsteps in the halls late at night that I hadn't allowed to surface into my awareness all made sense now.

"How do you know these things? Has this happened to you?"

He blanched, his half-breed skin growing even paler, but still he refused to answer. Saying more Chamuqwani bad words under my breath I answered my own question. *Of course it had.*

Recalling my earlier apple treat, I muttered, "Was it Praiser Tom; did he hurt you?"

"He's one of them I've heard of," he finally admitted, evading my question.

Oh, Kutima, back home I never knew you had such a courageous heart, I thought to myself. *All alone in this terrible place, with no one to stand beside you or guard your back, it must have been terrible for you. However did you manage?*

"The praiser is one of them, eh? Who else?" Under the table my hands balled into fists.

"I'm not going to tell you. And don't look at me like that, because you can't do anything to stop it—even if you use your Qwakaiva. Believe me I've tried—others have tried. No one will listen, and," he took a deep breath, then blurted out the rest, "And, I don't want you to be hurt—or maybe get killed."

I was silent for a long moment, thinking over his words, at last I ventured, "I think you are trying to tell me that Praiser Tom or one of the others you won't name has been humping Qwatola—and maybe Cohasi, too. Am I right?"

Keveneth sighed and nodded. "It's a possibility, true enough. And it must have been going on for some while if they are considering doing something stupid."

Oh, Kunai, escape, they'd been planning on an escape. Was that what Cohasi was waiting to talk to his brother about? Of course it was—damn them—of course it was. I shivered as another icy premonition slithered down my spine. But if that was true, what had gone wrong? Where was Qwatola? Why hadn't he waited for his friend to go with him?

Or, more to the point, why hadn't he told me. I probably would have tried to talk him out of doing something as foolish as running away without a plan or supplies, but no matter the personal cost to me I would have used all the power of my Gift to help him escape the attentions of the priest if he'd only asked.

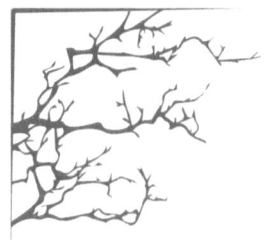

Chapter Three

I learned later that while Keveneth and I were studying a quiet but thorough search had been going on for the missing boy, organized by the director and Celibress Vomica. Discovering that our war brother seemed to be nowhere on the grounds of the school the director had sent a message to the village for hunting dogs to track the runaway.

While we'd been talking instead of working on my assignment, the sounds of the hunting dogs and their owner arriving in the yard sent me, Keveneth, and most of the children in the school to peering out the upper windows, hoping to discover what was going on.

The dogs were given a shirt of Qwatola's to smell and then the farmer released them to find the trail. They milled about the yard for only a few moments then caught the boy's scent and raced out of the stable yard, heading for the river.

I would have bolted after the dogs, but Keveneth grabbed my arm. "Don't! You will only get yourself into trouble if you run after them." He motioned for me to resume my seat at the study desk. "Follow them in your special way, eh?" he motioned with his lips to the cord around my neck. Taking his advice, I removed my string and quickly formed the pattern of the Seer's Pool. It took a moment for the image to form, my own fear and worry clouding the center diamond. Calming myself I pushed away my emotions and finally was able to find the missing boy within the pattern—and then I wished I hadn't.

Qwatola had crept out of the school after everyone was asleep last night as I'd feared, but he hadn't planned on running away. No, his goal was much closer. The dogs found him easy enough a little ways north of the grain fields, hanging from the limb of a willow elder near the bank of the river. Cohasi was too late. He'd gotten himself beaten up for stealing a horse to chase after a ghost. Choking on a sob I let the cord fall from my hands into my lap.

"What did you see, Siyatli dog turd?"

At the sound of a gruff voice my head jerked up, my eyes flying open. Matoqwa, Cohasi, Inishkim and Komonti had joined us in the study room while I was lost in my conjuring. As if summoned by my Gift Qwatola stood beside the grim faced brothers and placed a hand on Cohasi's shoulder.

Ignoring Matoqwa's question I spoke to the ghost. "Oh little brother, I'm so sorry. You should have waited—should have come to me—I would have helped you."

Outside the noises of the school went on as usual, some of the younger children talking excitedly about seeing the dogs, and the teachers in stern voices ordering everyone back to their tasks. Inside the study room the warband remained silent, waiting.

At last Keveneth took a deep breath and said in a soothing voice as if speaking to an upset child, "Tas, were you talking to Qwatola just now? Please tell us what you saw with your string."

<<Tell him I am sorry, Puhani,>> the ghost of Qwatola said. <<That evil priest hurt me, over and over—no escape—this was the only way. I know my brother would have run away with me,>> Qwatola gave me a sad smile and patted Cohasi's shoulder. <<But they would have caught us—brought us back—punished us, and alone in the Box he would have... It's better this way.>>

<<No, younger brother, I would have helped you. It's not better,>> I protested. <<You are dead and... and we will miss you.>>

Tears streaming down his ghostly face, he said, <<I'm sorry, Puhani, I'm unworthy. You can't help a dirty, unclean savage like me. I deserve the punishments that await me. But I will miss my family and all of the warband, too.>>

I shook my head, suddenly tasting his despair and knowing what he meant. <<No, what happened to you wasn't your fault. You aren't going to go to some stupid demon-god's fiery abyss because an evil priest did bad things to you. You are a Qwani'Ya warrior and our people aren't ashamed of you. Don't listen to the demons who tell you otherwise.

<<I can help you. I have been gifted the Qwakaiva to sing you home—back to our northern home—home to live among our ancestors.

When it's quiet and they lay you to rest I will come. Wait for me—please wait for me!>>

He thought about it for a moment and then smiled. <<I will wait,>> he promised

I took a deep breath, then rage welled up to replace my grief and failure. <<Which one of those evil priests hurt you?>> before he could answer I became aware of another shadowy presence nearby. The identity of the Spirit was shielded from me, but Qwatola obviously could see it.

Focusing on me again he shook his head. <<It's not important now,>> the ghost said and gave me his sad little smile again.

<<It *is* important,>> I insisted. <<This evil needs to stop. Other children will be hurt if I don't— >>

<<You can't stop them; you will only be destroyed, too, if you try>>

<<What are you talking about? Tell me who is it!>>

<<I'm sorry I can say no more,>> I heard him say as his spectral presence fragmented and disappeared.

<<Come back—please tell me.>>

Growing impatient with my silent communication with the ghost Matoqwa growled and punched my arm. "Tell us what you saw, Siyatli Dog Turd. Is Qwatola dead or what?"

Having no blanket I placed my hands over my face to shield my grief and nodded. "Yes, the dogs will find him soon. He is hanging from an elder willow near the river."

At first everyone was silent, stunned in spite of what we feared. Then Cohasi with a vicious swipe of his arm knocked our books to the floor. Keveneth let out a startled yelp and scrambled to pick up the scattered papers and books before someone who might have heard the clatter came to investigate.

Turning his back to us, Cohasi leaned his forehead against the wall his whole body shuddering.

"Cohasi, I'm sorry I didn't know that anyone was bothering him."

Without looking at me he swore and began pounding his fist against the wall. As his blows began to leave blood streaks upon its rough surface Inishkim grabbed his wrist to stop him.

"War brother, enough, this won't bring him back. We will take our revenge—I promise you," Inishkim soothed as he put an arm over his shoulder and led him back to our study table.

Cradling his fist Cohasi flopped into a chair and without looking at anyone, he got his emotions under control enough to finally explain, "I wasn't trying to run away this morning when Doff caught me. I just wanted to find my little brother—before... Damn that priest. I will kill him—"

Though I could feel his determination to do just that, I also heard the quiver in his voice and tasted his overwhelming grief upon my tongue. I shared it. Our little warband had lost the first of our number.

"Who are you talking about?" Matoqwa demanded.

"Who do you think?" Cohasi spat.

"Praiser Tom," I said into the silence, as a vision flowered in my mind. Oh yes, I could see how it was done, the smiles, the little treats, the "comforting" hugs when a child was ill or homesick, all done to gain the victim's trust—and then... We fell silent after that, each of us retreating into our own thoughts until the bell called us to evening prayers.

After everyone filed into the temple I looked back and saw Doff and a couple of his men carry a tarp-wrapped bundle on a blanket and pole stretcher into the barn. The exhausted dogs now leashed trailed in the farmer's wake. Refusing to answer any questions they deposited their burden and then went to report to the director.

That evening when he rose to take his place at the head of the assembly, Director Harriscot was well aware of the frightened whispers circulating through the room that couldn't be silenced by Celibress Vomica's threats. Though most of the children were only vaguely aware of what had truly happened, the evil lurking among us could be felt by even the dullest Chamuqwani attending.

Taking his place at the head of the room the director rapped his willow stick against the stand where he placed his god book. When all was quiet, he thundered to his audience, "Beware! There is a great evil amongst us and the Mighty Djoven is angry—very angry!

"Today a great crime has occurred. Mighty Djoven's holy law has been violated and the offender has been cast into the Fires to suffer for his misdeed. I know there are others among you who also harbor Evil in your hearts. Have a care all you offenders of the mighty god for his wrath is terrible!" Then he proceeded to give such a vivid account of the fiery tortures awaiting the Thunderer's transgressors that many of the children were in tears before he finished.

Without actually speaking of Qwatola's suicide and what had caused it, his sermon that night went on far beyond our usual prayer time, our meal being cold by the time we got to the dining hall to eat it. But truth be told no one had much of an appetite to eat anyway.

Later when evening chores were done Komonti, Matoqwa and Inishkim, three of the oldest and biggest youths at the live-away school, were held back from their usual bedtime routine. Matoqwa told me later that they were ordered by Praiser Jonash and Doff, to dig a long hole at the far end of the orchard. When the hole was deep enough to satisfy the priests they were ordered back to their rooms to wash up and get ready for bed.

Aware of Matoqwa's empty bed beside me when I finished my own bedtime preparations I sat cross-legged atop my bed and formed a pattern with my string to find out what was going on. I saw the men and boys take shovels and a pick from the storeroom and head out to the orchard.

Unfortunately I became too engrossed in my conjuring, unaware of Intercessor Fredderoth's approach until a sharp slap from his switch across my hands caused me to break my concentration, the cord falling into my lap. Swallowing a bad word I glanced up. "I'm sorry, Intercessor, did you say something to me?"

The bald spot on the top of his head a bright pink and an angry frown on his reddening face, he snarled, "I asked you if you had finished all your homework today, 297."

Had I finished my homework? With everything going on today school work was the last thing on my mind. Dropping my eyes, I mumbled, "I-I'm not sure, Intercessor. When the dogs came I—I got—distracted. But I will do better tomorrow," I hastily offered, hoping to please him.

It didn't work.

Glaring at my tattoos, he snapped, "See that you do. No more foolishness tomorrow or you will be staying a couple days in the Perdition Box while you pray for Mighty Djoven's mercy. Do you understand, savage?"

I nodded vigorously. "Yes, Intercessor."

His lip curled in a cruel smile as he glared at my tribal tattoos again, and then he wacked my hand a few more times, just to see if I would scream. I didn't cry out but I did let him know that his blow had hurt—because it had. One of my fingers was now numb and the long red streaks across my palm burned like fire.

I whimpered and forced tears to well up in my eyes. I'd learned from bitter experience that keeping silent only increased his punishments. I let him think what he wanted and saved myself worse torments.

Satisfied with the pain he had caused the intercessor finally moved on to inspect a new child's bed making, leaving me to cradle my hand and endure its throbbing pain. Ronalton smirked at me behind the intercessor's back; I ignored him.

When the hurt eased and I could move my fingers without crying out I put my cord back over my neck and lay with my blanket over my head. Not long after that a grim-faced Matoqwa came in, and dressed for bed without a word of explanation to Ronalton who demanded to know where he'd been.

"Ask the intercessor if you want to know so bad, dog turd," he snarled, his fists balled at his side.

Ronalton glared, but prudently decided it wasn't worth the intercessor's wrath to ask him.

When the lanterns were blown out and all was quiet, I turned on my side and whispered to Matoqwa, "I saw you digging a hole in the orchard, but the intercessor came in and broke my conjuring. Was that for our brother?"

"Probably, but that piss drinker Doff sent us back after we finished the hole, so not sure."

"I am. Ku-Keveneth told me that their god hates a suicide. He might pollute the ground in their precious graveyard if he were lying among the others."

Matoqwa grunted and not long afterwards I heard him snore. I couldn't sleep so easily, however. My now swollen hand throbbed, so after a time tossing about, I sat up and wrapped my blanket about my shoulders. With some difficulty I removed my string and reformed the Seer's Pool.

Focusing my intent on our lost brother a vision finally appeared in the center diamond. I watched Intercessor Jonash and Doff carry the body of our brother Qwatola to the hole in the orchard and without any ceremony dump him in. when they finished filling the hole they walked back to their beds, leaving the ghost looking confused sitting upon his solitary grave.

    <<Better to sleep with the friendly trees for company, far away from the demons and evil priests in Djoven's temple,>> I consoled the ghost.

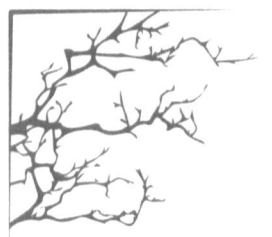

Chapter Four

In the days that followed it was as if Qwatola had never been among us. The staff at the school refused to answer the children's questions and severely punished anyone they heard talking about the suicide. It wasn't long before we all slipped back into the routine of daily life at the school. I suppose the priests wanted to keep the result of their crimes quiet, but of course everybody knew what had happened to Qwatola in spite of their precautions.

I wondered if the reason for their secrecy had to do with our friends at the Father Emperor's court keeping a watchful eye on us. Though, if I valued our lives, I dared not tell anyone outside the school about the conditions here.

In the hearing of others no one in our little warband spoke openly about the suicide, either, but I knew like me, our brother's sad end festered in the depths of our minds. Cohasi became quiet and withdrawn, ready to fight at the slightest provocation. Even his brother Matoqwa wasn't spared his outbursts.

Our Kukiya brothers Komonti, Kuweya, Inishkim and the cousins, coming from a more war-like people than my own Qwani'Ya band, took their revenge in part by secretly damaging personal items belonging to the priests whenever they thought they wouldn't be caught. It became a game amongst them, a way to demonstrate their warriors' prowess. And with each success they became bolder.

I feared for them should they get caught, but they no longer shared their thoughts with me and ignored my warnings. Remembering how I had disguised myself by wearing my cousin Xyilaha's dress in order to escape being burned as a witch when soldiers directed by a Kukiya malicer captured our food gathering party, they teased me, saying I was becoming very "womanly" and wondering when my breasts were going to grow.

After a while I let them go their own way and ignored them as best I could. I focused on my studies with Celibress Dinana and Kutima instead.

DURING OUR TIME AT the school we were always hungry. Inishkim and Kuweya, as representatives for the warband, had come to an "understanding" with Doff and some of the other men from the village who worked on the farm. If they turned a blind eye to our hunts for rabbits and other creatures that might damage the crops the school grew for profit and the kitchen, we would share our catch of quail and rabbits with them.

Everyone was careful not to speak openly of our need to carry out our promised vengeance, but it festered like a boil under the surface of our thoughts nonetheless. It was while a few of us were feasting on a meal of roasted gophers at the edge of the far grain field one afternoon that Komonti and Atuusca began tossing out ideas of how to take our revenge on the perverted priest.

"If we lured Praiser Tom out behind the orchard then we could beat him up," Atuusca was saying as I squatted to grab a piece of meat from the steaming pile on a woven grass mat by the fire.

"When we run we could steal horses before we grab him, and then just leave him to die among the trees." someone suggested.

"Yes, near our brother's mound. Let him know how we avenged him," Komonti agreed, smiling cruelly with his excitement.

"Good idea, no one would hear his cries for help out there—especially late at night," Iwaz said.

"If we stuffed a pillowcase in his mouth no one would hear him wherever we do it," his cousin Atuusca offered.

"Maybe we should bring a rope and lure him to the river instead," Cohasi growled. "Put a rope around his fat neck and show him where our brother died." Someone snorted a laugh then everyone fell silent, listening to the fire snap and crackle, mulling over his words.

Kill the priest? True we all would like to see him pay for his crimes, but murdering him was a dangerous solution to consider. We all could hang for such a misdeed, no matter how justified, and this time no pleading by Lord Bronworthy and his friends could save the guilty ones.

Since the suicide, Cohasi had become a bitter and angry young warrior. I saw the swirling colors of disharmony in his Spirit Fire and I was worried about him.

"That is an interesting way for us to take our revenge on the priest," Inishkim finally said. "But maybe right now is too soon after our little brother's death to risk. Like our Puhani always tells us, I too would counsel patience. The dog turd of a malicer will be too suspicious to go off alone with anyone even now."

"Not if someone pretends to be his cloocha whore he wouldn't," Iwaz suggested with a sneer.

"Are you offering to do it, sweetie," Komonti asked.

Iwaz scowled and turned red when the others laughed. "No, dog humper I'm not pretty enough," he growled. "I was thinking of someone else." Briefly he glanced in my direction then dropped his eyes, not daring to give me offence so openly.

Feeling my own face heating up I bit down hard into my share of the meat; the gopher's bones snapping in my mouth with a loud crack. I said nothing, but the anger and resentment, that a few moments ago was focused against the priest, I realized now was directed at me.

Ignoring them I continued to eat, but a shiver ran down my spine nonetheless. With a stab of insight I saw that they were furious with me for not using my Gift to help them escape, and now they blamed me for our war brother's death.

A knot twisting in my gut I finished my portion, standing I reached down, picked up several cooked gophers, wrapped them in an empty grass mat and tucked them inside my shirt. Not wanting to look at anyone I kept my eyes focused on the fire and said, "I have to get back before I'm missed. I'll bring these to Matoqwa and Ku-Keveneth."

Eyes stinging—from the fire, I turned my back on them and started across the field. Behind me someone murmured something too low for me to hear, then someone else laughed and the others joined in.

Goaded by my war brothers' snubs and growing contempt, I decided to keep my promise to Qwatola's ghost in the hope that I might appease the rest of my warband in some small way. Surely enough time had passed since Qwatola's death that it was safe for me to use my Qwakaiva and send the ghost home to remain with the ancestors I reasoned.

<<I have warned you, Young Siyatli, your Benefactor will not be pleased if you continue on this path. Your kindred's journey in life is their own, and each has his own lessons to learn.

<<Your time here is to help you separate yourself from the petty troubles of your friends and kin. You must learn to soar like a dragon and see the entirety of the pattern not a few small pieces.>> my crystal warned.

<<I've promised and it is the teachings of my Qwani'Ya people to help one another. I have to use my power to help them,>> I protested.

<<I'm aware that I will have to suffer the Great One's punishments if I disobey. I have pledged him my service but I can't leave Qwatola to be torn apart by that evil god's minions to save myself. It would go against my nature to do so. I need you; please try to understand,>> I pleaded.

<<No, it is you who needs to understand. If you are to survive and be of use to your people in future you must learn when to use your power and when not to use it. This is a time when you need to walk away.

<<Though young the boy is a warrior in his heart. He would not want you to risk the fate that awaits you if you make yourself vulnerable to the enemy's probes. The Crokno enemy are hunting you, Siyatli. Why can't *you* understand this and heed my warning?>>

A knot of uneasiness twisted in the pit of my gut. I knew I was swimming in a dangerous river. I felt alone and vulnerable, but I couldn't leave a young innocent like Qwatola to be devoured by Djoven's demons.

<<I'm sorry I must follow my own counsel in this,>> I finally admitted to the Spirit.

Uprooted, and grieving for all I had loved, my spirit had fallen out of harmony with my world. And this, I believe, is why I made several bad choices, choices that in the moons that followed changed my life as well as many others around me.

<<So be it then,>> the being intoned. <<But know this, too. If one of the Crokno's agents from the Beyond that have been sent to cause trouble in your world find and ensnare you, I won't be able to aid you. You will have to

rely on your human nature and your few inherited gifts from your father to save you.>>

The being fell silent and refused to answer when I tried to summon it again. My mind swirled like a whirlwind with indecision. What to do, oh what to do. I had tasted Kunai's displeasure before when I chose my family over the mentor he'd sent to instruct me. I had no wish to relive that painful experience. I was aware of my danger, both from disobeying my Benefactor and from Djoven's demons and other creatures who wished me and my people harm.

But on the other hand, was I strong enough to live among friends and relatives who were growing to hate me. I was a child of the Qwani'Ya people my life and the lives of my ancestors were rooted in the teachings of our land. We took care of one another, no one person could survive without family and friends. Together we were strong; alone we would die. Growing up among the clans I feared that without allies in this terrible, soul-destroying atmosphere I couldn't survive.

So, after mulling it over in my mind all that day I decided that the next night would be a favorable time for my conjurings. Sister Moon was past her fullness and the sky was clear and cool. If I waited till everyone was asleep I would have plenty of light to find Qwatola's grave in the quiet hours before dawn. Keeping my trousers on under my night shirt I slipped under my blankets after the evening prayers as usual and fell into a dreamless sleep.

The cry of an owl awakened me just as the sliver of Moon's light shone across my closed eyes. Breathing slowly as if I still slept, I listened to the sounds of the sleeping boys around me and allowed my Spirit-self to slide out of my chest and search for anyone else who might be awake.

Everyone slept ensnared in their dreams, so I rose and hurried to the door in my bare feet. All quiet in the hall I crept down the stairs and out the unlocked door that led into the garden behind the kitchen. I made my way to the orchard without being discovered then paused. The night air smelled of cut hay and rotting summer apples. A breeze stinking of river mud caressed my cheek then moved on to rustle the drying leaves of a pear tree. In the brush along the fence a fox barked.

Allowing my feet to lightly touch the ground before trusting all my weight to them, so I wouldn't give myself away to anyone else who might be abroad in the night, I moved through the trees searching for the ghost I hoped was still hovering by his grave waiting for me.

When I drew near the place where I thought Qwatola's grave must be, however, I found not only the ghost but a blanketed figure sitting on the ground nearby. He was only a dark silhouette in the moonlight, but too small to be one of the workmen or priests. It must be one of the warband, and I could guess who. Moving slowly, so as not to frighten him I approached the grave and sat beside him. We remained silent, each aware of the other; each lost in our own thoughts. Qwatola's ghost sat somber and voiceless on his grave facing us.

Feeling the essence of the Night settle about me like a comforting blanket I raised my eyes and spoke to the ghost, <<Thank you for waiting for me,>> I told him. Behind me Owl hooted. I looked up; she was perched among the branches of an apple elder, her silhouette bathed in Moon's silver light.

I took in a deep breath and shoved aside the Shining One's displeasure. I had to do this. <<I've come to keep my promise to you. I've come to sing you home to our Ancestors.>>

<<Home to the Ancestors?>> the ghost shook his head. <<I can't go to them. I'm not worthy—unclean—the ancient ones won't want me.>>

<<That's crazy talk; of course they will welcome you home to live among them,>> I protested. <<You have nothing to fear from the ancient ones. They know you are a brave Qwani'Ya hunter. It doesn't matter what an evil Chamuqwani priest did to you. Be at peace about that.>>

He thought about it for a moment, then asked, <<But what will happen if the demons lurking nearby follow me? I don't want those evil creatures to hurt my mother, or anyone in my family—>>

I snorted a laugh. <<As for Djoven's demons, don't worry, they won't bother you,>> I assured him. <<look around you, little brother. The night hunter will fly with you and protect you on your journey. See she is already here and waiting for you.>>

Qwatola glanced up at Owl and then nodded. Returning his attention to Cohasi, tears formed in his ghostly eyes. <<He comes here often to keep me company. The demons that torment me stay away when he is near. He gives me strength. Keep him safe for me after I leave.>>

<<I will do the best I can to protect him—all of them, but I can make no promises. His fate is his own to keep. You will see him again when it is his time; I can promise you that much, however.>>

The ghost smiled and nodded. <<I am ready, Puhani. Send me home; I want to see my mother again.>>

I placed a hand on Cohasi's shoulder. "Brother, I've come to keep my promise to him. Will you help me?"

He remained silent for a long moment, not turning to face me his eyes focused on the mound of soil in front of us. I knew Cohasi lacked the Qwakaiva to see the ghost, but perhaps he sensed his presence. Finally he choked out, "I will miss him so much, but I was too frightened to leave without my older brother," he admitted. "I suspected he was planning something stupid, but I ignored his pleas and now... This is my fault. Matoqwa was sick and—"

"It isn't your fault, brother, if you had run they would have sent for the dogs. They would have caught you both. And maybe they would have just handed you over to the soldiers to be hanged, instead of bringing you back to this living torment."

Cohasi let out a mirthless laugh and I felt my face heat. "I'm sorry, that talk about hanging was a stupid thing to say."

"Yeah it was, stupid Siyatli dog turd."

I murmured a laugh. "Yes I am, as you and Matoqwa keep reminding me." Feeling around in the dry leaves and grass under the trees I picked up two fist-size stones and handed them to my companion. "Here, this is how you can help me. These stone beings have offered to be our drum. If you remember the songs I will sing, you can join me, too. Now let us begin before Sun wakes, or one of the early-rising priests or a workman finds us.

As my trance deepened Cohasi did remember a few of the songs from when, after their hanging, I sang my adopted father and our captured warriors home, and he joined me. Framing sister moon's light between my fingers I opened the portal. Her silver essence grew brighter as I focused her Qwakaiva on the opening expanding out from my joined hands.

Dawn neared. It was time. Owl swooped down from her perch, and took our brother's spirit in her talons then flew away with him, heading for the pulsating circle of light I created. Still singing I watched her enter the rim of the portal's silver luminescence. My heart rejoiced at the sight and I sang a little louder.

Then just before she disappeared my concentration was shattered by a heavy blow to the side of my head that sent me sprawling into the dirt.

"Filthy savages, what's the meaning of this?" a familiar voice thundered over my head and he raised his stick to hit me again.

I didn't black out, so I'd heard him, but I didn't answer Intercessor Fredderoth's question; I refused to look up and that little act of defiance earned me more blows. When he stopped to catch his breath my head was pounding like a drum. Dizzy and confused I lay stunned on the cool earth gasping for air and trying not to faint as I spat dirt out of my mouth.

There were more sounds of a struggle nearby and then I heard Cohasi say, "Chamuqwani devils, leave us alone. We just wanted to say good bye to our brother that's all we weren't trying to run away."

"But you weren't in your dorm room either, filthy zaunk," I heard Doff growl as he hit him again.

"And you two were chanting some foul heathen prayer," the intercessor roared as he and Doff continued to beat us. "Mighty Djoven damn you to the fiery abyss for your blasphemy!"

I don't know how long the beating continued; all my Qwakaiva was focused on keeping myself conscious and not giving the priest the satisfaction of hearing me beg for his mercy. I paid for it with more pain, of course, but at the time I was so angry that it seemed very important to defy him—even if it cost me.

The Chamuqwani's intrusion had come at a critical time in my conjuring. Without someone to protect me while I used my Gift this interruption meant that now I had no way of knowing if Owl had been successful in carrying Qwatola's spirit home. My shame at allowing myself to be discovered, and my fear that I had failed, sustained my rage in spite of the added torment they inflicted on me.

When the sun had risen and the bell rang for morning prayers the intercessor and a couple of Doff's workers marched us, aching and bloody, back to the school. When we arrived everyone was lined up for morning prayers to add to our humiliation. They stared wide eyed and some of the braver ones murmured nasty comments under their breath as we were hustled into the temple.

Instead of directing us to our usual seats in the back row, that day we were made to kneel at the front of the room on either side of the stand where the director set his big, god book.

As I expected we were the subject of the director's sermon that morning. I kept my head down and didn't listen. I needed all my strength to keep from falling over from the pain. I knew what he was going to say anyway. "Dirty zaunk, filthy heathen savage!" he'd said it all before.

When the rant was finally over we were taken to the cells under the staff house, without stopping for the lumpy mush that was our usual breakfast. By that time I was beyond caring about food. I welcomed the moldy straw and the dark. As long as I could sleep, leave the pain behind, and escape into my dreams I was content.

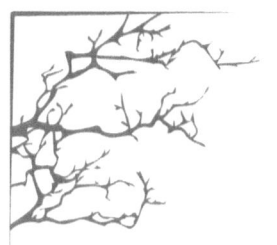

Chapter Five

O h my dearest ancestors I couldn't see. Was I blind? The darkness was suffocating when I finally dragged myself awake after their beating. My whole body ached; I wanted to slide back into the eternal oblivion tempting me back into the Dream, but I forced myself to ignore the pain and sit up.

Chest tight and a knot in my gut, my fingers frantically explored my face. I discovered that blood slowly oozed from a deep gash on my forehead. The trickle was adding to the crust already formed into a mask partially covering my eyes and nose. With a frustrated growl I picked at the drying mess; I could barely breathe. When I had scraped away the worst of the blood I could breathe better, but I hurt too much to move—to think.

Dizzy again I flopped back into the straw, but not to escape into my dreams. I needed to draw up the Earth's curative powers and start the recovery process. And to my surprise, the crystal being lodged in my chest roused itself to help me focus my Qwakaiva for the healing.

When next I surfaced my body hurt, but not as bad as it had earlier. I was still trapped, in the dark, but now I was well enough to do something about it. I had two objectives. The first was to check on Cohasi, and the second was to find us some food and water.

With those goals in mind I located my cell door and placed my hands over the lock. Using my Qwakaiva I felt around in its mechanism until I could shift its parts enough to open it. Once outside I traced my hand along the wall until I located another locked cell. Then I used my Gift to open Cohasi's door, too.

<<Shining One, can you help me conjure a spirit light?>> I asked the crystal lodged within my chest.

<<No, it would be too dangerous,>> the being answered. Aware of my dismay, it offered, <<I will lend you the Night Hunter's sight for a time. But be quick on your errands, or you will be discovered.>>

"Cohasi," I called as I opened his door. "Are you awake? How badly are you hurt?"

With my night hunter's sight I saw my Qwani'Ya brother curled on his side atop a mound of rotting straw. A blood crusted blanket was thrown over his head and shoulders. Kneeling beside him was the lonely ghost. Her bloody babe clutched in one arm she was bending over Cohasi and whispering something into his ear.

Her words were like dry leaves crackling under foot. I couldn't understand them, but my brother could at least make out some of what she was urgently trying to convey to him because he was answering her in a painful murmur.

<<Stop that!>> I demanded. Was I too late; had she done her worst and convinced him to follow her into death? Fear and anger as my goad I raised and pointed my left hand in her direction. Qwakaiva that only she and I could see shot from my fingertips to form a glowing orb about her and the child.

<<Leave,>> I commanded. With a despairing cry she and her babe disappeared. I breathed a sigh of relief. She was gone for the moment. Hopefully she now feared my power enough to stop bothering Cohasi until they came to let us out of this place.

Calling his name once more, I knelt beside him. Reaching out a hand I felt along his shoulder. He was shivering under the filthy blanket he had pulled over himself for warmth. "Cohasi, can you hear me; how badly are you hurt?"

"Leave me alone, please go away," he mumbled and tried to shrug off my hand.

I held on to his shoulder and shook it gently. "Cohasi, pay attention! It's me, Tas, speaking to you now, not the ghost who wants you to marry her. Wake up and pay attention," I demanded.

"T-Tas, is it really you? I can't see—"

"That's because we are in the Box, dog fart, but I can see you just fine using my Gift, so pay attention and answer my questions."

"All right, all right I'm paying attention, dog turd." With a groan he brushed my hand away and sat up. "What do you want to know?"

"How badly are you hurt, anything broken?"

He slapped my hand away when I tried to find out then proceeded to examine himself as best he could in the dark. "I don't think anything is broken." He took a breath and grunted, "—maybe a rib or two is cracked.... My head hurts—everything hurts." He groaned and lay back on the straw.

I covered him with the nasty-smelling blanket. "I'm going to go and find us some food and water," I said as I headed for the door.

"Want me to come with you?" he mumbled, though I knew he was still too injured to be of any use to me.

"No, I can do it. Stay and rest. If I don't get caught I'll be back soon."

I closed his door, but didn't lock it. Feeling my way to the stair I climbed. At the top I paused to listen.

<<There is no one nearby,>> my crystal assured me. <<It is late. They are all asleep for the moment, but you must hurry.>>

I knew from other raids to the priests' forbidden house that they kept most of the best food and tastiest treats for themselves, hidden away in their tiny kitchen and pantry. I slipped past the stairs leading to the bedrooms above and down the dark hall, being careful to avoid the creaky floor boards as best I could. Once inside the kitchen I closed the hall door with a sigh of relief.

My mouth was as dry as a desert, so I reached for a pitcher of water setting on the counter. I drained more than half of it before I remembered my injured brother. It didn't take me long to find several empty wine bottles and a nearly full pot of tea someone had left on the table. I chose two of the cleanest bottles and poured my tea and water into them. Quickly rummaging through the shelves in the pantry I found a container of cookies, a few apples and a half full jar of berry jam.

I discovered some leftover roast beef, but the meat was tough and hard to chew with my sore mouth, so I put it back. Cohasi probably couldn't chew it either, so I settled for a half-loaf of bread and some creamy, sweet butter instead. I put all my plunder in an old empty flour sack, grabbed my bottles of tea-water and let myself out into the hall.

Then I nearly dropped my precious bundle as I noticed a light reflected off the wall at the top of the stairs. Someone was awake and coming my way. Instead of racing for the cellar door and possibly being revealed by the lantern's light, I hurried to hide in the deep shadows under the stairs.

Crouching I created an image of black bats in a cave to conceal my presence. Then I watched a sleepy Celibress Vomica walk by in a long white nightgown and a drooping knitted cap. She reminded me of a ghostly, water bird, all bony hard angles and beaky nose as she continued on her way to the kitchen.

Once inside she left the door ajar, so I dared not pass to reach the cellar. I could hear her mumbling to herself as she set water to boil on the oil stove and rummaged through the cupboards for a late night snack. Discovering the mess I'd left I heard her swear like a soldier as she cleaned it up. Unaware of my presence she muttered about lazy priests who couldn't be bothered to clean up after themselves.

<<Dawn approaches,>> my crystal warned. <<You must return to your cell in the dark soon, or be discovered.

<<I know, but she might see me if I try to get by her with the kitchen door not closed properly... Can you help me?>>

<<I am helping all that I can,>> the Shining One answered, then fell silent, and remained so in spite of my begging. I could still see with an owl's sight, but that seemed to be all the aid I was going to get on this raid.

It felt like she stayed in there forever, but I dared not move until she was safely back in her bed. I prayed that no other person would awaken in the meantime and join her in a late night trip to the kitchen.

Though still dark dawn was indeed approaching when at last she came out carrying a steaming cup of mint tea setting atop a plate with some bread and cheese. When I was sure she was gone and back in her room upstairs, I hurried to the cellar door and slipped inside. The closed door at my back, I breathed a sigh of relief and crept down the stairs.

I opened Cohasi's door, glancing around to see if he was alone. Hopefully the ghost hadn't come back in my absence to bother him again... No he was safe, still huddled under his blanket.

Knowing he still couldn't see me I called out, "It's only me. I've brought food and drink," I added as I came and sat beside him.

"Wish you'd also brought a lantern," he grumped. "I can't see anything."

I chuckled and handed him one of the wine bottles. He took it and drank greedily. "Slow down," I warned, "or you'll puke it back up. And I'm not risking going back to get you more." I next handed him a chunk of bread slathered with butter and jam. He wolfed it down and I gave him a couple of cookies made with oat mush and raisins.

"How long do you think the dog humpers will keep us down here?" he asked between bites.

"I'm not sure, so keep back the apple and a bit of the tea-water and cookies I'm giving you in case they don't feed us or let us out today. If we have to stay longer I may not be able to get out again to bring more plunder." He grunted and crunched on another cookie.

When he finished he asked, "I hope our little brother is safe now. Did you manage to send him home before those damned priests found us?"

Just about to take a bite of my own cookie I paused with its edge nearly touching my lips. "I think so," I said, hoping I spoke true. "Owl with his spirit in her talons had just reached the rim of the portal when they surprised us. I think they passed through."

"But you don't know for sure."

Feeling my shame rise up to nearly choke me I took a bite of cookie and chewed. Finally I admitted, "No, not for sure; I'm sorry."

He grunted then swore under his breath and went back to eating.

Not wanting to answer any more questions I rose. "It's near dawn; I have to get back in my cell, before they find me. Don't be afraid—and don't listen to that ghost if she comes back to pester you."

My guilt and failure still twisting a knot in my gut I paused at the door before locking him in, and offered one last piece of advice. "When we get out of here act like you have repented of your sins. Their punishment worked. You are a good zaunk now.

"Don't try to beat up or kill praiser Tom; it will be too dangerous for you—or any of the warband to attack him. I will take care of it—for all of us. Qwatola's murderer will answer to me."

"You will do it; what made you change your mind?"

"I just did, all right? Since none of the others is talking to me much these days I need you to tell them."

By committing myself to sending Qwatola's ghost home I had already placed my feet upon a dangerous path. I was already doomed. No need for the others to share my fate, I reasoned. But oh how wrong I was about that.

"How? How will you accomplish it?" he persisted.

I said a bad word under my breath. I didn't want to answer, because I didn't know. But to avoid harm falling upon the others, I reasoned, I needed to be the one to do it. I was sure of that much.

"Never mind that, you just need to know that I will do it—for all the abused children he has hurt. And I will take our vengeance in the way only a Puhani can," I said and locked his door.

CELIBRESS VOMICA BROUGHT us lumpy mush and water later that morning. Grim-faced and silent she refused to answer any questions, just setting down her cold offerings inside our cells then leaving us alone in the dark to ponder our sins.

Later that evening Intercessor Fredderoth arrived. Flinging wide our cell doors he held his lantern high and surveyed the damage he and his men had caused. A cruel smile curved his lips and he nodded his satisfaction. Before he would give us the cold bean soup and stale bread he'd brought he stood outside our doors and preached to us about our sins.

While he ranted on, and on, we had to kneel and humbly beg for his, and the Mighty Djoven's forgiveness.

"Swear that you will be good little zaunks from now on," he roared, "or I will leave you to starve alone—in the dark—until you die!"

There was no danger of that, truly, I would use my Gift to let us escape, before that happened. But of course we tearfully swore to anything he wanted—every time he asked. We promised him anything we hoped might get us out of the box, but nothing seemed to satisfy his cruel nature.

It was easy to lose track of time when we were kept always in the dark. No one came to look at or bandage our wounds. Lying in filth and always cold as the days passed, I feared for our health, especially Cohasi's. He developed a phlegmy cough that troubled me. I worried the ghost dwelling with us might get her wish after all if his illness got worse.

In spite of constant headaches and a festering gash on my arm that was hot to the touch, I knew I could call upon my Qwakaiva to insure I wouldn't sicken to the point of death. But Cohasi lacked my Gift and so was more vulnerable to a life-threatening illness than I was.

At night when I was fairly certain we wouldn't be discovered I would open our cell doors so we could huddle together for warmth and I could secretly share my Qwakaiva with him as I'd once done with his brother Matoqwa. I prayed our ordeal would be over soon, before either of us was too ill or weak to recover.

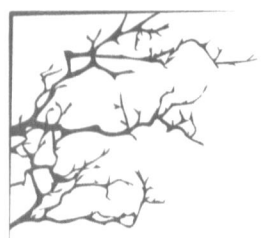

Chapter Six

As our time underground dragged on and on I was seriously considering a plan for us to escape, when at last our day of deliverance came. And much to my amusement, it was the subject of my murderous thoughts himself, Praiser Tom, who had been assigned to release us.

He entered the cellar just as the bell was ringing for morning prayers. Unlocking our doors he held up his light and motioned for us to come out.

"The director thinks you boys have stayed in here long enough to have learned your lesson, so you can come out now," he announced in a cheery voice.

We staggered out of our prison blinking at the light. Catching a whiff of our bruised unwashed bodies and filthy clothes for the first time, he grimaced. Wrinkling up his nose at our smell, he stepped back. Then studying us carefully with his arms resting atop his rounded belly, he said, "Well, I was told to bring you to the temple, but I think your first destination must be the bathhouse."

I had no argument with that plan, so following Cohasi up the stairs we trailed the praiser down the hall and out into the yard. I straightened as I noticed that most of the children still waiting in line to enter the temple were staring at us with mouths agape.

Some like Ronalton and his friends smirked when they saw our disheveled condition, but most of the children took a quick glance then dropped their eyes and looked away. Many of them had experienced harsh punishments from the priests or other staff and feared to look too closely at us. They might be next.

From their places in line, the warband gave us relieved glances as they filed into the temple for the morning prayers. Ahead of me Cohasi coughed, doubling nearly in half with the spasm. I hurried to catch up to him.

Throwing his arm over my shoulder, I helped him to stand when he caught his breath, then together we stumbled along after the praiser.

The water in the bathhouse was barely warm enough to take off the chill, but I welcomed its cleansing touch nonetheless. It felt good to rid myself of the caked-on blood and dirt at last. Once more in clean clothes, Praiser Tom would have sent us back to our usual morning tasks, but I stopped him.

"Praiser, please, boy 305 is sick, we in dark and cold a long time. Now he got bad cough." I motioned to Cohasi bent over tying his shoes and hacking up a gob of green phlegm. "Will you take him to see Doc, so he won't get sicker, eh?"

"Hmm." He considered us thoughtfully. Ignoring us Cohasi carried on with dressing and coughing as he worked. "And what about you, 297, do you want to go to the infirmary, too?"

Did I? I hadn't thought about myself when I'd asked. My headaches were gone, but the rest of my body still suffered from the beating. I feared he might suspect us of trying to both get out of work if I said yes, and Cohasi needed the doctoring more than I did, so I shook my head, and then said, "No, I hurt little bit, but I can go work now." I drew his attention to my wounded arm that had begun to ooze a little blood and green pus. "Maybe later I go."

He smiled, patted me on the head then gave me a quick one armed hug. "Good boy, that's the spirit. Our Mighty Djoven loves a boy who isn't lazy. I'm proud of you."

I suppressed a shudder; his touch made my skin crawl, but I smiled back at him then lowered my eyes as if shy, so he couldn't see how I truly hated him.

He patted my shoulder. "I think you are right about your friend," he agreed. "You run along to find Celibress Vomica and see what she needs you to do while I take 305 here to see Doc."

Still coughing Cohasi gave me a murderous glare as he followed Praiser Tom out of the bathhouse.

Left alone I took my time about hunting up the Celibress, managing to grab a carrot and wrinkled apple from one of the warband's hidden food cashes before wandering away to search for her.

Being smaller and slimmer than most of the boys my age at the school I usually wasn't assigned the harder farm and stable work that the older and bigger boys were expected to do, so in spite of my injuries I figured I could manage to make it through the day.

At the noon meal Cohasi was not at his regular seat. Hopefully he was still at infirmary resting on a soft bed. Except for a couple whispered remarks about filthy savages needing to repent their sins, made by Yohan, the bad-tempered half breed boy who was Ronalton's Second, no one asked about our absence.

I had no idea how long we had been in the Box or what everyone had been told about our punishment, but for the moment at least I wasn't singled out for more humiliations. Everyone just ate their soup and ignored my bruised face—which was fine with me.

On my way out of the dining hall when none of the staff were watching, Matoqwa roughly seized my arm and he and Kuweya hustled me into the shadows under the stairs for a little *talk*.

"What happened, dog turd—and where's my brother?" Matoqwa snarled in a voice barely above a whisper.

I jerked out of his grasp muttering a few bad words of my own. When he'd snatched up my wounded arm it had started to bleed again. Pulling my shirt out of my trousers I dabbed at the blood and pus dripping down my arm. "Leave me be, dog turd see what you've done. You didn't have to grab me, piss drinker, you could have just asked me, eh."

He let go, but didn't apologize. "So what happened—and where's my stupid brother?"

I made him wait while I finished wiping the blood onto my shirt and then tucking it back into my trousers. Finally I said, "Last I saw him after Praiser Tom let us out of the Box he was on his way to see Doc. He got a bad cough while we were held in that hole, so I convinced the praiser to take him to infirmary, before he got sicker."

Matoqwa folded his muscular arms across his chest and glowered down at me. "I suspected you planned to sing the ghost home, but why did you take my brother with you?" he demanded. "I would have gone and so would Kuweya here if you needed someone to help you."

"I didn't take him, dog turd, he was already at our little brother's grave when I got there," I protested. "And I planned to do the ceremony alone, so nobody else would get in trouble—but he was already there—so what was I to do, eh? He refused to leave when I asked him."

"So what happened," Kuweya asked nervously glancing up the hall through a gap in the stair treads where the director and Intercessor Fredderoth had paused to talk to another teacher.

While we waited for the group to break up and move away I told them in a quiet whisper all that had happened during the time Cohasi and I had been gone. They seemed satisfied with my explanation, and as soon as the priests left we each went our separate ways.

Cohasi was sitting at his usual place at the evening meal next day. He was still coughing occasionally, but he did look better than he had when we came out of the priests' cellar. As for me, I never went to see Doc. I chewed up some plants I knew were medicine and then plastered the green goo on my arm and bound it with some linen strips I stole from the infirmary closet.

OVER THE NEXT MOON we all drifted back into the school's usual routine. Plotting my revenge was still upper most in my mind but like any good hunter I needed to practice patience. I carefully observed my prey—and waited. Little by little my forbearance was rewarded. I could tell that Qwatola's suicide was affecting the man.

Outwardly he seemed the jovial praiser who loved to laugh with the students and sneak them treats when he could. He also continued to pretend he hadn't noticed a child breaking the school rules when Intercessor Fredderoth or Celibress Vomica wasn't around.

But to me his laughter seemed a little forced. He was also losing weight and there were now dark circles under his eyes and a nervous tremble in his hands from time to time. All these signs told me a different story—without me using my Spirit Sight I suspected he was having trouble sleeping.

We could only hope.

But was he feeling guilty for causing our war brother's death, or was he only afraid of being caught and punished for his perverted deeds? I decided with a cruel inward smile that I was going to find out by invading his dreams.

I had been guilty of such an intrusion several times before once my old mentor Chumco had taught me the way of it. By entering my mother's dream I had learned more about my unique parentage. And during our time trying to escape soldiers chasing us, I had communicated with my adopted father Nachoga and my friend Collin that way on more than one occasion.

Only this time I wouldn't enter to ask for help or offer a promise of future spiritual guidance. No this time, I would use what I had been taught for a darker purpose. I planned to twist the knife of guilt a little deeper and intensify the evil pervert's torment instead.

By hurting other children over the years—like maybe Kutima, and now causing at least one death by suicide, I rationalized that the praiser deserved whatever punishment I could inflict on him. I wanted to make him suffer—and maybe end his own life—like he had done to our brother.

My conjuring wouldn't be a physical assault that could be traced back to anyone he had wronged. My attack was far more subtle, and no one at the school had the Qwakaiva to detect my meddling. With my help, he would seem to bring about his own destruction. He would do it all himself—*to* himself. And no one could blame any one of the students for his tragic disaster when it came, I reasoned.

To rid my world of this priest and his evil I would willingly pay the price owing for this use of Qwakaiva given to me by my birth and by my Benefactor's teachings.

Ah, but to carry out my dangerous vengeance I needed to obtain a personal object belonging to the praiser, or something he had handled often enough to infuse with his essence. This had to be my next strategy of attack. And that meant that I would have to get much closer than I wanted, to someone I now loathed.

As the moons of summer cooled into the harvest moons/months of autumn I focused on keeping my head down and staying out of trouble. I was a good little zaunk—everybody said so. I did the tasks assigned to me, did my school work on time, and was rarely tempted to secretly use my Gift to annoy the bullies like Yohan and Ronalton that tormented the vulnerable children among us.

Along with being so "good" I managed to find myself near my prey several times during that period, but he was cautious and when he was left in charge at night, he never brought me—or anyone else to the on-duty priest's room—like I knew he had done with his earlier victims. Without being able to search his things meant it was much harder for me to get a personal item for my conjuring. He was being "good," too, much to my disgust.

Every time I saw Praiser Tom I offered him a shy smile and a quick touch if possible. And, as I hoped it wasn't long before he began returning my smiles and sneaking me treats when he thought no one would see him.

And then just before the first harvest holiday the chance I'd been waiting for finally presented itself. That morning along with Intercessor Fredderoth, Praiser Tom was summoned to the director's office for a meeting. I assumed the discussion concerned the upcoming work assignments and the festivities after the harvest's completion.

Not being invited to the talk that morning Celibress Vomica was in a foul mood. Furious about being excluded from the planning session, she managed to vent her displeasure on everyone unlucky enough to cross her path—including me.

Seeing me coming out of the dining room at the wrong moment she stopped me with a snarl and demanded that I sweep and mop the main hallway. I imagine she hoped doing "women's work" would be an insult to my male pride, and then if I protested she could seize the opportunity to vent her frustrations on someone other than the priests.

I was equally determined to giver no reason to punish me. So, I calmly retrieved the broom from the kitchen and began to sweep. She continued to glower in my direction, waiting for me to slack off no doubt, but when I ignored her and carried on with the task she assigned me, she grumbled something about filthy zaunks under her breath and finally stalked off, yelling for team A to get started on the laundry.

I had a healthy fear of this bitter old woman. Though I'd been lucky, so far, that she hadn't recognized me. She had been one of the mercy women travelling with my people on our journey south to the Preserve who accused members of my family of witchcraft.

When along the trail Intercessor Raymonel contracted a fever she hadn't come right out and accused me of being a witch—like Grandfather, but she swore to everyone that I was a liar and a thief. Seeing her at the school when we arrived was a shock. I had changed a great deal since she'd last seen me, but I tried to avoid her notice as much as possible nonetheless.

Whatever actually went on behind the closed director's door that morning the praiser wasn't happy with its outcome when the meeting ended. Face pale and hands shaking he stumbled blindly down the hall in my direction. Hoping this was my chance at last, I deliberately put myself in his path, causing him to bump into me hard. With a startled cry I dropped my broom and nearly fell to my knees. As if waking from sleep he blinked several times and stared at me in confusion.

Mumbling an apology under his breath he steadied me then stepped back. "I-I'm sorry, 297, are you all right?"

Whatever had been said to him I could tell he was upset, and maybe needed a sympathetic friend. So with my goal of revenge in mind I came closer and put a hand on his arm. "I'm all right—not hurt, but you look very sad, Praiser Tom. Are *you* all right?"

The praiser stifled a sob, then arranging his round face into a smiling mask that seemed more like a grimace he nodded. "Oh, yes, boy."

I gave him a skeptical look and came a little closer. "You be sad, maybe. I am sorry for that." I patted his arm. "I hope you feel better soon."

Was that a tear gleaming in the corner of his eye? Glancing around to see that no one was looking he gave me a quick hug, and then said, "You're a good boy, and very kind. Thank you."

He might have said or done more, but to my relief, a group of noisy children chose that moment to start down the stairs, and he hurried down the hall in the opposite direction. Overly confident in my power I allowed myself a self-satisfied smile and went back to my sweeping. I knew it wouldn't be long now. He had swallowed my bait and the hook was set.

My chance came the very next night when the praiser was left in charge of the boys on our floor. Later that same evening when all was quiet and most were asleep he came for me. He put a heavy hand on my shoulder, telling me in a whisper, that he wanted me to come to his room and "pray" with him.

Heart pounding in my chest, I suppressed a shiver of fear and followed him out of the boys' dorm room without a word.

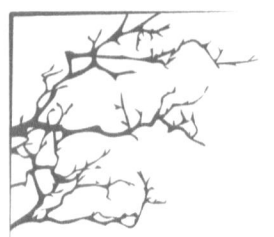

Chapter Seven

Once inside the on-duty priest's room down the hall from where the boys slept, he motioned me to sit on the bed and help myself to a plate of snacks he had brought from the kitchen to share with me. Always hungry, the sight of such an unexpected feast caused me to ignore my earlier misgivings. I needed no further urging to stuff myself on the sweet treats he was offering.

Only half listening as I gorged he blubbered on about how the director and the other priests didn't appreciate him. Sitting down beside me he stroked my cropped hair, and nearly pulled me onto his lap as he continued to drone on about the abuse he was made to suffer.

"I can't be always supervising the children while others escape to town. Director Harriscot just doesn't understand how much I need to get away for a while—I've been asking ever since—"

Piss drinker! Abused—him? What a laugh. Him suffer? Only the act of gobbling down another treat helped me contain my rage. *Self-absorbed turd,* I thought. *What about Qwatola, and the others you abused. They are the ones that truly suffered!*

Then I nearly choked on a bite of cream tart as he lifted up my nightshirt and ran clammy pale hands across my chest and belly. "Never mind why, my sweet boy, I just want a break from all this... and maybe you can help me with that, hmm?"

Choking down my disgust—both for him—and myself, I snatched up the last cookie and stuffed it in my mouth without chewing, to avoid another attempt for him to try and stick his slimy tongue in my mouth.

Angry and afraid I chided myself for my arrogance and stupidity. Some great hunter I was. Maybe I should have let the rest of the warband beat or kill him, because now I had foolishly entrapped myself along with my prey.

Growling with impatience the priest set the empty plate out of reach on the night table and held onto me with his free hand. I shook my head and tried to squirm off his lap. As I did, I pressed one of my elbows into his fat gut.

He grunted, but didn't release me and firmed up his grip. Fearful of making too much noise, and drawing the attention of Celibress Vomica, who was also on duty, I resisted him as best I could, but he was much stronger than I would have guessed for a man carrying so much fat.

Suddenly panicked I pleaded with the crystal being who I thought would always be my true protector if I was in danger. <<Shining One, please help me. I will forgo my vengeance as you advised. I will listen always to your wise counsel in future as my mentor wishes. Please!>>

As I feared the being didn't answer. With a sinking feeling in my gut I realized that this violation was a part of my punishment.

When I pledged my life in service to Kunai and his aims, I had felt myself blessed with his favor—a favor I had tested more than once. In spite of evidence warning me to be careful I had ignored how ruthless my benefactor could be if crossed.

Yes, I had been warned. I was alone, and abandoned—for now—and maybe forever.

Becoming impatient with my evasions at last, Praiser Tom showed the other half of his nature. "Stop fighting me you nasty little zaunk," he snarled and then slapped me hard across the face. "Did you think you could eat all my sweet treats, my greedy little piggy, without paying for them, hmm? Well I have needs, too."

Hands still squeezing into my arms hard enough to bruise flesh, the priest pushed me to my knees in front of him "Behave, or I will put you in the Box and leave you there until you die, you little whore. Now hurry up and take care of me."

So close to his unwashed body I wanted to gag, but dared not. He reeked of sweat and excitement. Inexperienced in such matters as I was at that time, even I could see that he was aroused too much to let me go back to my bed. My skin crawled at the thought, but I had no choice. With no Qwakaiva to aid me to resist further I stopped fighting and agreed.

I hesitantly lifted his blue priestly robe above his bloated middle and stroked his male twig. It was a sad twisted thing peeping out from under the folds of sweaty fat collected atop his pale fish-skin of a belly.

As he instructed me with gasps of mounting pleasure he leaned back as I continued to move my hand up and down. His twig grew purple and engorged, stinking like a rotten fruit as his excitement intensified under my efforts.

I withstood his attempt to penetrate me from behind, frantically trying to soothe him with my voice and my hand. I thought I had succeeded, but at the last moment before he poured out his sap, he took hold of my head and shoved his bloated twig into my gagging mouth.

Ramming it hard down my throat he pumped himself into me. And then with a final groan of pleasure he released me and flopped backwards on his bed. Still caught between his thighs I sank to the rug choking and spitting out the vile taste of him.

Fortunately when it was over I recovered my wits quickly enough to remember my purpose. Fumbling around for the cloth napkin I retrieved it from the empty plate. While he was still weak and vulnerable after indulging himself I wiped him clean. I stuffed the cloth, covered in his fluids, into the small-pants worn under my nightshirt.

It had cost me, but I now had what I needed to destroy him. I was anxious to go back to my room and begin. "P-Praiser, may I go back now? I'm tired."

I glanced up at my tormenter, hoping he would release me to return to my bed; I dared not leave without his permission. But his eyes remained unfocused; he was still ignoring me. "Praiser, may I go?" I repeated.

"Go?"

"Yes, praiser."

"Where?"

"To my bed in my dorm, please can I go?"

Unfortunately, as he recovered the priest's mood changed once again. "No, you can't leave."

Red-faced and glaring, he pointed an accusing finger at me, and demanded, "On your knees wicked, wicked boy!"

Hitting me again when I protested, he pushed me to the floor when I didn't move fast enough to suit him. His voice roughened by his emotions, he accused, "You are to blame for this sacrilege; once again my soul is damned, and it's all your fault!"

"My fault? I didn't ask for this,'" I protested.

I dodged his next blow, but instead of striking out at me again he covered his face and burst into tears. Thoroughly frightened by this crazy priest I begged him once again to release me.

"Not yet," he blubbered, tears flowing down his fat cheeks. When he had some control again he sucked back in the snot dripping from his nose, and said, "First we must pray, to Mighty Djoven for his forgiveness. You tempted me to sin again, you wicked zaunk whore. On your knees, evil child and beg the Great God's forgiveness. Repent, whore, repent!"

Joining me on the rug he clasped his hands together and said in a trembling voice, "Fear your God and master wicked savage. We must pray and ask Him to cleanse us of our sins or we will be condemned to his fiery pit for all eternity. Do you want to suffer and burn forever?"

Well, that wasn't likely to happen. When death claimed me, Owl would bring me home to my ancestors, I thought to myself.

But I could and would pray. Tears coming to my eyes I prayed, prayed to escape this nightmare. I said I was sorry, oh so sorry. I repeated whatever he told me to say, hoping somehow to satisfy him so I could finally escape this mad man and return to my bed.

BACK IN MY DORM ROOM at last I slipped the dirty napkin into the hiding place some child in the past had carved into the wall behind the head of my bed. Climbing under my blanket and sheet I curled up in a protective ball shuddering and trying to hold back my true tears.

I was exhausted, yet dared not sleep, the nightmare that had just happened to me I feared would haunt my dreams if I allowed myself to sleep. I felt so alone at that moment, alone and afraid, with too many obligations weighing me down. Cursing myself for my arrogance I wondered if I had the courage to continue.

My throat felt raw and my jaw ached from being forced open. The few sips of water left in the wash pitcher weren't enough to cleanse the bitter taste of his sap from my tongue. It clung to the back of my throat like rotting fish slime. In spite of knowing in my mind that I wasn't at fault, I still felt dirty and ashamed. So arrogant, so stupid, ashamed I couldn't beat him at his own game.

It was too late by then to creep out to the bath house to truly wash myself; someone would catch me, but I longed to immerse myself in some kind of water, be it a copper tub full, or the Waymon River flowing past the school. Enough water to wash away this terrible stain on my body and soul.

If what I'd experienced was only a small portion of what Qwatola had suffered, I could understand why he might choose to take his own life. He must have felt like there was no escape from the nightmare except to give himself into death.

<<Oh, little brother, I'm so, so sorry I was blind to what was happening right under my nose. I wish I could have helped you more while you were still alive. I wish I'd known then what I know now.>>

I was afraid of what he might do now that I'd shown myself to be "manageable" if not agreeable to his advances. Would Praiser Tom and maybe others of his perverted kind want me to be available for their pleasure, too?

Without my powerful crystal being's help could I stop them? Was I doomed to be nothing more than a cloocha whore after all? That last thought got me shivering again, turning my guts to water.

But I had been warned by my crystal guardian not to pursue this course of vengeance—advice I willfully ignored, so I had left myself no choice but to swim this turbulent river. I'd plunged in fearlessly and now I had to prevent myself from drowning until I reached a calmer shore.

But I would keep my promise to the ghost and the warband. I would destroy him—or die in the attempt. The priest was such a loathsome creature. I couldn't falter in my resolve—all the children he had abused—or might abuse in future, they were counting on me.

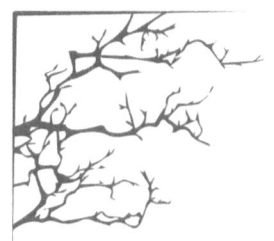

Chapter Eight

Nervous and unsettled, I was as twitchy as a fawn with cougar scent up its nostrils as I joined the line to march into temple for morning prayers. I feared meeting the praiser this morning and worried about how I was going to fend him off if he came for me again that night.

But as it happened that wasn't a problem. I didn't see him at all that day. After breakfast I was ordered out to the fields with the rest of the older children to help harvest apples and dig up more root vegetables to be loaded onto carts and sold in Town.

The praiser was too fat and lazy to work at the harvest, claimed he had a bad back. So, instead he'd been instructed to stay indoors and supervise work in the office while director Harriscot and administrator Rizdale went into Town to negotiate for the school's crop.

The priests planned to be gone a few days, and everyone knew, though dared not say, that they were selling food supplies meant to feed the children this coming winter, but in reality would be sold to put money in the greedy director's pocket instead.

Later, when I returned to my dorm room to change out of my muddy clothes before evening prayers I found a note and a half-empty tin of cookies hidden under my pillow.

Reading the note I shuddered. It said that I was a sweet, dear boy and he missed me. He also promised that he would come again for me soon, but with the director gone he had other duties to occupy him. With trembling hands I crushed the paper, wondering how long I had before that happened.

Deciding that tossing away good food was stupid, no matter who gave it, I slipped the tin into the storage box under my bed; I would share them with the little ones or the warband later.

FALLING INTO EXHAUSTED sleep each night after the day's harvesting I'm not sure how long I might have vacillated if the cousins hadn't pushed me into action at last. As in years past, the older boys and some of the girls were assigned the task of digging up root vegetables and picking apples along with the workmen hired from the village for the task. Then we had to haul the heavy bags and wooden cartons to the wagons that traveled back and forth to the dock by the river.

That day I'd been digging potatoes and I was hot and dirty when Doff called a halt for a quick mid-day meal. I willingly got in line by the pump to wash off. One of the girls handed me a chunk of bread slathered with pig lard for my meal when I finished. Then I crossed to sit in the shade behind the north wall of the barn.

Several of my war brothers were already sitting and eating their own tasteless meal. As I took a seat on straw piled up against the wall, they gave me side-long glances and mostly ignored me. It hurt, but I suppose I deserved that. I'd been too absorbed in my own troubles to concern myself with theirs for a while, so what did I expect.

Without any explanation from me I knew they were all wondering what was wrong with me, because I'd been so quiet and withdrawn since the night I sang the ghost home, and my reserve only worsened after the praiser took me to the on-duty room.

Then as I sat glumly eating Inishkim scooted closer to me and asked in a low voice, "I think you are worried about something, Puhani, what's troubling you? Or are you sick?"

I shrugged off answering at first and just continued to choke down the stale bread, but they were all watching me now and I realized I had to say something. "It's nothing—don't worry about me—and I'm not sick."

"If you're not sick then why haven't you carried out the vengeance you told my brother you would take care of, eh?" Matoqwa growled as he wolfed down the last of his portion. "Change your mind; want us to finish it?"

Out of the corner of my eye I saw Komonti snort and Atuusca looked in my direction and made a rude sign with his hand. Inishkim saw them too and made a cutting motion, silently telling them to stop. "Please tell us; maybe we can help," he offered.

Oh yes, I was worried, but none of them could help me—not now.

Continuing to study me as he finished his own lump of bread he finally pressed, "Are you worried about Praiser Tom coming for you next?"

That question earned another snort and a laugh from the cousins who shared a smirk between themselves.

"What?" Cohasi demanded. "What do you two know that we don't?"

"Ask him yourself, Qwani'Ya brother," Iwaz challenged.

Cohasi frowned then glanced at me, his expression asking the question he didn't voice. When I continued to eat and refused to answer Atuusca gave them a toothy smile. "Oh our Puhani isn't afraid of the priest or his attentions—not at all, I think."

Just then we all heard Doff shouting that the lunch break was over and it was time to get back to work. Knowing my face must be turning red under their attention I breathed a sigh of relief that the questioning was over and got to my feet with the others.

I started to walk away, and then I turned back to face them as Iwaz said quite clearly, "Oh, he's not worried about the pervert of a priest coming for him that already happened a few nights ago."

"It's true," Atuusca agreed. "We saw the tin of cookies that the praiser put under our Puhani's pillow. And, my girlfriend read to us the little love note he wrote to his 'sweet boy', too."

"No, he isn't afraid, brothers. I think maybe he likes the 'special' attention—and the treats too much to destroy his new 'friend,'" Iwaz said.

Cohasi stared at me with his mouth dropping open.

A menacing frown twisting Matoqwa's broken-nosed face into a frightening grimace, he demanded of the cousins, "Are you saying that's the real reason behind his failure?"

Atuusca shrugged. "Maybe—who can say."

Komonti let out a derisive laugh then joked. "There are cookies and other treats and he isn't sharing them with his brothers? Puhani I thought better of you."

Feeling the force of their contempt like a hammer blow I felt my face get even warmer. My fear and rage twisting a knot in my gut, I snarled, "You can get your own damned treats Komonti, and so can the rest of you dog turds—and I gave the tin to the little ones—I didn't want them after-after what he did. But I had to let him—-t-to get what I needed for my conjuring—"

"Sure you did—for your conjuring," Iwaz snorted and stepped closer to me. "I don't think I believe you. Are you sure that's true, cloocha-whore?"

He might have said more hurtful things, but I didn't give him the chance. My feelings suddenly bubbling over I stepped in, and like a striking rattlesnake I smacked my fist as hard as I could into his jaw.

He staggered backwards into his cousin, who pushed him right back in my direction. With an angry howl Iwaz came at me with fists swinging. All my fear, pain and rage suddenly finding a convenient target, I willingly met his charge with blows of my own. Lock together we fell to the ground punching and kicking, each of us trying to inflict as much damage as possible on the other.

I'm not sure how long we might have gone on with our senseless battle, but realizing we hadn't answered his shout to get back to work Doff and a couple of his stable hands charged around the barn looking for us. Seeing the fight in progress and the other boys standing around just watching, they wasted no time in breaking it up. Wading into the mess with blows of their switches and heavy fists they soon had us gasping for air and separated.

When it was over, Doff snarled, "What's this all about, you pack of heathen savages?" he glanced around the circle, waiting, demanding an answer. Everyone remained silent, eyes cast down, our expressions blank.

"Well?" when no one volunteered an explanation after several long moments Doff grew impatient with our show of defiance and his mouth hardened into a cruel line.

As he held me unresisting and trying to catch my breath, he cursed under his breath and happened to glance down at my bloody face. His eyes widened as he recognized me by my tribal tattoos. "You again?" he snarled, and shook me hard enough that I bit my tongue. "And here causing more trouble, too. What happened? Did you get lonesome for your cozy nest of filthy straw in the Box? Want to go back there?" When I didn't answer he shook me again. "What? I didn't hear you."

I spat out a mouthful of blood and stammered, "N-no, brother Doff. I don't want to go back to the Box. I'm sorry for fighting."

Doff grunted and stared at Iwaz still being held by one of his men. "And how 'bout you, noble warrior it won't be your first time in the Perdition Box, either. You missing your comfy bed?"

Needing no urging Iwaz shook his head no.

Doff grunted. Seemingly satisfied with his efforts to make us behave, he warned "Well if I didn't need all hands to get the harvest in right now that's exactly where I'd be sending the pair of you dirty little zaunks—and that's exactly where you'll go, and work be damned if I have any more problems with you. And, you will stay there till you rot, got that?"

We mumbled our agreement and Doff let me go. As he stepped back he glared at all of us. "Everybody get back to work. We've wasted enough time today on this foolishness."

Not daring to meet anyone's eye I grabbed the hoe I was handed and followed Inishkim into the nearest field to dig more potatoes. My shameful secret was out and would be common knowledge throughout the school soon enough, I decided. This event would become just another reason for Ronalton and his friends to torment me.

Body aching and bruised, for the rest of that day I worked and worked hard, channeling my fear and frustration into the brown soil. No one spoke to me; I was alone in my misery.

After I'd washed up and we were in line for the march to prayers, Inishkim, standing right behind me put a hand on my shoulder and murmured next to my ear, "Be easy in your mind, Puhani. Don't listen to the cousins' mean words. That whole family can be jealous and spiteful at times. We know what they claim isn't true.

"They forget too easily all the sacrifices you and your father have made for the People in the past. To offer oneself to such an evil man to protect others is a great deed; one that only a fearless warrior of heart could make for us. But remember, too, brave Puhani, you aren't alone here. We are your relatives and we will help you if you need us. Never fear."

Unable to speak past the lump swelling in my throat I just nodded and continued into the temple for the evening sermon. I was honored by his praise and grateful for his kindness. And I would tell him so when Celibress Vomica wasn't glaring at us.

A nervous Praiser Tom was waiting as we filed in and took our places. Wearing a blue priest's robe with food stains splattered across his mound of a belly. He stood beside the stand where the director always laid his big god book. The god's silver lightning bolt pendent that all Djoven's minions were required to wear blazed in the candle light like a warning of torments to come.

When he saw me enter, his lips curled into a shy smile. Iwaz and his cousin smirked, letting me know they had seen his silent communication with me, too. Remembering what he'd done to me I shuddered. My face reddened and I dropped my eyes. *Not tonight*, I begged him silently, *please not tonight.*

The praiser cleared his throat and wiped his sweaty brow with a rag he then stuffed back into a pocket. As the next highest ranking priest at the school I thought it would be Intercessor Fredderoth giving the sermons, like the other days since the director's absence, but evidently not. Maybe he was tired of us and decided to let the praiser have the "pleasure" of offering the evening's prayers for a while.

He stumbled through a rambling sermon that seemed to be as much of a torture for him as it was for us who had to endure listening to it. He rambled on about his mighty god, and how we should all confess our sins and beg for forgiveness. As he did so, he kept glancing at Celibress Vomica as if seeking her approval. Occasionally she would nod and he would stumble on for a few more passages then he'd glance her way again.

At last it was over and we were marched to the dining hall for our usual supper of soup and bread. I breathed a sigh of relief when it was time for us to return to our dorm room and wash up for bed.

I was still hurting from the fight and exhausted, but who knew when the director might return and free up the praiser to pursue *other* interests. I had to stop putting my conjuring off and do what I had promised. So with that intent on my mind I retrieved the napkin saturated with the praiser's sap from its hiding place and shoved it under my pillow.

When the lantern was snuffed out and I heard snoring surrounding me in the darkness I withdrew my prize. Crushing it in my fist I took a deep breath and composed myself for the work.

WITHIN THE DREAM I shifted into my seal form to swim the dark river. Conjuring an image of Praiser Tom's pale round face to guide my intent I found him easily. And with the teachings of his own demon god to encourage him, he readily swam into my net. Drawing upon what I'd witnessed in Qwatola's tortured dreams, combined with my own suffering at the man's hand, I created his own personal nightmare to begin his punishment.

<<Unclean, unworthy!>> I roared, using the director's angry voice.

He whimpered, but I refused to let him wake. <<Tempting the innocent into sin, nasty, filthy creature.>> At my urging, a faceless specter materialized and accused him from the shadows.

The specter chuckled. <<Did you think you could eat all my treats without paying for them, my greedy little piggy? Come here! I have needs, too, you know.>>

Sensing what was coming, the priest's belly cramped. He shook his head desperate now to awake. Cruel laughter mocked his efforts, growing louder. Still entwined in his dreaming mind I sensed him continue along the path I had guided him to follow with no further effort on my part.

The anticipation of forbidden pleasure bloomed, combining in equal measure with guilt, fear, and pain.

<<Nasty, sinful creature, come here. You know you want it,>> the specter purred. Praiser Tom whimpered, <<No, no, go away demon!>>

Ghostly hands stroked and kissed. <<Do you really want me to leave?>> the specter of his own imagining laughed as his weak flesh grew and hardened. <<No, that's not what you want at all, hmm? Perhaps this is what you really are asking for.>> The praiser grunted his breath coming in shallow gasps.

<<And this...>> Then suddenly he writhed spewing a molten river of brown liquid and sap down his thighs.

The priest shuddered and fell back, mocking laughter echoing through the dream. Begging the voice to stop—leave him alone, he next burst into tears.

But I didn't stop; he had to pay for what he did to me, and all the others he had hurt over the years. He needed to know how his victims *really* felt.

<<Unclean, unworthy!>> I roared again, this time using Intercessor Fredderoth's voice. <<You are a loathsome disgrace. Down on your knees beg for mercy. Repent! Pray!>>

<<I'm sorry, so sorry. Yes I will be good,>> he assured the voice. <<I will be strong; I will resist their tricks. I won't let those evil zaunk whores tempt me again—I swear! Forgive me, please!>>

<<Don't blame others for your weakness and your crimes, Filth,>> I accused, using Celibress Vomica's voice this time. He pleaded with her to understand—he was only a weak, sinful man. He begged for forgiveness—but I was merciless and denied him.

Then, in the way of dreams, his naked bloated body was standing in a copper tub, the opaque water about his knees.

With a sob he reached for the hard bristled brush hanging from its cord by the rim above the drain. Then he grabbed a bar of lye soap in his other hand. Still crying he rubbed the brush vigorously over the soap, its acrid smell, submerging the blood and fecal stench.

Ignoring the discomfort of the hated brush he applied the stiff bristles vigorously to his skin. <<Have to wash the sin off—before anyone finds out—have to get clean,>> he muttered in a desperate sing-song voice.

He washed and washed, arms, legs, chest, belly and below. His skin, by his own imagining, turned even whiter, like the dead skin of a reptile and sloughed off in great chunks, leaving his body raw and bleeding.

I watched in fascination and horror as he imagined his bloody flesh swirling down the copper drain. Skeletal hands of bloody bone clutched the brush tighter as he continued scrubbing frantically. Sending him a picture of the hanged Qwatola as a parting *gift* for his enjoyment I left him to his torment and slipped out of his dream. Letting go the power I sighed and drifted into a dreamless sleep. I would have lots of work to do next day and I needed my rest.

IN THE MORNING WHEN Intercessor Fredderoth came to rouse us I awoke at peace, anxious to get started on the day's activities. Self-righteous in my belief that I was doing the right thing, I promised myself I would continue my assault on Praiser Tom through his dreams until he killed himself, or he went crazy and he was locked up somewhere far away from anymore children he could hurt.

I kept that promise and to my own satisfaction I saw the man fall apart before my eyes as the winter progressed.

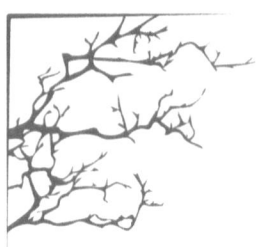

Chapter Nine

That winter dragged on and on, tormenting us with harsh blizzards and bone-chilling cold. Travel to the village was often impossible. We were cut off for days at a time, with wood for the stoves doled out sparingly and food rationed, even for the staff.

It became apparent to everyone as the winter continued that the director had sold too much of the crop for his own gain and now the whole school was suffering for his greed. The hired staff threatened to quit and a few of the priesthood complained, warning they would contact the head of their order if something wasn't done to improve conditions for *their* comfort.

Like everyone else I shivered in my ragged hand-me-down jacket and wore my extra pair of socks over my chapped hands to try and keep them warm while I did the work assigned to me. Belly empty, I huddled in my blanket each night, barely able to fall asleep. I wished I hadn't chosen a bed so close to a window that even with the shudders barred couldn't keep out the chill.

When the director was finally forced to pay for supplies out of his own purse, or face a scandal and possible recall in disgrace, little of the extra wood and food trickled down to the hungry ones in the dorms. Things didn't improve much for the children and there were several deaths among us as the cold moons lingered—including that of Cohasi.

Ever since our confinement in the Perdition Box for so many days in late summer Cohasi had developed a reoccurring illness that refused to go away completely in spite of Doc's medicines and my attempts to find the right herbs to help him. And as the cold worsened he developed a fever and began coughing up blood. He was dead before the sap flowed upward in the trees that year.

Being so close since their babyhood Matoqwa took his brother's death hard, but outwardly he showed little of his grief to anyone—including me.

But I noticed his headaches increased in their number and severity after his brother's death. Matoqwa often lashed out at everyone, which, of course, earned him more punishment from Intercessor Fredderoth or Doff.

The ground was too frozen to bury the ones who died during the winter, so a place was made for the shrouded bodies in an unheated store room where farm tools were usually stored. They would have to wait until warmer weather thawed the ground for a proper ceremony. I suspected that Matoqwa visited that store room late at night to sit with his brother. And though he never asked me, I risked myself once again to sing a Qwani'Ya brother home.

Matoqwa never openly acknowledged what I'd done, or the added risk I'd taken by using my power to sing Cohasi's ghost to rest with our ancestors, but he and the others somehow knew. We weren't exactly close war brothers again, but I stopped feeling unwanted when I was assigned a work detail with them.

As the winter progressed, Praiser Tom's unpredictable behavior also increased in severity. Gone was the cheerful friendly priest who loved to laugh and offered treats when Intercessor Fredderoth or Celibress Vomica wasn't around. He muttered to himself, ignored children stealing and breaking other rules right in front of him and neglected to appear for duty as often as not. At all hours of the day or night he could be found shivering and kneeling in prayer on the cold temple floor.

Both the staff and some of the older children whispered that he was a devil-haunted man that had been witched. Even the ones who were known to be his 'special' friends avoided him as much as possible.

Unnerved by what I had put into motion, I had mixed feelings about the matter. I despised him and rejoiced in his suffering, thinking it a just revenge for what Qwatola and many unknown others had suffered because of his unnatural appetites. And yet as I watched him sinking into the madness I'd had a hand in creating, a part of me couldn't help but pity him. I wished the director would send him away, or that he himself would do as Qwatola had done and end it—for both our sakes.

Things finally came to a terrifying conclusion one evening as we were settling in for the night. Several times as his behavior became more and more unpredictable the praiser had tried to corner me and I feared I knew that he wanted comfort from someone who would help him satisfy his unnatural hunger. But fortunately for me he chose times when it was easy enough to stage an interruption so that I was never alone with him.

He continued to beg off work as often as he could, claiming to the director that he was too ill. But that fatal night the director had had enough. The angry shouts coming out of his office as the praiser entered could be heard all over the school.

"I've had enough of your whining and malingering, Praiser!" Director Harriscot roared. "I'm through coddling you. You aren't ill; you're just lazy. It's time—more than time that you got back to your duties."

So, the result of the director's angry reprimand was that Praiser Tom was denied the refuge of his bed and assigned the unwanted job of patrolling the school corridors that night along with Celibress Vomica.

When he arrived for the last bed-check at my dorm room he seemed in a bad way. Pale and trembling, he motioned for me to follow him out into the hall when he completed his inspection and led us in our nightly prayers. I realized that he had trapped me at last. It was going to be impossible to avoid him any longer. With mixed expressions on their faces everyone watched as I rose to obey.

Knowing as well as I did myself what was probably on his mind Kutima was frightened for me, while others in the warband, like Matoqwa looked angry and ready for a fight. They knew the most probable reason he had singled me out and weren't happy about it.

They might have wanted to protest, but I made a sign to stop them from interfering. I had created this problem for myself and I wasn't going to let others suffer for my stupidity. Hoping my expression showed nothing of the revulsion churning in my gut I arose and followed him into the hall.

As I passed Ronalton I could see by the light coming from the woodstove him mouth the word whore and heard Yohan's muffled laugh. In the darkness I felt my face flush, but didn't give them the satisfaction of looking back to offer my own insult.

As I had feared from the beginning it was common knowledge among the boys by winter that I was now one of the praiser's "special friends." At first he continued to leave small gifts of food under my pillow, hoping I guess, to entice me to his bed on my own. But as the winter dragged on and food became scarcer, and his demon-ridden madness worsened, his attentions stopped. To protect myself I also tried to remain among other children as much as possible to avoid being singled out by him or anyone else with his perverted bent.

But that night was different; I could feel a "wrongness" in the air about us and I feared it. Once in his room with the door closed he crossed to his bed and sat down heavily on its side.

On the nightstand were the remains of a recent meal. My stomach growled with its emptiness. Meat and bread, and a sweet tart. Even in his distress he managed to fill his fat gut, leaving none for me, the greedy pig.

Swallowing hard I remained just inside the closed door hands clinched into fists at my sides, unsure what he expected of me and afraid to ask. If he thought I was going to touch him without even offering me something for my discomfort I was definitely going to fight him—no matter if I ended up in the Box for my trouble, I decided.

Silent and unmoving we remained like that for a long time. Then he finally found the courage to lift his head and looked me in the eye. "You're a good boy, 297, and very kind. I've watched how you try to take care of the children younger than you and do your work without complaining. I know our mighty god favors you."

Oh by the blood of my ancestors I hope not. I shuddered; what was this crazy priest trying to say to me?

When I remained silent, he nodded to himself as if I had agreed with his assessment of me. "Yes, you are a good boy and blessed, too. I'm sure you won't torment me when you hear my confession, or blame me. Please will you pray for me, boy?"

Pray for him? What a laugh. But I would gladly curse him—already had. "I don't understand, pray for you, Praiser Tom, and hear your confession? I-I'm not a priest—or even a brother—shouldn't you ask—"

Choking on a sob he covered his face with his pale hands, tears leaking through the web of his fingers. "N-no I can't. Please, there's no one else," another desperate sob. "No one else..." Then he broke down, crying uncontrollably.

From my place by the door I stared unsure what to do next. When I remained silent and unmoving, he found his voice again and begged, "Please, have mercy, dear boy, I am a weak, loathsome sinner, but you are such a sweet boy. I can take care of you if you let me—give you lots of nice things. Won't you come closer and..."

His eyes implored me to comfort him, come to him. My arms now folded across my chest I remained silent, glaring, my lips curled into a snarl of disgust. When the silence between us had gone on long enough I finally broke it.

My voice dripping with my contempt I said, "Pray for you? After you raped my Qwani'Ya brother over and over till he took his own life to escape your unnatural attentions? And now you want me to pray for you? You disgust me, priest.

"Yes, I will pray for you, pervert. I will pray to all the spirits of this land for your death." He cried out as my harsh words struck him like arrows shot from an avenging bow, but even though I was trembling inside, afraid of what he could do to me if he regained his wits, I was beyond caring.

"Unnatural, evil man, did you think I wanted or liked what you made me do?" I snapped. "I did not—I hated every moment of your touch. I hope you burn forever in the fiery abyss of your god."

I turned and reached for the door handle, my rage choking me, nearly uncontrollable. I feared what I might do next if I stayed any longer in that room. But just before I opened the door a strangled cry from the bed caused me to turn one last time.

Praiser Tom was still sitting on the edge of his bed, but he had reached for the knife lying on the side of his plate. When he saw he had my attention once more he looked me in the eye, gave me a mirthless smile and drew the sharp knife across both wrists. Frozen like a deer caught in torchlight I stared openmouthed as red blood streamed down his hands and arms in a growing flood.

Finally I got my wits about me and rushed out into the hall screaming for Celibress Vomica, or someone to help him. The Celibress heard me from her post on the girl's side and came charging in my direction.

Red-faced and breathing hard she demanded when she came to a stop right in front of me, "What's the meaning of this noise, boy? Why aren't you in your bed?"

Trembling and afraid I would be blamed for the crazy man's death I wordlessly pointed behind me into the on-duty priest's room.

Muttering something under her breath she angrily pushed past me.

With a startled oath she was back in another moment and grabbed me. Spying Ronalton peeking out of our dorm room she shouted for him to run get Doc from the infirmary.

Her bony fingers clawing into my shoulders she shook me and demanded, "What have you done to the praiser, you nasty little zaunk?"

"N-nothing, Celibress Vomica, I've done nothing," I protested. I held out my hands to show her that there was no blood on me or my clothes.

She stopped shaking me and really studied me. I shuddered. If this angry and bitter old woman finally recognized me from our march south to the Preserve...

But in the next moment she was distracted by Doc's arrival and she released me to show him into the room. They closed the door so no one else could see what was happening.

By this time the commotion had roused the boys in the nearby rooms. I saw curious faces peering through half-opened doorways and a few of the braver girls were peeking from the stairs. I ignored the inquiries whispered in my direction, but I dared not leave—I knew they would have more questions for me when they came out.

Finally when Ronalton was sent to inform the director and tell Doff to bring a stretcher Kuweya and Matoqwa ignored Yohan's command to stay inside our room. Along with Komonti they ventured out to ask me in a whisper what had happened. "Is the praiser dead?" Kuweya murmured

"I've seen no ghost, so I don't think so," I said.

Komonti let out a bark of a laugh. "Too bad, Puhani, better luck next time, eh?"

I made a face, and told him to keep his voice down. Then I told them quickly and quietly what had happened. At the sound of more footsteps they snuck back to their rooms. As he stepped inside Kuweya turn to me and gave me the hand sign of respect that was often given to a Puhani of power. I nodded, but in my heart I wasn't sure I deserved it.

It wasn't long before the men returned. Entering the room where doc and the celibress still labored over the dying man they bundled him on the stretcher and began carefully carrying him down the stairs to infirmary.

When they were gone the Celibress returned her attention to me. "If you meant no harm to the praiser, what were you doing in that room, answer me that, boy?"

How much to tell of the truth…? "Praiser Tom told me to come with him back to his room after prayers were over," I finally stammered.

"Why? Why would he do that?" she shook me again. "Speak true now or be damned to the eternal fires forever."

"I don't know, Celibress. He said he wanted me to pray with him." When I said those last words an understanding flared in her eyes and then was gone. She obviously was aware of what the praiser had been doing to the children here and didn't like it.

Letting go of me as if my touch now soiled her, her lips thinned into a hard line. "What else did he say to you in that room? That still doesn't explain why he would do something like—like that." She pointed back into the bloody room.

"I don't know, Celibress, truly I don't. He said he wanted me to hear his confession. I told him I was no priest. But when I turned to get Intercessor Fredderoth he cried out, grabbed the knife on his tray and cut his wrists. And, and then I shouted for help. I swear, Celibress Vomica that's all I know." She was staring at me so intently as I choked out my explanation that I feared she had recognized me. Then her eyes widened and I knew she had.

"Nasty little zaunk, I remember you now. You and your witch of a grandfather nearly killed Intercessor Raymonel and now here you are trying to kill another of Djoven's good priests."

I was terrified by then. If anyone here believed her accusation and contacted the council of the inquisition they might send someone to investigate and I could burn—or hang—or both.

Deciding to try and lie my way out of this I shook my head vigorously and then pointed to the tattoos on my face. "I am Kukiya boy. I not go on march south."

"Then how do you know their language and why are you so friendly with them? Don't the bunch of you call yourselves a 'war band' in your heathen language?"

As I'd been talking to the Celibress, Director Harriscot had come up behind me unnoticed. As his frosty blue eyes captured me in their malice I felt the evil I had noticed before in him pierce my chest. Though he had no Qwakaiva to conjure, this dried up stick of a man possessed the power to do great evil in the way of selfish and greedy men. And now, once again he had his attention drawn to me.

Spies, they were everywhere, and I had been warned. "We live on Preserve together," I offered, hoping to avoid more punishment. I stared wide-eyed, unable to speak further.

It didn't matter, because Celibress Vomica had plenty to say—about me—my family—and the praiser. Reciting over and over what she claimed were my evil deeds I couldn't tell how seriously he took her accusations as she ranted and raged about god-cursed witches and how they were out to destroy the priesthood and her in particular.

Fortunately for me she had no idea of my real crimes, so when the director asked me if any of her outrageous accusations were true, I could honestly say they were not.

The director at last put me out of my misery and ordered me to my bed. As he ushered the Celibress, still ranting, down the stairs I heard him say, "No, Celibress, I don't think that boy had anything to do with this unfortunate accident. We all know the praiser has been—ill, for some time."

I couldn't hear her response, but the director's deeper voice carried up to me quite clearly. "Nonsense. If the boy was as evil as you claim I'm sure the good Intercessor Raymonel wouldn't have pleaded so hard for his admittance to this school."

Once again her answering comments were lost to me as they reached the next floor and headed down the corridor towards infirmary. I took a shaky breath and crept back into my dorm. I didn't need to hear her; I could guess well enough what she might say. I had been spared further punishment for the moment, but I knew in my heart it wasn't over.

And I was afraid.

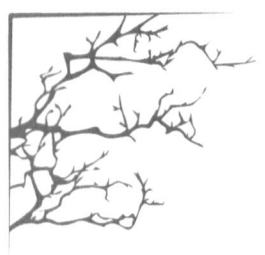

Part Three
Chapter One

PRAISER TOM RECOVERED physically from his attempt to take his life, but his madness only worsened as the cold weather dragged on. After leaving infirmary he was confined to his bedroom in the staff house until warmer weather made the roads passable and he could be sent elsewhere. At times he had to be tied to his bed when he tried to kill himself again. His howling and screaming sent shivers down the spine of anyone passing by outside who heard him.

This, of course was a big inconvenience for the rest of the priests who had to care for him and take over his assignments as well as their own. For the children this meant that some of the morning and nightly duties, like morning bed checks and bedtime prayers were left to trusted head boys and girls to oversee.

I'm not sure how it was for the girls, but in our dorm Ronalton, who had always been a bully and a dog fart became nearly unbearable after he was given added responsibilities. He had been allowed to have a discipline switch and he used it often on the ones whom he didn't like or those he thought were slow to obey his orders. Keveneth, of course, became once more his victim, as did I, still being small for my age.

Over the years I had had lots of practice ignoring bullies and their taunts, so I did what he ordered and took his occasional lick without complaint. Keveneth, however, wasn't so lucky. It was easy to fall back into old habits of fear and submission, and like any predator the head boy sensed it. He tormented him mercilessly when none of the warband was near. I suspected he was back doing Ronalton's homework again, though he refused to admit to it when I asked.

And I, to my shame, had been reluctant to help him by invoking my gift ever since Celibress Vomica had recognized me. But then one afternoon things became intolerable and the warband, including me, were forced to intervene.

When the older and stronger boys were sent to bring back a fallen tree that could be chopped up for future firewood, Keveneth was ordered to join us, now that his health had improved by drinking my herbal brews. Though he was the best reader at the school and did better than most with his numbers, since the harvest he was often included in the heavier farm work, when Celibress Dinana didn't need him to teach the younger children.

That day Ronalton was in a foul mood. It was cold and Doff had left him in charge of the final loading onto the wood cart when he was called back to the school to help restrain the praiser again.

As soon as the man left Ronalton started in on us, shouting for us to hurry. Thus far to my knowledge the head boy hadn't dared bully or use his switch on one of the warband. Knowing we stuck together, he feared the consequences of such an open act of war, no doubt.

But that afternoon was different. The wind singing in the branches of the bare trees whispered of danger coming and I'd felt the "wrongness" all about us as snow cloud beings massed and the air chilled.

I don't know if it was the cold or with the praiser gone he had gained confidence that the priests needed him and would ignore his cruelties, but for whatever reason he decided to take out his frustration on the weakest of us, which that day happened to be Keveneth.

Ever since Celibress Dinana, at my urging, had forbidden him from doing Ronalton's school work the bully had wanted revenge for getting him punished.Now that the priest and the staff were short-handed I guess he figured he could get away with threatening Keveneth again.

With only a thin pair of socks to protect his hands from the cold and the rough tree branches Ronalton decided that he was slowing down the loading with his clumsiness. Ronalton began threatening and hitting him with his switch and swearing at him to hurry with his pile of wood or he'd tell the intercessor to put him in the Box.

My own hands were numb with the cold; I could barely feel my fingers, so I could understand how easy it was to drop a piece of wood now and then. Keveneth endured the abuse without crying out when he was whacked, which seemed to anger that dog turd of a head boy even more. And the added abuse to his half-frozen hands, of course, caused him to be even slower and clumsier.

When we were back inside and a bit of warmth was coming back into my body I came over to Keveneth with Matoqwa following, and demanded to see his hands. "It's nothing," he protested and tried to shove his reddened hands into the pockets of his trousers.

Reaching out I grabbed one to have a look. It was an unhealthy white at the fingertips while on the back there was a series of red slashes, some oozing blood as they thawed in the warm indoor air. "That doesn't look like nothing to me," I growled.

Looking over my shoulder Matoqwa swore in Chamuqwani and glared around murderously, searching for Ronalton.

Inishkim alerted by the three of us standing together by the stairs came over to investigate. "That looks bad, brother," he said after also examining Kutima's hand for a moment. "I think you should go to infirmary and let doc see it. You wouldn't want to lose the tips of your fingers."

"I'll be all right. I'll get some water and just soak my hands for a while till they warm up."

Spying the pretty Celibress Dinana, who I knew liked him, standing by the entrance to the dining hall, I urged, "Go, brother, show her your hands and tell her you want to see doc. I'm sure she will let you."

Inishkim put an arm over his shoulder and speaking quietly to him walked him over to talk to her.

"That head boy dog turd is wrong if he and his pack think they can get away with that," I heard Matoqwa grumble as he watch them approach the Celibress. She studied what they showed her and then she waved Kutima and Inishkim up the stairs to infirmary.

Surprised by his reaction I turned to him, and asked, "What are you thinking, war brother?"

"I'm thinking that it's time—more than time, that dog humper is taught a lesson." He snarled.

My mouth fell open, too startled to speak. Finally I said, "You surprise me, Bear, back home you were as likely to pound Kutima yourself as defend him."

He snorted and gave me a disgusted look, as if I was stupid. "Well, that was then, and this is now. The breed is still a bossy dog fart sometimes—as are you, but he is from home, and us Big Ice Lake boys have to stick together, right?"

In my mind I heard the echo of Cohasi saying those same words to me on more than one occasion. "Right," I agreed, choking on the lump of sadness now forming in my throat. "So I repeat, what are you thinking?"

THAT NIGHT WHEN ALL was quiet and the halls empty of nosy priests, five boys arose from their beds with strips of blanket wrapped around each hand and their faces covered by empty grain sacks with holes for eyes cut into the cloth. They picked up the sleeping Ronalton, now as stiff as a log by my conjuring, and half carried, half dragged him down the stairs and out into the cold night with no one the wiser.

Eyes wide with fear and unable to move or speak, he gave us little trouble. As an added precaution though, someone blindfolded him when we reached the yard. The night was bitterly cold, the wind picking up as the approaching storm massed for an attack. Fortunately for the head boy maybe, we would have to be quick about our punishment. But the weather would hide our tracks and no one was going to venture out to catch us—even if I let Ronalton howl his head off, so that was good, I guessed.

Once away from the school windows and safe behind the bathhouse where no one could see or hear them the five were joined by two other masked figures, one carrying a willow switch similar to the one Ronalton himself had been using. It didn't take long—everyone was too cold to drag his torment out. No one touched his face, but he should have a cracked rib or two and lots of nice bruises in the morning.

Before bringing him back inside, however, a muffled voice spoke with the growing storm as its echo. "No one cares if you and Yohan remain head boys, as long as you and your pack of mangy dogs don't abuse your power. Change your cruel ways," the voice warned.

"Because if we have to come back to remind you," a harsh voice said from the darkness on his left. "You might not survive next time."

"And if you think to tell one of Djoven's devils what we did, remember this, too. We will come for you again. And just like tonight, no stupid priest will save you, piss drinker," another unrecognizable voice promised.

When the beating was over and the blizzard finally beginning to dump its load of snow on the blood, we carried the whimpering and shivering head boy back to his bed and tucked him in like a babe for the night.

Before releasing him from my power we covered his head with his blanket then slipped back into our own beds. The masks and bloody wraps we had used to cover our hands were hidden away in the bath house for future use if needed.

Next morning Blizzard still whined and blew his snow outside. Everyone was cold and slow about waking. To my surprise the director announced that there would be no school which meant we could all stay in our beds to try and keep warm if we wished. Hunger drove most of us to the dining hall for our small portion of mush and hot tea at some point during the morning.

Ronalton chose to remain in his bed and snapped at Yohan. "You're in charge, so after morning prayers send someone to get me some tea and mush—I'm not feeling well." Yohan looked at him with mouth agape, but led us in the morning prayers and then did as he asked.

Catching sight of me sitting atop my bed dressed in several layers of clothes with my blanket thrown over my shoulder for added warmth, Yohan shouted, "297, get your lazy behind up and go get me and the head boy some breakfast."

I'd been just about to twist my cord into the Seer's Pool pattern to check on my baby sister Kitahtla and the rest of my outlawed family, but I rose instead. Inwardly laughing at the irony of the situation I hoped my face was expressionless. I replaced the cord around my neck and I headed for the kitchen without complaint.

Maybe at some time in the future we might need to teach Yohan the same lesson we had given to his friend, but for now I wasn't giving anyone an excuse to throw me in the Box.

When it came time that afternoon to shovel the mountain of new snow that had collected in the yard there was a call for all the older boys to pick up shovels and help. As I'd feared Intercessor Fredderoth did discover that Ronalton had been badly beaten.

But Ronalton himself could tell them little about how many, or who had assaulted him. And when all the older boys were lined up and their hands were inspected by the director it was even more of a puzzle because no one displayed injuries that would be visible after giving someone a severe beating.

That, of course, much to my horror, got Celibress Vomica muttering about witches again. Especially after Ronalton got up the courage to confess to being unable to speak or even move while the assault was taking place. The Celibress, of course, accused me of magically causing the attack, and dragged me into the director's office for a thorough questioning. Unfortunately Ronalton couldn't prove I had anything to do with it to the director's satisfaction.

But to appease Celibress Vomica's nagging I'm sure, I was made to kneel in the cold temple for an entire night, wearing one of Djoven's lightning bolt pendants. I was instructed to repent my sins and pray that the god wouldn't strike me dead for being an evil heathen savage.

Throughout my punishment the bitter old woman often appeared with her willow switch to check on me, and administer stinging blows to my hands and back, which she claimed she did just to make sure that I stayed awake, kneeling and praying the entire time. I doubted the director had ordered the extra cruelty, but I endured the added suffering without a sound. My hands especially ached mercilessly for several days afterward, but I had the small satisfaction of knowing that each of us suffered a cold and sleepless night.

In the morning when I was released from my vigil and I would have removed Djoven's sign she put up such a fuss that the director gave in and ordered me to keep wearing it. Once before I had been forced to wear one of the Chamuqwani god's pendants, and I only survived the fever it cursed me with, because Grandfather had been wise enough to remove it before it killed me.

This one was pretty harmless, or so I thought at the time, just a piece of metal not infused with any god or malicer's power, but I would regret my stupidity before summer was over.

At the time, however, I didn't put up a fuss when Celibress insisted I continue to wear the annoying thing. I was exhausted and hungry and all I truly wanted was to get out of the cold drafty god house. If it eased her mind and kept her from acting further on her suspicions about me, I was content to give in to her demands and let her think she'd won.

Nonetheless I vowed to myself to stay out of trouble as much as possible when I was dismissed to return to my tasks and school work. But after a hasty meal I wasn't allowed to rest and sleep, as I'd hoped. No, I was instructed to join a work party sent out for wood.

When my jacket fell open as I lifted a large round into the cart Matoqwa and Kuweya saw the pendant and their eyes bugged wide. Remembering Matoqwa's violent reaction when he first saw me wearing Djoven's glyph back on the Preserve I balled my hands into fists by my side as I faced them and tensed for another attack.

"Don't you two start in on me about my new jewelry," I growled at them. "I haven't converted. You've all heard the rumors going around that an evil malicer is cursing the school. And you can also guess, Bear, that I'm her first choice for that honor."

Matoqwa glance from me to Kuweya and they smirked. Then Kuweya said, "So, if it eases Celibress Vomica's mind to think that she's protected from your heathen savage witchery if you wear the damned thing, then you wear it, eh?"

Relieved they weren't going to fight me or call me a traitor I relaxed my fists. "Something like that," I admitted and smiled. It felt good to be back in favor with the warband again. We had shared so much together, in our outlawry and here at the live-away school. I had missed our former closeness without even being aware of what had been absent in my life.

But all too soon our slacking off had been noticed and Doff shouted for us to get back to work, which we did willingly enough. You stayed warmer working than standing around talking.

WARM WEATHER CAME AT last and snow melted. Willows greened by the river and fish swam to the surface of quiet pools to gulp down insects and frog eggs. Trees bloomed in the orchard, their branches heavy with sweet-smelling pink flowers. The warband when sent to do farm chores often took the time to graze like our deer relatives on green shoots popping up among last year's leaves that the ignorant Chamuqwani called "weeds".

Overhead I watched with tears in my eyes as ducks and geese headed north in the cloudless blue sky. I wanted so badly to go with them. But I dared not think too long about that. I was still here at the live-away school and unlike several others I had survived another brutal winter among the Chamuqwani. A vision of Cohasi's face forming unbidden in my memory, I reminded myself that I should be grateful to be alive and not let my heart dwell on something beyond my power to change.

Yes, I told myself, I had much to be grateful for. Ronalton was being more careful about how he enforced school rules, and I was certainly grateful for that. The Perdition Box remained empty, because no one in the warband had the energy to torment enemy boys or get into trouble with the priests and I was thankful for that, too.

At the school and on the farm there was always lots to do. For us boys there were seeds to plant in the rich brown earth fences to mend and pigs and new calves to help feed and tend. In the school and the yard the girls were kept busy with washing and airing out blankets and other bedding as well as mending clothes and sewing new ones, using materials donated to Djoven's temple, "for the poor savage children."

Like everyone else I fell into bed each night exhausted by the day's work. Yes looking back I realize it was a good time. It was the calm before the storm, as the old people would say.

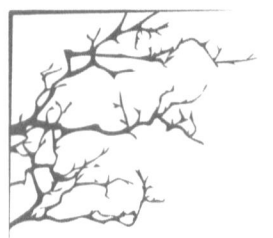

Chapter Two

As soon as Sun dried the mud on Road the director sent Administrator Rizdale and a couple of the farm workers who lived in the village to Town with Praiser Tom. Keveneth told me that they were taking him on Train to another god house far away where they would take care of him.

In spite of the rumors about a witch cursing him the staff had told the children he was ill and would be coming back someday when he was feeling better. Except for the youngest among us no one believed that he was ever coming back, but we all liked the going-away party with pudding cake and canned berries that we were given in his honor.

With the treats still rounding our bellies we dutifully lined up to sing him a holy song and wave him farewell as he was settled on straw in the back of the supply cart.

Like some big over-grown baby Praiser Tom was wrapped with blankets in spite of the warm day so I wasn't able to get a good look at him. To keep him clean they had shaved off his brown hair and beard. The gray eyes that stared back at us were vacant and unfocused, drool glistening in one corner of his slack mouth.

"He looks like a big fat baby sitting up there," Iwaz murmured.

Komonti snorted. "A baby too big for a woman to carry so they have to use a cart."

Iwaz swore. "Maybe if everybody is lucky they will dump him off the bridge on their way down river."

"He's going to Saint Royston's monastery for those who are ill or insane," Kutima supplied, using his know-it-all voice.

Back home Matoqwa used to punch him when he tried to impress us with his learning. Now he just spat on the ground and gave Keveneth a disgusted glare. "Shut up, dog turd. Who cares where he's going as long as it's away from here."

"And he can't hurt anymore children," Kuweya added.

"I agree, brother, but what's wrong with him?" I heard Atuusca whisper. "He looks so, so—weird."

"He's probably been drugged so he won't cause any trouble to his minders on the trip," Inishkim said, stroking his chin in thought.

Awe, fear, pity and remorse, looking upon the result of my conjuring for the first time since he'd been carried away bleeding, I felt a mixture of emotions churn in my gut and a shiver slide down my backbone.

I had been gifted powerful Qwakaiva both from my Qwa'Nayhi Seal father and from my Benefactor Kunai. I had sworn my life to serve the People and not to use my gifts for personal gain. I wanted only to do good in my world and help my people survive these terrible times, but often it was so hard to know what was right.

What I did to the praiser—was that doing good or a violation of my oath and my power? The man was a pervert who hurt children. He had abused his position as a priest entrusted with vulnerable ones assigned to his care. Didn't he deserve what I'd had a part in doing to him? Didn't he...? I told myself yes he did deserve what I conjured for him.

Ah, but was I the one his fate had destined to carry out that judgement?

The Great Kunai didn't think so, if the crystal being given to me as protector and guide was speaking true. I had disobeyed them all and I trembled inside wondering what consequences for me and those I cared about might be waiting for us in the future.

WHEN THE WAGON'S DUST had disappeared on the horizon a wave of relief flooded me and everyone else at the school. Without being consciously aware the mad man's presence had been a nagging irritant no one could reach to scratch. With him gone the school fell into a lazy rhythm enjoying the warm weather and the ability to work and play outdoors.

To my surprise Doff and Celibress Dinana organized ball games after the evening meal on more than one occasion. During the games the boys were broken up into teams with the girls hovering on the sidelines to watch and cheer their favorites. I caught Inishkim as well as Matoqwa, Komonti and Kuweya making flirty eyes at a few of the older girls when Celibress wasn't looking.

Inishkim...Before joining the outlaws his Kukiya parents had converted and allowed their priest to begin teaching him the Chamuqwani language and how to read their god book. After coming here he, like me, saw the wisdom in studying the enemy through learning to read, as well as speak their language.

Inishkim himself was a thoughtful, sensible youth not easily given to emotional outbursts. He had run away from his convert family and was living with an uncle in Golannah's band when I first met him. But I'd only seen him occasionally and didn't know him well before our capture. Here at the school his quiet appeals for the more excitable among us to see reason had helped me calm a bad situation many a time. I liked him and hoped I could call him friend.

I wasn't sure how he was able to do it, but my war brother had found a way to pass messages and meet secretly from time to time with the girl he fancied named Jamiya. She was a slim brown girl from a people whose tribal lands were further east from the desert preserve where we'd been sent. With long legs and a full-lipped mouth that could smile flirtatiously or thin with displeasure she was the one who had captured my war brother's heart. I didn't care for her much, but I wished my brother good fortune on his hunt.

So when I kept noticing his wistful looks when he saw the girl washing clothes or sweeping the steps I asked him about her one day when we were alone and working next to each other. After a little prodding he shyly admitted that he hoped to marry Jamiya one day when we were freed from this terrible place.

Though old enough to be interested in girls myself I looked younger than my actual age of sixteen—and I was shy. It was no wonder that the bolder ones among the girls our age would be interested in my taller and stronger war brothers. But there was this one girl with raven hair and dark eyes who gave me a shy smile whenever she dared. Unfortunately for us I had no time to pursue a love interest that spring, and later it was too late.

IT WAS HOT AND SUNNY the day the supply cart returned and my life changed forever. I had been working in the big field garden with Kuweya and Kutima-Keveneth when a cloud of dust heading our way from the village caught our attention. Doff was nowhere in sight, so we stopped working and shaded our eyes to see who was coming.

"I think it's administrator Rizdale and the cart sent to bring back supplies from Town," Kuweya said after focusing on the murky veil for a while.

"You may be right, brother," Keveneth said. "When I was passing by his office yesterday I heard Director Harriscot say they were due back any time."

Yes, that was probably the truth of it, I thought. Then a shiver ran down my spine as the dust cleared for a moment and I saw that leading the supply cart was another vehicle, a dark carriage with the lightning bold sigil of the temple on its door.

"Who is that, I wonder?" Kuweya said, voicing my own thought.

"Probably another priest to take over for Praiser Tom," Keveneth guessed. "I also heard the rest of the staff is complaining about the extra workload since the praiser fell ill."

"Maybe... but it looks like three or four people inside there, not just two," Kuweya said as he continued to watch the approaching vehicles.

"Hmm, I think you are right, brother," I said.

It was steaming hot that day and I had welcomed the break in our routine. Like my brothers I was mildly curious, then a spirit voice on the breeze murmured in my mind, <<Beware, young Siyatli, the enemy comes.>>

His physical form was still blocked from my human eyes. I focused my Gift on the carriage and saw the malevolent power radiating from someone riding inside. I trembled and drew back as a knot of fear tightened in my gut. My crystal guardian also became aware of the malicer at the same moment, and I felt it shrink down to the size of a grain of sand inside my chest. I had been warned...

Suddenly unable to stand I sank to my knees wishing I could sink into the brown Earth. I must have made a sound as I dropped because my companions broke off watching the approaching newcomers to stare at me.

"Tas, what's wrong?" Kutima-Keveneth asked. Then when I didn't answer he turned to Kuweya and said, "Maybe the heat today has got to him. Help me get him into the shade by the barn."

The barn! "No, no I can't go over there," I said as I staggered to my feet. "I'll be alright. Picking up my dropped hoe, I turned my back on the commotion by the stable yard.

"Tas, where are you going?" Keveneth called after me. "Praiser Jonash will want us to help unload the supply cart soon."

Not turning back, I shook my head and kept moving deeper into the field. Behind me I heard them talking amongst themselves but didn't stop. My thoughts were in chaos I wasn't thinking clearly. All I knew was that I had to hide—run away before he noticed me and...

A few moments later Kuweya, also carrying a hoe, past me and began digging up weeds further down the row where I was working. When he was close enough that we could speak quietly, he asked, "What's wrong, Puhani?"

How could I answer; what should I tell him? Swallowing down the fear threatening to overwhelm my reason I finally said, "One of Djoven's powerful malicers is in the carriage. And—and he's come for me. I was warned..."

Kuweya swore in the enemy language and jabbed his hoe into the ground viciously tearing up a young seedling along with the bushy weed he was unearthing. At last he said, "What does your guardian say about this? Will it protect you?"

I shook my head. "No. It tried to warn me not to use my Gift so openly while among the enemy, but I didn't listen. And now it is afraid, too. It is hiding and won't answer my call."

He was quiet for a long time just weeding. Over by the barn we could hear the sounds of welcome as the cart and carriage arrived and Doff began shouting orders for the boys to start the unloading. At last he said, "You used your power to help others in spite of knowing your danger.

"You saved us from the hangman, healed our wounds and avenged our dead at great cost to yourself. So if your guardian fears this malicer and can't protect you, then maybe it's time the warband protects you."

I stared openmouthed. I wasn't sure they *could* save me from the malicer, but I felt humbled, and honored that they would want to try. Feeling the lump in my throat once again, I choked out, "Thank you, I am honored. What do you have in mind?"

"I'm thinking that for the moment we need to go back to help with the unloading before someone gets to wondering where we are."

When I glanced over to the barnyard he chuckled at my expression. "Don't worry, Puhani. The malicer you fear has probably gone inside the priests' house by now. He will be tired from his trip. We have time to make a plan."

"What kind of plan?"

"What Komonti and the cousins have been grumbling about for moons now. Escape, what else?" he patted my shoulder and motioned for me to precede him back to the barn. "I will speak to Komonti and the others on your behalf, so don't worry. The weather is good now we will go soon."

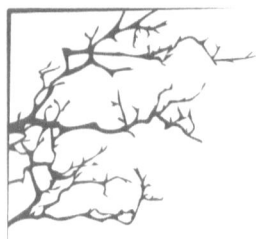

Chapter Three

Kuweya was right. By the time we arrived at the barn the newcomers had been collected by the director and were gone to the priests' house to get settled in and rest. We joined a line of boys waiting beside the cart and were handed down bags of grain and other supplies. Then Praiser Jonash directed us to carry our loads to either the barn or the storeroom by the kitchen, depending on what label was on the bags we were given.

Everything was unloaded and stored away by the time the temple bell rang to call us for the evening sermon and prayers. As we lined up to march to the temple Matoqwa and Komonti being two of the tallest in the warband put themselves in front and behind me. We took our places in the back row as usual and as soon as I was seated I lowered my head and arranged my hands as if in prayer.

Through my fingers I studied the priests sitting on high-backed chairs at the front by the altar. There were two. One was a plump dark-skinned man with a shaved head dressed in blue robes and wearing the usual silver pendent with the lightning sigil of their god on his chest.

His eyes were a deep brown and his full lips curved up at their corners as if it wouldn't take much to make him smile. I didn't dare unshield enough to use my Gift to see his spirit fire, but he looked harmless enough. Though I knew from experience that looks could be deceiving. I hoped for everyone's sake he would turn out to be no pervert and kind.

The other man sitting by the director, I knew without needing the power of my gift, was the one I needed to fear. He was dressed in a robe of dark red, the color of old dried blood. He wore the lightning bolt pendent, like other priests I'd seen, but his was a gold color surrounded by a triangle made of iron. His skin was as pale as cream, though his cropped hair was dark. He had deep violet eyes, a long chamuqwani nose and a cruel mouth framed by a dark mustache and short beard. Though it was obvious he did no work in the sun, his tall slim body didn't appear unhealthy.

Keveneth's father had sent him to Saint Yon's after his mother died and his chamuqwani father was transferred to another trading post. I wished he was sitting with us so I could ask him about the stranger's god sigil and clothing. It obviously meant something important, judging by how the other priests were acting.

Taking his place beside the director the newcomer regarded the people assembled his hard eyes assessing, judging us. I prayed my shield would hold because I could feel his malice even in the darkness where we sat. As if already aware of the danger, and sensing my distress, my war brothers moved closer as if to protect me.

Celibress Vomica was also studying the assembly with a smug expression twisting her thin mouth. I wondered if she had contacted the priests in the Father Emperor's town without the director's knowledge, because to my surprise the director didn't look pleased to see the priest dressed in dark read, either.

The director was all smiles when speaking to the man in blue, but when the priest in red addressed him, I caught the look of fear cross over his lined face and I realized the director was afraid. Though I didn't like the man, I feared with the stab of a foretelling that this stranger brought with him a great danger for everyone living at the school—including the director and the meddling celibress.

At last all were settled and the director rose and took his place behind the stand that held his big god book. He cleared his throat and began, "Bow your heads, everyone, and let us pray."

We bowed our heads and listened to a long rambling prayer telling us to repent of our sins and to be thankful for the Great God's many blessings. We had heard it all before so like most everyone else I stopped listening, and focused my Qwakaiva on becoming invisible like white rabbit hiding in a snow drift when the wolverine is near.

Before the director let us go to our meal he introduced us to the newcomers sitting beside him. Motioning for the priest in blue to rise he said, "Children, this is Praiser Liucas. He will be taking over the duties of Praiser Tom, whom we all wish a speedy recovery."

The new priest bowed to the director then turned to face us, a smile lighting up his face. "Good evening, everyone, praise the Mighty Thunderer, our god. I am so happy to be here and meet you."

His dark skin and his accent reminded me of the black soldier who had married my aunt Tuulah and taken her back to his island home across the big lake he called ocean. He was a bit difficult to understand at first but he seemed a good natured man who had all the children smiling by the time he finished speaking and sat down.

That was not true of the director's other guest. As the man in the dark robe stood, the director announced with a slight tremor in his voice, "And this is Grand Intercessor Hoyt. He has been sent to us by His Divine Holiness because the High One has heard of our troubles, and the deaths that have occurred among us. He fears for the safety of our eternal souls and has sent this good priest to discover the Wicked, lurking among us who have caused such evil, and bring the guilty ones to suffer the God's fearsome justice."

The Grand Intercessor acknowledged the director's introduction with a nod and rose so all could see him. He didn't speak to us directly, but his piercing stare as he studied us had many whimpering and shaking by the time he finished and resumed his seat.

It was a worried assembly that filed into the dining hall that evening. After meeting the grand intercessor everybody, including the staff hired from the village seemed fearful and anxious, except Celibress Vomica, of course.

When she surveyed the hall checking for children misbehaving, she found me sitting at my table with my hands clasped waiting for the prayer to bless our meal. Looking me rudely in the eye she gave me a gloating smile.

So it really was you, you bitter old hag, who has called upon your god's wicked malicer to punish me, I thought. *Well we shall see, eh?* You may have brought more trouble here than you planned on. I straightened and stared right back, giving her a toothy smile of my own that displayed my canines.

Though I refused to give her the satisfaction of seeing my weakness I lay awake most of the night tossing with worry. Hoping to speak to my seal father so I could warn him of my danger, I tried unsuccessfully to communicate with him by swimming the Dream, but I couldn't find him.

Fearing this malicer was stronger and more experienced than I was, I didn't dare continue my search for father so I reluctantly stopped. If I kept trying I reasoned this enemy malicer might be able to find and hurt some of my relatives or my chamuqwani friend Collin through their link to me. So I kept my anxiety inside and tried to go on with the tasks assigned me as if nothing was wrong.

Over the next few days Praiser Liucas worked hard at being friendly and nice to everyone, but the tension at the school remained thick enough to cut with a knife. It became clear as the days dragged on that the grand intercessor was at the school to investigate more than the Celibress Vomica's rants about witches.

Intercessor Hoyt had the director give him a room on the first floor down the passageway from the dining hall to use as his office. He also had administrator Rizdale bring him some of the big ledgers that Kutima said contained the school's accounts. And that, of course, got the director and some of the others involved in his schemes to steal our food and supplies very worried.

I knew Celibress Vomica had pointed me out to the grand intercessor that first day, but so far he had made no attempt to single me out and question me. That of course, made me even more nervous.

Thinking about it later I realized he was waiting on me to reveal myself and do something stupid—which I eventually did.

THE BERRY MOON WAS nearing the full when Kuweya whispered to me as we stood in the line for evening prayers. "We go tomorrow night. Gather your things and be ready, Puhani."

I felt my mouth drop open in surprise then I quickly closed it and hoped my expression revealed nothing of my inner thoughts. Since his arrival the grand intercessor had been focusing on the director and his books. No one knew what secret reports he was sending off to the priests higher up in his order, but here at the school the director and his friends were keeping to the priest house as often as was possible and allowing Intercessor Fredderoth and the new praiser to preach the daily sermons.

This of course had lulled me into a false sense of security. Maybe he wasn't here to find me, maybe he was just here to stop the thieving, or so I tried to convince myself.

I had been told not to worry, that the Kukiya would handle everything. I just needed to focus on keeping out of trouble—not doing anything that might land me in the Box. I hadn't realized they had gone so far with their plan as to have a particular night in mind. Spying Celibress Vomica watching us out of the corner of my eye, I gave Kuweya the barest of nods and followed Inishkim into the temple.

A few days after Kuweya's revelation to help me escape, Inishkim sought me out for a private talk when we were working in the garden again. When we were far enough away from the others that no one else could hear us, he said, "I hope you will not think too badly of me, Puhani, but I'm not leaving with you and the rest of the warband.

"You already know I want to marry Jamiya. She doesn't want to leave, so I will stay and finish out my time here. I wish you well and a safe journey back to the desert. I'm sorry to abandon you and my war brothers, but I give you my word I will not betray you. This I swear."

Not looking up from my own work I considered his words as I calmed my own feelings. I was shocked, and yes, a little hurt by his confession, but how could I blame him. A brotherhood born from outlawry and war, since coming to the live-away school the ties binding our little warband together had been slowly unraveling."

"I am saddened by your decision, war brother," I finally told him, "but I respect you and your choice. Do you know when they plan to leave?"

"No, and I don't want to know. They will want to question me and Keveneth afterwards, no doubt. But I can't tell them—even under torture, if I truly don't know anything, eh?"

I let out a mirthless chuckle. "Torture—to find some run-away boys? I hope it won't come to that, brother," I said. *But who could say with such evil men,* I thought privately.

He gave me a crooked grin and continued hoeing. "I hope so, too."

Matoqwa I suspected had told Kutima, or Keveneth as he kept insisting I call him, about their escape plan, because after his last return from Infirmary he had told me that if I ran away with the others he wouldn't be joining us.

Over the long winter his reoccurring cough had returned and now with the warmer weather he had developed what Doc called asthma, which he said was a reaction to some of the flowering plants growing in this southern land around the school.

"I never had this problem when we lived in the north," he told me one evening when I visited him in Infirmary. "But here everything is so different than what we lived with at home, I guess I'm having a hard time adjusting."

When I questioned him further he also admitted that his father was plagued by the same coughing and sneezing illness when he was younger, too, which was why he took a posting by Big Ice Lake in the first place. I would be sad to lose track of him again after we left, but he gave me permission to contact his dreaming mind, like I sometimes did with my Chamuqwani friend Collin, so we could stay in touch in the future.

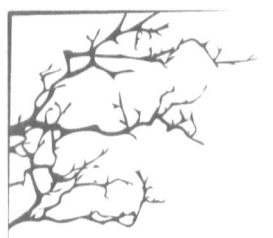

Chapter Four

Moon was climbing her way up the tree branches outside my window when a desert fox's bark awoke me. My breathing even, I lay still for a long moment, allowing my senses to explore the night around me. All was quiet hopefully everyone was asleep. Near the cold woodstove I could hear Ronalton and his friends loudly snoring.

The fox barked again. In the bed beside me Matoqwa rose, slipped off his nightshirt and now dressed in layers of his day clothes, crept to the dorm room door and then out into the hall. No one stirred or called an alarm.

As he passed me he saw that I was already awake and gave me a hand sign to wait before following. When he was gone I saw that the others sleeping in our room had already left. Their beds lay empty mounded up with dirty clothes to imitate the forms of the absent sleeping boys.

When I heard the fox bark again, this time from further away, I rose as silently as the others and headed for the hall. As I passed Keveneth's bed I saw that he was awake. He gave me a hand sign to wish me good luck. I nodded and followed the warband into the night.

I retrieved my small blanket roll from its hiding place by the bath house and hurried to catch up with the others. When they saw me, they quickened their pace across the field where the milk cai fed, heading for the band of willows bordering the river.

When I overtook them I caught my breath and murmured, "Where are we going? Aren't we going to take the horses? They will have the dogs after us as soon as the director can send for them."

"Yeah he will, Siyatli dog turd," Matoqwa growled and gave me a disgusted look. "So that's why we are going on River. Think you can remember how to paddle a boat, eh?"

"We need to keep moving," Komonti hissed and without looking back to see who was following he headed into the trees.

"There aren't enough horses at the school for all of us to ride," Kuweya explained as he lifted aside a low branch for me.

"And they are fat and stupid," Atuusca added, coming right behind me. "Couldn't run if a wolf pack was nipping at their heels. We will steal better horses later."

Moon was higher in the sky by the time we got to where Matoqwa and Atuusca and Iwaz had concealed a weathered chamuqwani boat that looked it might tip us into the water given the first breath of Wind. "Are you sure this old grandfather will carry us?"

"Have to. " Iwaz said. "But if it is too low in the water we can throw you over and let you swim, seal boy."

"Ha, ha, very funny, dog turd."

Matoqwa saw me studying the craft and snorted. "It will do. We don't need to go far just enough distance to throw any dogs off our scent." He motioned for me and Kuweya to help him turn the boat over.

Well it might do that, but not much more, I decided as I lifted the bow and helped him walk the leaky vessel down the muddy bank and into the water. "Where did it come from? Is anybody going to miss it?"

"Nobody has so far that I know of," Matoqwa said. "I found it about a moon ago when Doff allowed me and Kuweya to try our luck fishing. It was just drifting in the water. I swam out and pulled it to shore. Then we hid it in the brush. I thought it might be useful one day."

"And so it has," Kuweya said as he stepped into the tippy vessel.

For a moment I thought I really was going to have to swim, because it was tight with all of us crammed into its flat bottom. The Kukiya, being a horse people were both nervous and unskilled at this type of travel, so it was left up to me and Matoqwa to do most of the paddling that night.

Moving away from shore we allowed the current to take us as we slipped under the bridge by the village and headed towards the trees on the opposite bank. A heavy mist covered the river as dawn lightened the sky, which I coaxed to follow and conceal us as we continued along the river.

From the sounds echoing through the fog I could tell we were traveling through a land thinly settled by the enemy, so we took advantage of the cover to keep paddling far into the morning.

Knowing my own strength was waning I spoke to the spirits of the land on our behalf, <<Honored relatives, will you please help us? We are people fleeing evil men. Show me a place where we can safely camp and rest for a while before we continue our journey to our home.>>

A silver sun was just managing to burn through the fading mists when a grandmother willow spoke to me from the nearby shoreline. <<Here, young siyatli, hide your vessel among my trailing branches. You may rest in peace among the pines and grasses on the bank above.>>

Fearing what the malicer might do now that I had escaped, I decided to try and contact Kevebeth through our newly established mind link. It would have been easier for me if he and I were both sleeping, but I managed to snatch a few bits of information, even though he was awake.

<<The grand intercessor has left the school, and nobody—not even the director knows where he's gone,>> he told me, his troubled mind constantly mulling over his fear for us. That news sent a tremor of fear through my dreaming spirit-body. Worried that the malicer might be lurking in the Dream, hoping to capture me I returned to my sleeping form, but I slept poorly after that, unable to shake off the fear that he was hunting for me and might not be fooled for long by our attempt to throw off pursuit by traveling on River.

It was late afternoon the mists rising up to float atop the water in cottony patches as Sun sank below the treetops when I awoke. The others seemed to be still sleeping. My empty stomach rumbled, so I decided to set aside my worries and do a little fishing for all of us, before we moved on.

Taking off my long trousers I waded out into the river while still keeping within the concealment of Grandmother Willow's trailing branches. Allowing the water to settle I held myself perfectly still and let my Qwakaiva reach out and savor the life around me. I breathed in the pungent smells of growing things and river mud. All was quiet nearby.

Across the river a doe with nostrils flared crept down the bank to drink. When she sensed all was safe she allowed her fawn to join her. Far away down river I could hear men calling to barking dogs, but I sensed we had nothing to fear from them for now. The priests wouldn't have known we had a chamuqwani water vessel, so once we floated atop River the dogs would have lost our scent, throwing the search into confusion

Then my stomach rumbled, reminding me of my purpose. Murmuring a low chant I reached out with my gift and called the little swimmers to come to me. <<Ha-ai-ya, silver swimmers.

<<Ha-ai-ya, my little relatives

<<I am hungry, my war brothers are hungry.

>>We are fleeing a great evil and need your help.

<<Come to my hand and make the great gift of your life so that we can have the strength to escape our enemies.

<<We need the gift that only you can give me, if you are willing.

<<Ha-ai-ya, silver swimmers, come.>>

It didn't take long before I had caught and killed several fish that willingly swam into my out stretched hands. When I walked back into our camp in the pines up the slope the others were awake.

The Kukiya made faces at my offering of gutted fish strung on a willow branch. Taking them from me Matoqwa laughed when he saw their expressions. "What did you expect a seal boy to bring us, eh?"

Komonti snorted and stalked off to look for fire wood. "Next time one of us will do the hunting," I heard him grumble.

Matoqwa and I looked at each other and smiled, because we knew, that in spite of the desert people's dislike of fish they weren't going to refuse their share when we cooked them.

It didn't take long for us to have a small fire going its light concealed in a hollow dug into the ground near the edge of the pines. We cooked and ate quickly anxious to be gone. As we lifted our boat into the water Komonti grumped, "How long are we going to travel on the water like this? I'm tired of sitting cramped up and my bottom wet and cold all night."

"You could always take a turn at paddling. That will warm you up," Matoqwa suggested with a soft laugh. Komonti swore and someone else chuckled, but I couldn't tell who it was in the darkness.

"Right now this is our safest way to travel," I said before someone started an argument. "The people at the school don't know we have a boat and no dogs can follow us while we remain on River."

"But what we really need are horses," Komonti argued. "No dogs will be able to catch us if we have horses."

"He's right about finding horses," Atuusca added. "I doubt this old boat will last much longer, before it sinks. The place where I was sitting got wetter and wetter as we traveled last night.

"And, I don't know how to swim like you northerners if it dumps us into River," Iwaz said.

"I repeat," Komonti said. "We need to find some horses."

Though a knot of unease twisted in my gut at the thought of leaving River and its concealing fogs I knew we must. If the hunters didn't find us River's journey would pass through high blue hills in a few more days and there was no way the boat or my desert-born brothers could survive a bout of rapids.

And when we did leave River, I would once again, be forced into using my Qwakaiva to insure we truly did escape, I realized. I would just have to hope that we were far enough away from the malicer by then that he wouldn't be able to notice me.

"Be at peace, brothers," I offered. "If we don't sense any horses as we travel tonight, when we rest tomorrow I will ask a friendly hawk to lend me its sight so I can find horses and discover more about the land we need to travel to get home."

Setting out once more upon the river and hidden by the night and the mists we allowed the current to take us where it would. This river had carved its way through a wide tree lined valley dotted with small woods, fields of grain and grassy fenced land where when let out of their barns animals grazed.

I could sense with my Gift that River's water ran deep, with a slow and steady current at this point in its travel towards a bigger river many days ahead. But just to make sure there were no hidden dangers under its placid surface I coaxed two young river otters away from their play to travel near us for most of the night. They agreed to warn me if there were submerged logs or other snags in our path.

As they left us at dawn they told me about a sizable chamuqwani village not far ahead. Though we were still mostly hidden by the morning fog I could sense other boats were out upon the water fishing, so I felt an urgent need to find a safe hiding place for the day.

I returned the wave of a fisherman in a small boat floating through the mists not far from us and breathed a sigh of relief when he kept moving, intent on his own paddling. Soon many more chamuqwani would be awake and someone could give an alarm anytime now.

When we were far enough past him that we were once more concealed by the fog, I murmured to my companions, "The otters have told me that there is a large chamuqwani village close by. Keep watch for a safe place where we can rest and hide till night.

"I don't know if word has spread this far for the chamuqwani to be watching out for brown-skinned runaways, but it would be better if we aren't recognized." Komonti murmured his agreement and they all focused on, searching the shoreline.

We paddled on for a while before Kuweya pointed. "Over there." We were passing through a section of brushy tree covered bank at the time and not far ahead a shallow stream ran into the larger river. "Maybe we can hide the boat up that creek and find a place to hunt and rest in the trees where no one traveling on the big water can see us." Matoqwa grunted and steered the boat in that direction.

This patch of trees was thick with thorny berry bushes and other shrubs but the trees seemed to be growing only along the water. We were walking the heavy boat up the shallow stream when we sensed a brighter light coming through the trees in front of us and milk cai calling to one another from the grassy field beyond.

Water was sloshing about in the bottom of our vessel, making it heavy to carry over the slippery rocks in the streambed. Deciding to haul it no farther than the bank nearby we tipped it over on the mud just above the waterline. Exhausted and hungry we sank down on the bank beside it to catch our breath.

"How long are we going to remain on the river, floating in this dam leaky chamuqwani boat?" Iwaz grumbled, wiping sweat off his forehead with a muddy hand.

I shrugged. "I'm not sure. As far as we can, I guess."

"Until we find horses," Komonti said, repeating his earlier argument and glaring at me as if that lack was my fault. "The boat is getting bad and I don't want to walk. On horseback we can travel much easier through the enemy's country."

"Yes horses," Atuusca agreed. "But until we find them, where is the river taking us, Puhani, do you know?"

Well not exactly, I thought, *just far away from my enemy will be good enough for me. No that isn't right I need to think clearer than that. I can't just run scared without a plan, or I will get some of us killed—and the rest of us hanged.*

"Remember we had to ride on Train and then on a wagon for a couple days to get to the school. We are far away from the Preserve. They will expect us to head west straight away, so we can't do that—not at first anyway," Matoqwa reasoned.

"What should we do then, oh wise chief?" Iwaz mocked.

Matoqwa's face darkened with anger, but before he could do or say anything Kuweya changed the subject and asked me, "Have you had a foretelling to guide our journey, Puhani?"

Did I know where to guide them? I shook my head. "No, not really, but I will ask." Feeling the heavy weight of their trust settle upon my shoulders I closed my eyes and put that question to the spirits of the land around us.

After a long moment I opened my eyes and said, "River has been carrying us south because it is anxious to join one of its relatives, an older river flowing into a big lake. When we leave River my Gift tells me the spirits say we should go east and then north for a few days where there are not so many chamuqwani villages, before we head west to our desert home. The enemy won't expect that. It will give us more time before they are on our trail."

"Hmm, maybe that is a good idea and maybe not," Komonti said, not convinced. "In my dreams lately the spirits of my land have been calling to me. They warn me that to stay in this foreign land any longer than is necessary will mean death for me and my Kukiya brothers. Maybe I will travel with you, Puhani—for a while, but soon like Sun I am traveling west."

There were murmurs of agreement to his words from the Kukiya and with a shiver of another foretelling I knew it wouldn't take much for them to leave and go their own way. "Let's make camp and find something to eat before we decide anything that important," I suggested.

Kuweya yawned. "Good idea I could eat one of those milk cai I hear in the field I'm so hungry."

Iwaz laughed. "Better not kill one, dog turd, or the chamuqwani will be mad at you. Just stick to finding a nice fat rabbit or two for now."

"Or at least until we have horses to carry meat and ride away on," Atuusca teased.

I couldn't help my own lips curving into a smile at their joking. "Be easy in your mind, brothers. When I've rested I will find a friendly bird to help me and I will scout for the enemy—and yes, Komonti, for horses," I promised.

I FOUND WHEN I FLEW with an old crow that we were indeed camped near a larger chamuqwani village. South of this one there were several more chamuqwani towns with the metal tracks nailed into the earth that Train traveled. Fortunately for us River's banks would continue to be dotted with patches of trees and fields of grain and animal pastures for a while yet.

The farm near where we camped had no horses, so after we slept and ate a meager meal of rabbit and greens we agreed to drag the leaky boat back into the main channel and continue through the farm country that night, hoping for better luck in the days ahead.

By the end of the night, however, the river's current was moving faster and our vessel was sinking lower into the water. It was growing difficult to steer so just before dawn we reluctantly maneuvered it close enough to the bank that we could grab our blanket rolls and wade to the wooded shore beyond. Not bothering to beach the boat we offered our thanks to it for carrying us this far, and then just pushed it out into deeper water, allowing it to find the current again and travel on without us.

As we watched it disappear into the mists someone suggested that the chamuqwani might think we had drowned and stop looking for us, but I doubted that was true. Though I wasn't sure why, I knew the grand intercessor wanted me—wanted me bad. He wasn't about to let me slip through his net this easily, and that certainty made my guts turn to ice, fearing what he might be planning if he caught me.

Though it was light by that time we were all ravenous, so over my objections the Kukiya decided they were going hunting anyway, leaving me and Matoqwa to make camp among a cluster of aspens out of sight from the water. After that task we gathered firewood and some early berries and leafy greens we knew were edible. I managed to catch us a couple small fish to eat, and then there was nothing for us to do but wait until they came back—if they came back.

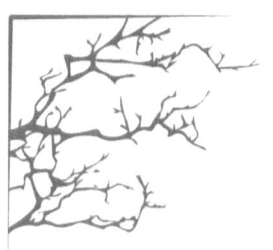

Chapter Five

Sun had passed the midpoint in his journey and still there was no sign of the Kukiya. Allowing our small fire to die out we sat across from each other not daring to speak out loud the thought we were afraid to share. The Kukiya weren't coming back. They had found horses and were heading home without us.

Unable to sit still any longer Matoqwa jumped to his feet muttering several chamuqwani bad words under his breath. "I'm going to have a look around," he announced without looking at me.

I yawned. "Be careful. I would hate to lose you, too."

He turned back to face me. "So, do you think those dust eaters have really left us? Komonti has been talking about his dreams for a while now—and those dog turd cousins... It would be a blessing to see them gone." He shook his head in disgust and swore again.

Then as a new thought came into his mind he asked, "Big fuckin' Kukiya warriors always boasting about stealing horses, could they have been caught? Have you seen something; are we—all of us in danger?"

I shook my head. "No, I've had no warning of danger—for any of us. But I will look later if they don't return. Right now," I yawned again. "I'm too tired to do it."

"Go rest then. I'll set out a few rabbit snares by the creek, but I won't go far," Matoqwa told me. "Get some sleep; I will keep watch for a while."

After he left I managed to fall asleep but I didn't rest well. My dreams were troubled by a shadowy spectre threatening me with horrifying images of death and torture that he planned for me and my relatives if I didn't return to the school—immediately. Shouting my defiance I fled the spectre, forcing myself awake with a gasp.

When I sat up it was almost evening. Sun nearing the end of his daily journey had painted the treetops with a golden light. Sleepy birds were cooing to each other in the trees and the noisy little creek was babbling happily to itself down the bank. All seemed well.

Matoqwa had returned, but had fallen prey to his own exhaustion and now sat propped against a sturdy aspen grandmother fast asleep, snoring through his broken nose. The axe he'd taken from the school was resting by his hand. Deciding not to wake him I arose quietly intent on checking the traps he'd set earlier, or if there was nothing in the snares, doing a bit of fishing, before waking him.

I was heading in the direction of the willows to check them when a splash and clop of a single horse's hooves coming up the stream sent me to the ground again. Peering between the branches of a berry bush I saw a lone rider heading up creek towards us, but he was still too far away for me to see if he were enemy or friend in the dim light.

By this time Matoqwa had heard the approaching horse and was awake and crouched beside me. "Is it a chamuqwani do you think?" I mouthed, my voice not carrying over the noisy stream.

"Not sure, but if so we can take him and grab the horse," he murmured.

I nodded, agreeing with his plan. As I grasped the heavy stick I could use like a club I cursed my foolishness. I should have remembered to erase our tracks from the mud before I slept.

He was about to slip away so we could attack from different directions when someone called to us using the Kukiya language and the horse began climbing the bank towards us. Fortunately for us, it was no enemy rider but Kuweya, sitting atop a fine brown mare.

Dismounting, he tied his new horse to a willow and came over to us smiling. Tossing a rounded sack to me, he said, "The farmer's pigs chased me out of their pen for taking some of their food, but after finding the horses we had no time for hunting. The pigs were too fat to catch me, but then I had to be quick, before those stupid chicken-birds gave the alarm when I took their eggs. Sorry there isn't more."

When I looked inside I found some stale pieces of brown bread and a few eggs. I wiped off the dirt from a piece of hard bread, took a bite, grabbed a raw egg, and then passed the bag on to Matoqwa.

"We should eat quickly and then go. The mare might be missed soon," Kuweya said.

Swallowing another bite, I asked, "What about the others; shouldn't we wait for them?"

Kuweya shook his head. "The others aren't coming," he said taking the nearly empty bag back from Matoqwa. "We only found four horses."

Matoqwa growled a chamuqwani bad word and glared at the Kukiya warrior as if our missing brothers' betrayal was his fault. "Only four horses, eh? So why didn't you go with them, too, dust eater?"

Kuweya reeled back at his use of the insulting name as if the Bear had slapped him. "Maybe I should have if you speak to me like that, dog humper," he snarled. Then taking a deep breath, he continued in a calmer voice, "I came back for you because I refused to abandon brothers in trouble who might need my help. That wasn't the way I was raised.

"I tried, but there was no changing their minds. Komonti kept insisting that we needed to head for home, and the cousins chose to follow him. He said we would be too slow riding double, so we should just go."

Feeling another foretelling twist a knife in my heart I knew Komonti had been right to listen to his dreams. Furious and threatening a terrible vengeance the evil priest was near. It was too late for me—and anyone who stayed with me—there was no escape.

"Kuweya I am grateful and honored that you would risk so much for my sake, but I fear Komonti was right to go—and maybe you both should leave me and catch up to them," I said quietly.

Forgetting their own budding argument, they turned to stare at me. "What? Why?" Matoqwa demanded.

"Because there's no hope for me now," I said and heard the resignation in my voice as I uttered the words. "I spoke with Kutima briefly while asleep," I explained. "Grand Intercessor Hoyt has left Saint Yon's. The priests don't know where he is; but I know. He is coming—for me—and will find me with his magic soon enough. You should go."

Kuweya turned to untie the horse. "Yes, we should go. We need to stop fooling around and get moving."

"Fuckin' right," Matoqwa agreed as he hurried to gather up our few belongings scattered around the campsite. When he had everything tied on the horse he turned to face me his arms folded across his chest. "Get up, Siyatli Dog Turd!"

I was still sitting by the dead fire my doom settling like a heavy blanket around my shoulders when they finished. "Why should I get up? Don't you understand; he's too strong for me—and I don't want you two to be hurt—or killed. Just go—please!"

My war brothers glanced at one another, a silent communication passing between them. Their faces grim they came to stand on either side of me. "Get up," Matoqwa growled, repeating his earlier command. "I don't care what kind of power you think the dog fart of a malicer has. I'm not letting you give up and just let him take you.

"I told you several times before when you were acting stupid, that us boys from Big Ice Lake have to stick together. You're all I have left from home and I'm not going to let you throw your life away. Now you get on that horse or we put you on it—and tie you there."

I was humbled by their commitment and afraid their sacrifice might cost them their lives. I got up with no more argument. "All right I'll go with you, but I'll walk—at least for now."

Before leaving the creek we checked Matoqwa's snares and found two fat rabbits and a small quail that could be our next meal. Kuweya told us there was a road beyond the next field so we agreed to travel within the trees passed the nearby farms and then once it was dark follow it.

Throughout the night we took turns riding the mare, hoping we would come across more horses once daylight had returned.

BY THE NEXT MORNING we had found no more horses, probably because we were still traveling through a big forest, a land emptied of its original people, but not yet settled by the chamuqwani invaders. Stopping long enough to cook a meal we decided to sleep until Sun was high in the sky. No one had passed our camp while we rested, so even though it was daylight we agreed to keep on going, knowing that we were most likely being followed.

Not sure how long we could remain safe hidden among the trees I ignored my fears and agreed to take the risk of using my Gift again and do more scouting through a bird's eyes, if they tied me to the mare.

Unfortunately for us it took a while for me to find a willing bird to coax out of the trees. In case a predator was hunting nearby the many little song birds near to hand didn't want to leave the protection of the leafy branches to fly high enough for me to see much of the surrounding land.

I assured them that no hawk or eagle was in the wood at the moment, but they were too frightened to listen. Finally a bored young crow agreed to fly with me for a time when I promised him the guts from our next kill.

As the day dragged on I was still tied atop the mare, my two war brothers walking by her side. Lolled by the afternoon heat and too tired by then to be paying as much attention to our surroundings as they should, they were caught off guard when the soldiers came charging around the next bend in the path heading straight for us.

Hidden until then by the malicer's conjuring, the crow and I had just spotted that same group of horsemen. Hastily dropping back into my body to warn my brothers I found I was too late. The mare I was riding had heard the approaching horses and called out a greeting to them, which was quickly answered. Their presence discovered, the soldiers discarded any pretense of an ambush and came charging towards us.

While I was still catching my breath from the fast transition back into my body, Kuweya gave the mare a stinging slap on her rump with the end of the rope he'd been using as her lead. He let go at the same time and the mare took off. I had no time to grab her lead, before we were pounding back down the trail we had just ridden.

At my back I could hear men shouting and the war cries of my brothers as they fought the enemy. Never a good rider and now tied to a runaway horse I had no way of helping them, so I just held on and prayed she wouldn't stumble and drop us both to the ground. I feared they had decided to offer their lives in payment for my freedom. Thank all the ancestors it didn't come to that.

I didn't get far before the air about me crackled with power. The Thunderer God's token I'd forgotten to remove when we left the school suddenly burst into a white-hot flame that burned into my chest. With the stink of burning human flesh choking my nostrils I screamed. As I fell sideways, nearly slipping under the mare's belly I ripped the heated metal chain from my neck and flung it into the bushes.

I had just managed to pull myself back onto the mare's back when a soldier dressed in black with a lightning bolt patch on his chest grabbed the horse by her rope halter, bringing her to a stop.

He drew his thunder weapon and pointed it at me, then he noticed I was already tied to the horse and couldn't give him any trouble. He smirked. "Well, me lil' bucki. Looks like ya' aint goin' anywhere on yeer own from now on." He let out a roaring laugh, amused by his own wit. "Cept ta yeer own hangin' maybe."

The grand intercessor was waiting for us when we trotted back to the rest of his men. Dressed in a well sewn black riding outfit with highly polished knee-high boots he studied me carefully with his power from atop a tall gray stallion. Though I doubted if anyone but me could see them, on each of his shoulders perched two of Djoven's ugly little demons, similar to the ones carved into stone on the large temple I'd seen when we passed through Town.

When they realized that I could see them their distorted faces burst into toothy smiles. <<Nasty little witch, we promised you we would repay you for your disrespect someday. And now here you are at last.>> They gleefully jabbered about what they planned, displaying their claws. <<You belong to us now—our master has promised us. When our master eats your soul all up we will feast on what's left of you—forever.>>

My captor brought me to a stop in front of him and saluted. The grand intercessor's lips twitched as if he wanted to smile when he saw I was already tied to my mount. Trying to ignore the demons threats I couldn't stop the trembling coursing through my entire body. But I did manage to give Djoven's priest and his pets one quick defiant glare. Then I dropped my eyes to prevent him ensnaring my spirit with his power.

Glancing around instead to see how my war brothers had fared I was relieved to see that both were still alive. Bound and bloody they stood guarded by more of the black-clad soldiers waiting, like me, to see what the grand intercessor planned to do with us now that he'd caught us.

All was quiet among the trees for a long moment. Even the little ones of the forest recognized the danger and were silent. At last the intercessor fixed his piercing black eyed stare on me and spoke. "That was very clever of you to escape upon the river. You had Harriscot's huntsman pulling out his hair when his beasts couldn't find your scent."

He gave an amused chuckle. "And then when the meddling old hag told everyone back at the school that you had escaped using your heathen magic they all were certain you were a fiendish heathen witch. They prayed most fervently for me to find you."

He laughed again, sending another shower of fear cascading down my spine. "Too bad I don't plan to tell them it wasn't magic that allowed you to escape so easily. Wherever did you acquire a boat, hmm?"

I doubted he really wanted an answer, so I kept looking at the ground by the mare's feet and didn't reply.

"If you had continued on the river for another few days I might have given up on you and let you run free a while longer, but then the celibress reminded me that you still might be wearing my god's token and sure enough, you were."

At his words my heart sank to the ground. I had unknowingly been the agent of my own destruction. Thinking it a harmless piece of shiny metal, and with so much else on my mind, I had forgotten that I still wore it. The priest, however, knew its potential and was able to empower the token from afar to use against me.

Drawing my attention to it brought back the pain he had already been able to inflict. I didn't dare to look to see if its outline had been branded into my skin forever, but I feared it might be so. And that terrified me even more. I feared I would never be able to escape this alien god's power.

What an ironic joke it would be if my uncle Royston and his family had been right to convert after all. Me betray my ancestors and convert? My spirit shuddered at the thought, and the brand in my flesh throbbed in sympathy.

"The question I need to answer at the moment is what to do with you now that I have you. Should we go back to the school where everyone hates and fears you? Where they would happily pound the stake and lay the wood for your burning, if I let them.

"Or should we go straight back to my home temple in the capital city where we can have many—talks before your fate is decided. I would welcome your thoughts on the matter, little witch. What shall we do, hmm?"

Like a big cat toying with its prey he didn't want my answer, and so I wouldn't play his game and give him one. I just kept staring at the ground and remained silent.

I was saved further taunts when the soldier with a long black beard and the most gold and silver patches on his uniform cleared his throat and said, "Your Reverence, I am sorry to interrupt, but it grows late. Shouldn't we be getting back now that you have your prisoners."

The grand intercessor seemed startled by the reminder, but nodded. "Yes, you are correct, captain. Now that I have this tattooed heathen witch under my control it *is* time. We *should* be getting back to the inn so we all can rest before our long ride tomorrow. You did well and you and the men will receive a bonus for your service."

"Thank you, Reverence, the men and I will appreciate that. Then he frowned, a puzzled look creasing his forehead as a new thought came to him. "Do you mean to take back only the zaunk tied on the horse?"

"Yes, he is the witch; he alone is important to me."

"But what about the other two runaway buckies who came with him?" the captain asked. "What do you want us to do with them?"

Growing impatient with the delay the intercessor's face turned grim. "I don't care what you do with them," he growled. His pets gnashed their teeth in a threat display, echoing his annoyance. "They are just savages; they have no devilish magic to corrupt the god-fearing. Let them go if you want."

"What?" the soldier spluttered. "We can't do that! They have already stolen a horse and the great god knows what other mischief they will get up to if we just release them."

"Then kill them. I don't care. Let's go."

The intercessor was turning his horse around when I spoke for the first time since my capture. "No." I had projected enough of my Qwakaiva into that one word that everyone fell silent, staring at me. "I won't let you kill them."

Switching to the mind speech I faced my adversary and said, <<If you have my war brothers killed I will fight you with all the power I have. I might not best you, but I will never quit until I die or you burn me, Evil One.>>

Hoyt chuckled deep in his throat. A cruel smile curved his lips as he moved his horse a little closer to me. <<Burn you? Who says I plan to do

that?>> Allowing the meaning behind his words to twist the knife of fear in a little deeper, he said, <<No, I have other plans for you.>>

<<Other plans?>> I snorted. <<Going to have your pets eat me instead?>>

Sensing the fear hidden behind my show of bravado his cruel smile grew wider. <<Maybe, if you don't surrender what you are hiding to me. Maybe I *will* let them play with you a while. Then maybe you will be more—biddable, hmm?>>

What did he really want from me, if it wasn't to watch me burn?

As I was puzzling out the meaning of his threat he shifted topics and asked, <<I am curious. Why do you care what happens to such puny, inferior creatures, hmm? These youths have no real power. They may have been helpful with your escape but what good are they to you now?>>

<<They are worthy young men and I owe them much. They were willing to give up everything—including their lives for me in that last fight. I won't betray their sacrifice by standing by now and let your soldiers kill them. If they die, I die—by my own hand, if I must.>>

I faced him defiantly and looked him in the eye. <<So, it is up to you, Malicer. Do I go back as a willing captive, causing you and your men no further trouble, or do I go back as a piece of dead meat?>>

His demons screeched, barely able to contain their rage. Echoing their fury the grand intercessor's face turned a vivid shade of red and I feared I had pushed him too far.

Idly I wondered if he would give into the little monsters' urging and strike me dead where I was. At that point I didn't care. My death here and now would probably be quicker than whatever he was planning, and certainly better than the pyre and the stake, the death Djoven's priests reserved for all those they name witches.

Controlling his rage he gave me a mirthless laugh, silencing his pets with a flick of power that made them disappear with cries of pain. Turning to the captain, he sighed and spoke. "The heathen witch has promised to behave if we don't kill his companions. So, tie them on a pack horse and bring them with us. I may have a use for them after all."

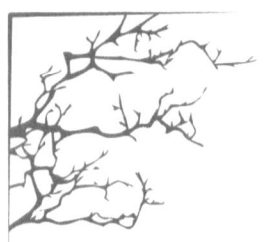

Chapter Six

It was full dark when we rode into the village by the river where the captain had paid for his soldiers to camp in the stable yard. To insure his comfort the intercessor had arranged for a room in the big house on the other side of the stable.

I was secretly amused when the keeper of the house discovered the soldiers had brought three zaunk prisoners back with them. And when the fat man overheard a couple of the men talking about one of the prisoners being an accused witch he nearly threw us all out. Intercessor was furious when he heard the uproar. He threatened to haul the house master off to a jail cell if he didn't settle down and get on with making him a meal.

The house master agreed that the intercessor and the soldiers could stay, but the question still remained what to do with us. The master insisted that we couldn't stay inside his big house, because no zaunks were allowed anyway and—especially zaunks accused of using heathen magics. That meant we couldn't bed down with the horses either, for fear I might put a spell on them so they sickened. And no amount of threats by the captain or the grand intercessor would change his mind.

Though no one was happy about the final resolution of the matter it was decided that we would stay locked in the local Thunderer's temple for the night with the soldiers taking turns on watch outside the barred door.

A surprised and trembling old priest met us when we arrived unannounced at his temple. We were just being unloaded from the horses when he came hurrying over to bar our way inside. By then the still furious grand intercessor was in no mood to have anyone dare to oppose his will—especially a lowly village praiser and he angrily told him so. Bowing nearly to the dirt, the priest humbly stepped aside.

Looking up as we were roughly escorted inside I noticed that the grand intercessor had posted his pets atop the roof just to make sure that I didn't try to escape by using my Qwakaiva.

He needn't have bothered. The malicer could post all the demons of the Thunderer's fiery abyss atop the temple and I wouldn't have cared. I was too exhausted and hurting to try and escape. Sitting on one of the hard benches where a soldier had tossed my blanket roll I covered my head with my blanket and rocked, allowing the tears to flow unchecked in the privacy I created with the cloth.

Even though my war brothers were with me they had no Qwakaiva and couldn't understand my pain in body and spirit. I felt abandoned by my crystal guardian, my seal father and my Benefactor Kunai. I was alone, afraid and miserable.

Not long after we entered the temple I heard Matoqwa and Kuweya pounding on the door and walls, demanding that our captors give us some food and water. The soldiers threatened them with a beating but they didn't stop. The soldiers were in a bad mood because after the hard ride to get to the village, instead of a night's rest some of them would have to stand guard over some "dirty little zaunks." They weren't happy about it and planned to see we suffered for it, as if their situation was our fault.

The priest, who turned out to be a kindly old man, finally understood what my war brothers wanted and convinced a soldier to return to the big house and bring us food and water. The grumpy man returned not long after with a pail of water from the horse trough, a loaf of hard bread and some boiled eggs.

The smirking soldier might have just tossed everything on the floor inside the door, but the old man protested so at last he agreed to let the priest bring the food and water inside while he watched us with his hand on his thunder weapon from the doorway.

Noticing how battered we were the priest glared at the guard, clicked his tongue in disapproval and then went back to his home to find some medicines and bandages for our wounds.

When our guard protested giving us his medicines the old priest defiantly faced him and said, "Young man, we are all children of the great god, and like his sister, The Mother of Mercy, who teaches that all sinners deserve our pity and care, these young men—no matter what they are accused of deserve my help."

While all the fuss was going on I had remained shrouded in my blanket, only partially paying attention to what the others were doing. When the priest left, promising us a better meal in the morning Kuweya came over to me and touched my shoulder. "Sit up, Puhani. You need to eat and I want to look at your wounds. I need to see what he did to you."

I didn't want to show him, I was ashamed of my weakness but he insisted. When I gave up and at last let him see he hissed in surprise. "By my ancestors, what has this evil malicer done to you?"

"I haven't been able to dare look at it," I confessed in a small voice. "Tell me, is it what I fear? Has he branded me with the lightning sigil; has he claimed me already for his devil god?"

"The lightning sigil is blurred in its form, but yes it is there," Kuweya confirmed. "Does this mean he has stolen your Qwakaiva, too?"

I shook my head. "I don't know," I admitted, and I didn't want to find out. The brand marking me now as his property, felt as if it was still worming its way deeper into my being, hungry, searching. I shuddered; I wasn't sure how long I could resist.

By that time Matoqwa, too, had come over to see. Cursing under his breath when he saw the mark he came back a moment later with a wet cloth and a cup of water for me to drink. "Guess this means you aren't going to be much help when we escape, eh?"

I made a face and snorted. "I told you to leave me. I knew I wasn't strong enough to oppose him. You both should have listened to me."

"And you should have listened to me, too, dog turd. Us boys from Big Ice Lake—and the desert gotta stick together. We'll find away, so stop wallowing in self-pity. Even if you're branded you can still fight him. With your fists if necessary, he won't expect that."

I agreed just to shut him up and took a drink. The water tasted brackish and smelled of horse, but I drank it anyway. I ate the eggs and bread they forced upon me, but I didn't feel much like answering their qwestions after that. I just curled up in my blanket again and tried to dream my way to a mountain stream where I could lay down in her soothing cool water and let her take the pain and fear away.

LOST IN MY OWN MISERY I don't remember much about our trip back to Saint Yon's school. I learned later that because of a possible investigation concerning some of Djoven's followers taking place in the father emperor's capital the grand intercessor decided to return to the school until the threat had been resolved and the city quieted down. After all the school had "the Perdition Box," a convenient place to stash me and question me at his leisure.

Hoyt timed our arrival after dark when the students would be in the dorms preparing for bed. As we were being unloaded from our tired horses Director Harriscot and Administrator Rizdale arrived and they didn't look pleased to see us.

"Grand Intercessor, this is an unexpected surprise," the director stammered. "I thought you were going straight back to the capital once you captured your—uh—heathen witches."

Dismounting and handing his stallion to Doff Hoyt faced the director and chuckled. "You hoped I would no doubt, director, but plans change according to unforeseen circumstance. Not to worry, however, I have already sent off my report to the High Divine, concerning your care of this fine school. I'm sure you will be hearing from the temple's executive council soon enough."

That news didn't seem to reassure the director because his face suddenly turned an even paler shade of white than usual. "Yes, well, that is most welcome news, Grand Intercessor Hoyt. And of course, you are always welcome to our humble lodgings." Glancing thoughtfully at me and my brothers, he asked, "What do you want us to do with your prisoners while you remain among us?"

"The tattooed little witch is mine. He will remain confined in your cellar accommodations until a temple guard can be sent for from the capital as an escort for our return," Hoyt said, also turning to study us. After a long moment he added, "The other two prisoners just took the opportunity to run when given the chance. You can do with them what you like. They aren't of interest to me or the Temple."

"There were six students who escaped. What has happened to the other three? Are they dead?" Administrator Rizdale asked.

The grand intercessor shrugged. "I have no idea where they are and care less. Those two were the only ones with the witch when we caught up to him."

Doff and intercessor Jonash who were in charge of the farm work at the school had come up while the priests were talking. When they heard about the loss of three of their best farm hands they didn't look happy.

"The harvest will be upon us soon, praiser Jonash," Doff murmured. "We are going to need all the help we can get—even those two rebellious buckies. Don't let the director—" Praiser Jonash cut him off with an angry slash of his hand, before Doff could finish his thought.

Frowning, the director turned his attention back on me. "Grand Intercessor, I have some concerns about the safety of my charges and my staff if this foul creature continues to be lodged here. Shouldn't you continue your journey in the morning after you have rested?"

Hoyt snorted a laugh. "Anxious to get rid of me, are you director? And as for my prisoner he has been among you for what...two and a half years now? I doubt if you are in anymore danger with his return than you and your school were in all that time."

"Yes, he *was* here, and it cost us dearly. We had food and equipment broken or stolen, a head boy badly beaten and a praiser go mad from unnamed causes, because we didn't recognize the danger he presented when he was among us." the director countered.

Muttering a curse under his breath Hoyt stalked over to me and lifted up my shirt to display his brand upon my chest. "Look upon our god's work. This foul heathen witch is under my control. He isn't going to give anyone trouble now." The director scowled, but accepted the grand intercessor's assurance without further comment.

"Director, what do you want us to do with the prisoners he doesn't want? It grows late," the administrator reminded him. He shivered and tugged his cloak tighter around his shoulders.

Director Harriscot sighed, "You are right. With the grand intercessor's permission, put them all in the cellar cells for tonight. We will discuss this more in the morning." Turning back to the priests' house he added. "I will have Celibress Vomica fix up a room for you again. Cook will prepare a simple meal for you and your party. The soldiers can camp in the stable yard for the night."

As I suspected we weren't included in that offer of food and a bed. The soldiers did allow us to keep our blanket rolls, so when we were ushered into the cellar we wouldn't freeze.

Since there were three of us and only two darkened cells it was decided to lock Matoqwa and Kuweya in the two cells while I was tied with a physical and magical tether to the post at the bottom of the stairs. I could move far enough to pee in a corner under the stairs, but I couldn't reach the cell doors to free my brothers, or climb to where I might let myself out of the cellar and escape.

Once all the priests were gone and we were left in the dark the grand intercessor's nasty little pets appeared to torment me.

<<Hello, little witch. Do you taste good? Our master has given us permission to see if you do.>>

Using a few chamuqwani bad words I told them to go away and leave me alone. They only chortled with excitement, swooping in from time to time to bite or scratch me with tooth and claw every time I would have dozed off during the night.

Finally near dawn I had had enough. Deciding to test what Qwakaiva I might have left, the next time they came at me I spat out bolts of spirit fire that sent them howling in retreat. <<And don't come back, you nasty little pests, or I will give you more of the same,>> I warned. <<The seal pup still has fangs, so maybe it will be *me* who eats *you* up.>>

The effort cost me dearly, and I wasn't actually sure I could follow through on my threat, but Djoven's demons feared me enough to retreat for the rest of the night.

I was awakened sometime later in the morning when I heard the cellar door being unlocked. I decided to conceal myself in the shadows under the stairs while I collected my wits enough to face another adversary. To my surprise it was Celibress Vomica carrying a heavy tray filled with a jug of water, cups and three bowls of mush.

Not seeing me for the moment she unlocked each cell and handed in a bowl of the usual burnt mush and a mug of water to the prisoner inside.

When she discovered that only my war brothers were confined her eyes grew round with fear, afraid I had used my power and escaped, no doubt.

I wanted my breakfast more than I wanted to tease her so I stepped into the lantern light where she could see me. "I'm right here, Celibress. May I have my mush now?"

She reddened when she at last saw me, and then her expression hardened and a cruel smile curved her thin mouth. Before giving the bowl of mush to me she looked me in the eye and then deliberately spat into it. "Hungry, foul heathen creature? Well, eat this."

I took the bowl, sat it on the floor and then quickly snatched the cup of water off the tray before she could spit in that, too.

I drained the cup then poured the rest out of the pitcher and drank that as well. Placing cup and pitcher back on the tray I handed her back the mush. "I guess I'm not as hungry as I thought."

Dropping the tray onto the step she screeched in outrage and slapped me hard across my cheek. "Filthy little zaunk. I'm glad the grand intercessor caught you at last. He will punish you for using your heathen magic on decent god-fearing people. I will dance for joy at your burning."

"Decent god-fearing people, eh? Who are you talking about, Celibress? Praiser Tom who molested me, and my brother Qwatola so often he killed himself to escape his attentions?

"Or maybe you are talking about the director and his friends who sold most of the food meant to feed us last winter, causing starving children to die? Are those the decent god-fearing people you are speaking of? If they are, I'm glad to still be a heathen zaunk witch."

"Shut your foul mouth, zaunk. I won't listen to your lies." She knew I spoke true, but hit me again nonetheless.

Spitting blood on the floor from my bitten tongue I faced her defiantly. I was angry now too, and if I was going to die, I might as well voice some of the resentment that had been building up inside me ever since the enemy forced us to leave our northern home.

"Zaunk, why do you call us that mean word? I asked you back on the march south why were you traveling with us if you hate my people so much? Are you just a cruel person by nature? Does it please you to be mean to defenseless children assigned into your care? What happened to you to make you so bitter?

"Or, was it because you love Intercessor Raymonel so much that you chose to follow him on his mission among the savages—even though we terrify you?"

As I was speaking her eyes widened and her face contorted into a frightening mask. Before I could finish she slapped me again, this time hard enough to make my ears ring. "Filthy witch, I hope you burn forever in Djoven's fiery pit," she hissed. "I curse you—"

She was about to hit me again when the grand intercessor spoke from the top of the stairs. "Celibress, celibress, what has come over you? I can't have you abusing my prisoner like that," he said as he came down to us.

"But intercessor, the foul heathen witch said—"

"It doesn't matter what he said. You were to bring the prisoners their morning meal—nothing more."

"But this evil creature was telling lies about—"

"I said you were to bring food and nothing more. I will deal with him now. He will be properly punished for his crimes against our Mighty God in due time." As she growled under her breath and started up the stairs I showed Hoyt my bitten and clawed arms. "Along with your pets tormenting me all night does your punishment also include eating food she spat in before giving it to me?"

"No, it does not." Hoyt whirled around and glared at the retreating woman. "Celibress, is this true?"

At the tone of voice he used, she paused halfway up, trembling with fear, but remained silent, not turning to look at him. The grand intercessor's face darkened with rage. He waved a pale hand and one of his pets materialized and bit savagely into her arm. The old woman cried out, nearly dropping the tray.

"Don't make me ask you again, Celibress," he warned. "You won't like it if I do, I assure you."

"Y-yes, it's true," she hissed, staring wide-eyed at the blood and teeth marks that had suddenly appeared on her arm.

"That is not what you were instructed to do, Celibress. Now go get him proper food. If I have to discipline you further..." he left the rest of his threat unvoiced, but she understood it and hurried off to replace my meal.

THE CELIBRESS RETURNED soon enough, but not with mush this time. The cook had already thrown the leftovers from breakfast to the pigs. Not daring to disobey the grand intercessor she brought me sweetened tea, and several slices of toasted bread coated with berry jam from the priest's own kitchen.

As I ate Hoyt studied me with a feral intensity that I tried to ignore. I savored the unexpectedly delicious food, trying to make it last, but still it lay like a rock in my gut. I was worried what he was planning for me next. I feared it would involve a lot of pain. He might burn me in the end, but first he wanted something from me, but I had no idea what.

When I'd finished he took the plate and sat it on one of the empty shelves lining the cellar's stone walls. Returning to me he held the lantern up to my face and studied me carefully in its light.

"Yes, I can see the signs of your other worldly heritage in your eyes. Mother or father? What creature from the Beyond gave you life, I wonder? Hmm..."

He traced the dragon tattoo on my jaw with a slender pale finger. "This glyph, though stylized and crude, suggests to me that the dragon Kunai claims you. Was it someone from clans sworn to him that had a hand in your making?"

The brand on my chest suddenly throbbed with renewed vigor as he probed my defenses with his power. I didn't answer, and stared defiantly back. Fortunately for me one of the first lessons I mastered was how to shield my thoughts and my Spirit from such an enemy attack. He was older and far more experienced than I was; he might break me with time, but I wasn't going to make it easy for him.

As he drew back his probe and I was able to focus on something more than my defense, the insight came to me in a white-hot flash.

He must have seen the revelation mirrored on my face, because he demanded, "What did you see? Tell me!"

I couldn't help it; I began to laugh. He shook me hard, repeating his question until I got myself under control. The mirth still threatening to take me again I managed to say, "I thought you were some fearsome enemy warrior shape-shifted into human form, but you're not that at all. You're just a half-breed, of sorts, just like me.

"True you are older—and more experienced than I am, but you probably have no more Qwakaiva than I do myself."

Echoing his earlier question back to him, I blurted, "Mother or father? What other worldly being had a hand in *your* making, eh?"

He muttered and ungodly curse, his face contorting in anger, then he chuckled, relaxed and sat down on a hard-backed chair facing me. "You are very clever. It was my mother, damn her. She left me with my drunken human father for many years before she appeared to claim and teach me. And what about you?"

I sat down on the lower step and decided to answer. "It was a father for me; my mother was a woman of the Qwani'Ya people."

He nodded. "Someone has taught you a few tricks. Was it him?"

"No. I have met him a few times, but mostly I have had other teachers."

Hoyt snorted a laugh. "Well you might not be so grateful for his attentions when you get to know him better. The people from Beyond can be unpredictable—and cruel when it suits them. My mother is a bitch and a hard task master, but I also have to give her credit. She taught me well."

I thought about it for a moment, then said, "I'm not sure cruel is the word I would use to describe my experience with the Beyond people—as you call them. I think they are just different, and we can't judge them by human standards."

"Even now when they have abandoned you for me to do with as I please, you defend them. Why is that?"

I shrugged. "I defend them, because just like my Qwani'Ya relatives they are my people."

"Your people." He snorted his disgust. "If you were to swear your allegiance to my Crokno master and make me your teacher and benefactor I would never abandon you to the enemy like your father and Kunai have done to you."

In a way he had spoken truth. It did seem like all those I loved were either dead, or had abandoned me. And now this powerful being, a half-breed like me, someone who could understand what I was feeling spoke compelling words that were sweet to hear. He offered me love and acceptance if I would surrender and welcome him past my shield.

But behind the sweet flavor of his words, when I thought about it for another moment, I sensed a bitter after-taste that would destroy me if I gave in to his soothing promises. The image of my young sister Kitahtla suddenly appeared in my mind to help me resist his temptations.

Then I also realized that he was still using his power on me—only in a different way this time. Deciding he wasn't going to get me to surrender with a direct assault that I would resist, maybe to my death, he was now playing on what he perceived as my weakness. If it got him what he wanted he would pretend to offer me kindness and love instead of pain and violence.

But love and kindness wasn't weakness to my way of thinking. The ties that bound me to my ancestors, my land and my people gave me power and strength. My sister was no longer a baby to be carried in my auntie's cradleboard, but I loved her deeply. Even though I couldn't be with her right now I had promised my adopted father Nachoga before the chamuqwani hanged him that I would protect and care for her as best I could—even from afar.

When I watched her in the Seer's Pool pattern I made with my string I saw a toddler with honey gold skin that told of her mixed race heritage. Though a bit too thin, her outlawed adopted parents were always on the move, her golden cougar eyes, so like her father Nachoga's were bright and smiling.

How could I even consider forsaking her, and jeopardizing my people's well-being to follow this alien half-breed? I thanked her for giving me strength and returned my attention to my adversary. He had been quiet, allowing me time to consider his proposition—a poor strategy on his part.

Changing the subject I asked him. "Why are you one of Djoven's priests? Why would you commit yourself and your power to such loathsome people when you could do so much good in this troubled world?"

He gave me a mirthless laugh. "Good is such a malleable word. It has so many different aspects, depending on your perspective. My and my people's perspective is that to do 'good' as you put it would be to destroy this world, before the human cancer spreading upon it has time to infect other worlds within the flow of the starry river.

"And what better way to bring about our noble goal of annihilation, than to become one of Djoven's enforcers. Oh, these stupid humans will do my work for me, given enough time. I am merely helping the process along as a grand intercessor of one of their most destructive religions."

Shocked, I felt my mouth drop open. "But you are part human yourself. How could you work for the death of your own kind?"

He snorted. "My kind, hmm? I owe no allegiance to the drunken father who sired me then beat me nearly every day until my mother returned to claim me. No," he snarled. "I have no tender feelings left in me for, 'my kind'.

"But what puzzles me is why you should care. You have enough otherworldly blood flowing in your veins that, like me you could survive in the Beyond. Why not return there with me and let this world destroy itself—which it will in the end."

Since he seemed willing to talk, and to stall for time I asked another question, "Thank you for telling me. My Benefactor has never spoken to me of your people other than to say I had enemies in the Beyond as well as among the chamuqwani.

"I think I understand your reasoning—and maybe a little of your resentment towards the human side of your nature, though I must confess I don't share it. But my Qwakaiva also tells me that there is something more. What aren't you telling me? What do you really hope to get from me, before you hand me over to burn?"

He chuckled. "You haven't mentioned your lineage, but now I can guess you are one of Co'yeh's lot; they all have a powerful gift of divining what is hidden. Which Qwa'Nayhi Seal man poked your human mother? Was it Whale Hunter, Star Swimmer, or the mighty Enemy Slayer? They all have lusty appetites for copulation with whatever female they encounter."

He was baiting me, trying to make me angry. I could feel my face heating with his insult and had to take a calming breath before answering.

"Who fathered me isn't important at the moment. So I ask again; what do you want from me before I burn?"

"Burn? Who says I want you to burn? If you were to join me I would tell my stupid superiors that I have converted you. And now—under my tutelage, of course, you will use your Gift to help destroy the temple's enemies. I only want what I said, for you to join me."

<<Not true.>>

For the first time in nearly a moon the crystal guardian lodged in my chest spoke to me in a small voice I could barely detect. <<He wants me, and the link to Kunai I can provide the Crokno if you surrender to him. Beware, and don't let that happen—even if you must die to prevent it.>>

So, the crystal's warnings and my determination to use my Gift to help my relatives had a far more ominous consequence than I suspected. Well, if I had to give up my life to save my relatives and my world, so be it.

I sighed, hoping my expression conveyed my disappointment with his answer. "You are right about one of my Gifts and that is how I know that you are lying again. You do want me to join you, but only because I would give your Crokno relatives another possibility to destroy Kunai and his plans to heal my world if I did—and I can't let you do that.

"I know little about the chamuqwani people who raised you. However, I do know from bitter personal experience they can be greedy, cruel and unbelievably blind to the unseen world all around us.

"I can sympathize with your hatred, and I suspect that was the very reason your mother chose to mate with one of the pale-skinned people of the empire. And like the chamuqwani, you yourself are ruthless, cruel and strong. With the added Gift you have inherited from her lineage the Crokno have created a perfect weapon to conjure chaos among us.

"But whatever else I am, first and always I am a child of the Qwani'Ya Tsa'adi. My ancestors lie in this earth and my roots run deep. I could never betray my people, and my land. In spite of your *generous* offer I cannot accept. I would never betray my Benefactor and my world."

As I'd been speaking I had sensed his growing agitation. "Then if you won't give me what I want willingly, I will have to *take* it."

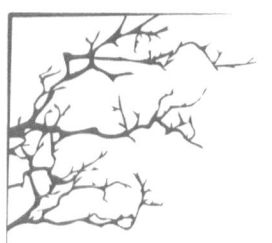

Chapter Seven

I barely had time to strengthen my shield before he attacked with a fury that had me howling in pain within moments. His onslaught was brutal, merciless and seemed to go on forever—as did my screaming.

I could hear Matoqwa and Kuweya pounding on their cell doors and shouting for him to stop, but no amount of noise halted his thorough assault on every aspect of my being. I screamed and didn't care who heard me—I wanted someone to hear me, both at the school and in the Beyond. I wanted someone—anyone to make him stop.

And at last my rescue came from an unexpected source. Suddenly the cellar door was flung open and the director roared, "Enough, Intercessor, you must stop this—NOW!"

With hand upraised, Hoyt paused. Turning to the man silhouetted against the hallway light, he snarled, "Close that door, damn you! How dare you interrupt my interrogation session?"

"I dare because you have no right to terrorize my students and my staff in such a manner. The children studying can hear you and are hysterical and my staff can't control them. Do with your prisoner as you like when you return with him to the capital, but as long as you remain at my school, you will conduct yourself in a restrained manner, Reverence. Do I make myself clear?"

"Quite clear, Director Harriscot," Hoyt answered through gritted teeth.

I thought he might direct some of his power and strike the director down where he stood, but a little calmer by then he merely stomped up the stairs and out into the afternoon light. Barely glancing at me, quivering and gasping on the bloody floor the director closed the cellar door and left me to my misery.

From the darkness the muffled voice of Matoqwa said, "Tas, are you all right?"

Stupid question. Still catching my breath I couldn't answer.

Then he swore again and growled, "I'd like to kill that evil malicer for what he's doing. Damn it, Tas, speak to us. How badly did he hurt you, Siyatli dog turd?"

My voice rough from screaming I took a shuddering breath, and managed to croak out an answer. "Bad enough. But I suppose I'll live—for the moment anyway."

My pain was intense; my spirit felt raw and bruised, and I ached in every muscle and bone of my physical body. Sitting up I groped for my blanket to wrap around my shoulders. I was cold—so very cold.

My brothers were silent for a long moment then Kuweya asked, "We could hear some of what you two were talking about. I'm certain he will be back, Puhani, can you defend yourself against him another time?"

"I-I don't know," I admitted. "He is very strong and skilled with conjuring pain. I may have to kill myself if he presses me too hard. I won't let him use me to destroy everything and everyone I cherish."

"Hmm..." Kuweya thought about my answer for a while, and then voiced his thoughts out loud. "That is a very honorable intension, but it may not have to come to that. When he comes to question you again remember the Prophet's teachings we learned when our families stayed with him at Saluuli Lake. Pray and ask Iyantsha to help you withstand this evil malicer. Pray, my brother, pray."

The Prophet was a great Kukiya Puhani who I'd met while living with my outlaw relatives off the Preserve. I knew he had suffered much to receive the blessings and healing Gift he now shared with the People. He drew his puwa/power from a different source than did my father and I, but our Gifts were compatible. I had helped him in the past with many healings of the sick and injured. I would act on Kuweya's suggestion. Iyantsha would help me if he could—I was sure of that.

"I will do that, brother, thank you for reminding me."

"Praying is good," Matoqwa agreed, "but we need to get you and ourselves out of this place and back to our own people as soon as possible. Let's talk about that, eh?"

Before speaking I checked to see that the grand intercessor hadn't sent his pets back to spy on me. After a thorough search and finding no trace of them, I said, "When we arrived and the priests were arguing I overheard Doff complaining about the loss of so many workers for the harvest, so he may be able to convince the director to release you two before long.

"I know that as a good student, Administrator Rizdale often gets our brother Keveneth to help in the school office. If you can, tell him to secretly send a letter to our friend Collin Golbraith and let him know what's been going on here at the school—and what's happened to me."

When I heard Matoqwa grumbling about stupid chamuqwani, and how could they be of help, I cut him off. "Collin, he's the one who got his friend Lord Bronworthy to stop Judge from hanging us—remember?"

And he might be able to contact my father to help—since I dare not.

"We have to try *something*, eh? And letting our friends outside the school know what is really going on here is our best plan." I insisted.

"All right we will do our best," they promised.

AS THE SILENCE AND the blackness closed around me I covered myself with my blanket and tried to sleep. My body hurt with a soul-deep ache that gave me no rest. However, neither the grand intercessor nor his pets bothered me for the rest of that day, for which I was grateful.

Next morning I was also grateful to see the new priest, Praiser Liucas coming down the stairs with our morning meal. I was hungry and looking forward to my lumpy burnt mush, doubting that the praiser would spit in it.

I decided he must be a kind man by the way he spoke to Kuweya and Matoqwa when he opened their doors and handed them their morning meal. He wrinkled his nose at the smell and clucked his tongue in disgust at the filthy conditions he could see inside the cells. Then he assured them they would be released soon.

When it was my turn he was a little hesitant to approach, setting the bowl and cup on the floor rather than come too near me. Trying to ignore the fear I could see swirling in his spirit fire I picked up the cup of water and drank it down. "Thank you," I said. "I am very thirsty. May I have some more if there is any left in the jug? No one came back to offer us food and water yesterday after my—interrogation."

I slid the empty cup along the floor closer to him. "You can just leave it on the ground like before if you are too frightened. I don't mind."

Startled, he hesitated a moment then took up the cup and filled it from the near-empty jug. Taking a deep breath he came closer and handed it to me instead. I took it without touching his hand, drained the cup then handed it back and picked up my spoon and took a mouthful of the mush. "Thank you."

Instead of climbing the stairs he studied me for a long moment while I ate, and finally got up the courage to ask, "You say dat I'm 'fraid of you; why you tink dat?"

Swallowing a mouthful of mush I shrugged before answering. "My elders have taught me that all living beings are surrounded by what we call the spirit fire. This aura, or halo as Djoven's priest say, changes colors with our emotions. I have been blessed with the gift to see them and I was taught their meaning by my grandfather."

I expected him to grow more afraid and then angry as I spoke, but he surprised me by only becoming more thoughtful. At last he said, "Grand da, hmm...My granny use ta tell me tings like dat."

I chuckled and gave him a smile. "That's good to hear. My aunty married a black man who talks like you." My smile grew a little wider as I decided to tease him a bit. "Maybe we are relatives of a sort, eh?"

He jerked back his head as if I had slapped him. I thought he might hit me, then he relaxed and laughed. "You jokin' wit me, yes?"

"A little maybe," I admitted with another smile. "But it is true that my aunt Tuulah did marry a black man like you and I'm sure my aunty will be happier in her new island home, knowing the teachings of your old people are so similar to ours."

At my words his eyes opened wide "You aunty really marry someone from de islands?"

"Yes, she decided to marry a soldier, who she met on our march south to the Preserve. When he finished being a soldier he took her with him back to his home across the big lake he called 'ocean'. Is the lake really salty and as big as he said?"

He let out a booming laugh. "I never tink of de ocean like a big lake afore. But tis true, de wota tase salty."

We talked for a little while longer, but he had other duties, so he left promising to return later. I wasn't sure how much to trust him, he was one of Djoven's priests after all, but I hoped by talking to him he realized that I wasn't the fiendish monster Celibress Vomica and the others were telling him I was. Planting that seed might become useful later.

The praiser didn't come back till he brought the evening meal and by that time I was the only prisoner left in the Perdition Box. As I had predicted my war brothers were let out of their cells later that morning and I was escorted into the one where the ghost and her bloody baby stayed.

Along with my meal of soup and lard-covered bread, he did bring me an extra blanket and a jug of clean water. Wolfing down my portion he leaned against the door frame and studied me.

He was little more than a dark shadow framed by the lantern hung on the post behind him, but I sensed something was on his mind and he wanted to talk again. I waited, wondering if he had the courage to ask me what was bothering him.

When I had nearly finished my soup, he took a deep breath and blurted, "Da peoples here dey say lot bad tings bout you. Dey say you make praiser afore me go crazy. But wen me talk you afore I no tink you devil—or witch like celibress and grand intercessor say. I no understand. Why dey say much bad tings bout you?"

I placed my spoon in my bowl and considered my answer carefully. "I think it is natural for anyone to fear what they don't understand. People like me were given special gifts by the Life Giver. And with the power entrusted to those like me, also comes a great responsibility to protect the People and use our gift for good, that's how I was raised, and that's what I try to do."

"But what 'bout de praiser? Did you make him crazy, like dey say?"

"Yes, in a way I did," I admitted.

He was only a dark silhouette against the light, I couldn't see his expression, but I could sense his growing anger and hoped to calm him by saying, "Praiser Liucas, you are new to this live-away school. Like the muddy water in a flooding river there are many things hidden beneath the surface in this place that can harm or even kill, so be careful. I had my reasons, believe me or not as you will."

"Reasons, like what?"

"Well, for one thing Praiser Tom was a man who liked to take children and make them suck his twig or do other bad things to them that your god has forbidden."

Once again he jerked his head back as if I had slapped him. I saw his mouth harden, but before he could say anything I hurried on. "I know this is true, because he did these things to me, and he did the same to others confined to this prison for children, too.

"My brother Qwatola—uh—298 hanged himself to finally escape the monster's attentions. Because of my Gift, I alone in this place could stop him—and so I did."

I saw the shock blazing in his spirit fire, but the sour discoloration of doubt was there as well.

"If what you say is true, why you no tell intercessor or director so dey stop him?"

"Because the director knew—most of the priests and some of the celibress know, too, but they didn't stop him, because they were afraid, or they like to do bad things to children, too.

"But others who the praiser hurt before me did go to the director to tell their story. Instead of punishing his praiser the director got angry, said the boys were lying, and punished *them* instead.

"So when the praiser did those things to me, too, I saw no point in telling the director, because he wasn't going to listen. And knowing all that, I chose to accept the danger for me personally that using my Gift so openly might mean. I did what was necessary to prevent him doing more harm."

I gave him a mirthless laugh as a new thought came to me. "You don't have to believe me, though. Ask Celibress Vomica. I'm sure she has had plenty to say about me. But I know too that she doesn't approve of many of the secret things that go on here. So you know she won't lie to you if you ask her. But for your own safety do it where no one can hear you."

He shook his head and relocked my door, leaving a troubled man.

PRAISER LIUCAS DIDN'T return next day, or the day after. It was either Brother Doff or intercessor Fredderoth who came with my food—and they wouldn't answer my questions or stay to talk. The grand intercessor, too, left me alone, for which I was grateful, but also his absence troubled me, and I spent much of my time worrying about what he was planning for me next.

Alone in the blackness I lost track of time. My body was recovering—slowly, but still hurt. In spite of the extra blanket I was always cold and found it hard to sleep.

Since I had been confined to her cell my ghostly companion and her baby were always there to pester me and keep me awake unless I got angry enough to shoe them away with my Qwakaiva.

I searched for Keveneth in the Dream to learn the news, but every time I tried Hoyt's pests were there to follow, or attack me. I was forced to give up and stay in my dark prison—bored.

To amuse myself one day I asked the ghost girl, <<Was praiser Tom the father of your baby? If so, then be at peace. He has already been punished for his 'sins'.>>

<<No, it wasn't him.>> She looked at me with frightened eyes.

<<Who then, please tell me.>>

She shook her head and refused to answer. I might have gotten her to tell me with a little more coaxing, but we both heard footsteps on the stairs and she disappeared.

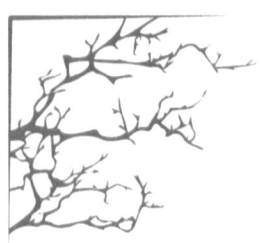

Chapter Eight

To my dismay it was the grand intercessor himself who returned to torment me. Opening my cell door he made a face at the smell, and then ushered me out and tethered me with his power to the post at the bottom of the stairs again.

Bringing closer the hard-back chair he straddled it backwards and folded his arms across its wooden back. "It's been several days since our last talk. Alone in the filth and the darkness down here were you bored without the other boys to talk to?"

"No, I still have the ghost and her baby to keep me company."

"Yes, the ghost," he drawled. "I bet her conversation was—stimulating."

I just stared. His malicious sarcasm wasn't worth an answer.

When he realized I wasn't going to rise to snap at his bait he tried another cast. "Did you miss me, little witch?"

I sat cross-legged on the ground facing him. So he wanted to talk first before beginning my torture. "Not particularly, but I knew you would be back."

"Yes, that's true. I can see your foretelling skills are still working quite well." He gave me an ironic smile. "And does your *Gift also* tell you whether or not you survive our next session, hmm?"

Not wanting to play his game I dropped my eyes and didn't answer.

He let the silence go on for a while before saying in a serious voice, "You don't have to make this harder on yourself, you know. If you gave me the token Kunai has entrusted to you, and swear your allegiance to me and my Crokno masters it will end here and now."

I looked up and shook my head. My guts turned to water, but I managed to stare him in the eye, eyes of a deep, unfathomable violet, so like my own. "You know I can't do that. You wouldn't betray your own kin if you were in my place, so why ask it of me?"

He nodded, acknowledging my point. Then he considered me again, before saying, "You think your acts are virtuous, beyond reproach because you see yourself as a noble warrior avenging injustice and doing only good in the world, don't you? When you destroy an enemy you're only—protecting your people—right?"

His expression hardened. "Well as I told you before 'Good' is such a malleable word. It can justify the deeds of whoever invokes it."

I shook my head denying his implications. "Not true. Good is good. What I did to the praiser—was needed—and they were deserved punishments for the suffering he caused."

"Ah, but were they really? Let's consider Praiser Tom and one of the other predators here you missed."

Not sure where he was going with this I reluctantly nodded. "Praiser Tom was a monster. He hid his evil under a mask of kindness, but only because he wanted to hurt children."

"Yes he did bad things according to your reckoning," Hoyt agreed. "And along with causing your relative's suicide he also hurt *you*, too, didn't he?"

I glared. Where was he leading me? I sensed a trap behind his words, but couldn't find where it was hidden, so I refused to reply.

"Answer me, witch!" Hoyt growled, and there was a touch of power in his voice that compelled me to reply. "Y-yes he hurt me, he forced me to—but that's not why I entered his dreams to torment him. It was to save my brothers—and other children," I repeated defiantly.

"How noble of you." He snorted a mirthless laugh. "If that's the convenient fiction you tell yourself let's talk about perversion and the men and women who indulge themselves with them. Too bad your divinations on the matter failed to reveal to you this one. He is a far more dangerous predator than the whining praiser."

Exerting his power once more he poured into my mind horrifying images of Administrator Rizdale molesting several students, including my friend Kutima. And along with the images I could hear their cries and taste their pain, as well as the administrator's pleasure in their suffering."

With all my strength I broke away from the horror he invoked for me to witness. But was the vision a true retelling of past events or something the grand intercessor conjured to entrap me?

"Unfortunately you didn't know about that one. Killing him would have been a true blessing for the unnamed children you so desperately want to protect." He shook his head in mocked sympathy. "Too bad you will never get the chance to avenge your old friend—and the ghost girl, now that you are mine."

Huddled on the stone floor, my whole body trembling, he saw his arrow had found its mark so he aimed and shot another. "So, let's talk now about Praiser Tom and his—perversions, shall we? How do you think he learned his predatory ways, Hmm?"

When I didn't answer, just continued to hug myself with head bowed he flicked a finger and pain stabbed into my chest from the brand he had given me. "Answer me, rebellious witch, or I will give you even more pain."

Gasping I jerked my head up to face him. "I don't know—and don't really care. Such deeds come naturally to one such as him, I guess."

"Do they? And what about you; does tormenting a man to insanity come natural to you? Are you any different than him, really? I charge you to examine the motivations behind your use of your power in the past. Haven't you done far worst crimes than poke a boy in the ass?" He clicked his tongue and shook his head, in mocked disapproval.

A part of me knew he was toying with me, attacking my defenses in a different way this time, but another part of me feared he spoke true, and the revelation cut deep into my sense of self-worth.

He must have seen the knowledge in my horrified eyes and smiled. "Haven't you killed mercilessly when it suited your plans? What about all those dead soldiers at the river ford and the ones who died in the ambush back in the desert? Did they deserve their deaths by your will? How many of them were innocent and just following their leaders orders?"

"They were enemy," I snapped. "Their orders were to kill my people. I had every right to help defend my relatives with my Gift."

"Every right, hmm...I wonder if their families would agree with you? And what about the innocent settlers to your land who just want a better life for their children and are slaughtered without mercy by Kukiya warriors?"

"I never killed any children—nor did my father's warband. Greedy miners, soldiers, it is the chamuqwani who kill innocent children," I shot back.

"Oh, are you sure? But if you like, let's talk about those innocent chamuqwani children. Wasn't that the fate of your own adopted father? What happened to his 'real' family? Did they spend years mourning the loss of a precious son, or were they killed when their farm was burned and the livestock stolen?" he gave me a toothy smile, enjoying my confusion. "Do you see now how 'good' changes its shape depending on who invokes it?"

I shook my head refusing to acknowledge his point to either him or myself. "The chamuqwani who steal our land and kill or confine us and then starve us, are greedy monsters.

"Our land was given to us by Mother Earth and Father Sky to protect and cherish. The chamuqwani have destroyed their own land and now they want to take ours. They don't deserve a better life. They need to go back to *their* own land, the land Earth Mother gave to them, and I don't care whether they were happy or not when they lived there.

"And as for the soldiers...Every man or woman who agrees to follow the war trail knows that death is waiting for them at the end. To follow that path is their choice—my choice, too. I did what I needed to do to protect my People when I used my Gift."

"How very noble of you," he said. "What a convenient fiction you tell yourself to justify murder."

Murder... his words forced me to recall an act that even to my mind I would call murder—though I still feel my actions were justified. Against Rattlesnake's advice I had also gotten myself involved in an old family feud amongst the Kukiya, and then killed without mercy the chamuqwani trader to avenge my adopted father's capture after the trader betrayed the warband to the soldiers.

But Hoyt either didn't know about that, or didn't think it mattered. Not wanting him to grab that knowledge from my mind, I remained silent and wouldn't meet his eye. I wasn't going to give him more arrows for his bow. Trembling, my emotions in chaos I refused to answer his questions.

He waited, then realizing I wasn't going to play his game any longer he gave me a mirthless laugh once more. "Well, my little witch, if you had looked beyond your own self-imposed obligations and your war brothers' stupidity, you would have seen this..."

Placing his hands on both sides of my head so I couldn't fight him, Grand Intercessor Hoyt poured into my mind images of the praiser as a young boy and then a youth being molested by many shadowy figures.

<<As you can see, our fat priest learned from the best. First under the tutelage of his own father and uncle, and then when he was trained to like his perversion he tried to escape his unnatural urges by joining Djoven's priesthood.

<<Ah, but even there among Djoven's faithful he found no refuge. A predator can always recognize easy prey. His torments continued and his own desires flowered under the ministrations of several priests who hid their unnatural desires under the robes of their sanctity. At last the transformation was complete and he became one of them.>>

He caressed my cheek and smiled, sending shivers of terror cascading down my spine. <<As you will be, too, my sweet, little morsel, before I'm done.>>

Kneeling beside me he brushed his hand across my twig, and his cruel smile grew wider as he noticed my reaction. Placing his lips upon mine he murmured into my mind, <<Yes, as you will be, too, before I'm finished with you. You will be begging me for more. You will agree to swear your allegiance to my Crokno masters. You will want to give us the token belonging to Kunai. Yes, you will gladly help us destroy him and the father who has abandoned you.

<<Why? Because after I finish with you, you will crave the sweet release that only I can give you. You will do anything I ask of you to obtain my favors. That's why.>>

Pulling my mouth away from his questing tongue I shook my head vigorously, denying him with all my Qwakaiva as he used his power to enhance the pleasure radiating with a cruel intensity throughout my whole being. <<Leave me alone, malicer. I will end my life before I give in and forsake all that I cherish.>>

<<Really? Even now your body betrays you.>> he smirked and exerted his power once more. A ripple of desire followed his hand as he traced a line of fire from my brand to my twig. <<I don't think I believe you, my lovely siyatli.

<<Why do you resist me, my sweet little witch? You know you like what I'm doing; you know you want more. Relax, give in to your desires. We are what you said, both half-breeds of a sort; you are no different than me. We can rule this dying world together, if you will only surrender,>>

I am different, I'm not evil like you, I'm not, I'm not! I kept repeating to myself these words, but I was finding it harder and harder to resist his skillful control over my mounting pleasure.

<<Ah, yes, I can see you like what I am doing my tasty morsel. Don't try to deny it you do, oh yes you do.>> Wrapping his slender pale hand around my enlarging twig he stroked me rhythmically, cooing to me and kissing me on my chest where his mark burned, intensifying my delicious arousal.

Then as he became aware of a new insight he raised his head to look me in the eye and crowed, <<Ah, my sweet morsel, you have been keeping a little secret from me. I had no idea...>> he laughed again and kissed me. <<But now I see that you have been taught some of your magical lessons by one of your former mentors like this, yes? And just like now, you liked it—liked it very much. How delightful, this is going to make my task so much easier. We are going to have so much fun with your taming aren't we, my lovely, little witch?>>

Then he pushed me onto my back upon the dirty stone floor. <<And just like the praiser whom you despise, when I'm done, you, too, will hunt the innocent for what you will learn to crave.>>

Horrified I shook my head. <<No, no I don't want anything from you.>> Though If I were honest with myself I would have to admit that what he had divined was true—in part.

Chumco *had* used pleasure as a way to strengthen our bond, but still that didn't make me like Praiser Tom—I never would—never.

Everyone I had used my Qwakaiva to harm had deserved my attack. I kept repeating that denial to myself as he flooded my being with unbelievable pleasure. I wasn't going to doom myself and become his slave and victim. I had to resist, had to fight—and keep fighting him...

But to my eternal shame I did like what he was causing me to feel. I wanted him to let me spill my sap, and then build me up to the crest of pleasure and release again, and again.

<<Yes, that's it, give into your newly aroused hunger, yes... Show me how much you want it...>> he cooed.

Did I want this, did I really? *Oh, my ancestors—somebody—anybody help me resist!*

A sane part of my being kept insisting that if I surrendered to this unholy pleasure who was I but another monster who deserved to die?

But, if what the Crokno breed had shown me was true wasn't the praiser as much a victim as the children he abused? Looking at this from the Crokno viewpoint, attacking the praiser's dreams and causing his mind to crack open, wasn't I just another abuser of the helpless and vulnerable?

Many children are abused in your world, but they don't grow up to be abusers of the innocent in return. The priest was an adult with the power to choose. He could have curbed his harmful behavior. But instead of mastering his urges he was weak and chose to take the easier path, a strange voice in my head argued.

That was true, I answered. *But I was the one gifted with the Qwakaiva that could do good or destroy. And going against all my grandfather's teachings and my spirit guardian's warnings what had I done with the power entrusted to me?* I asked.

You did some good and some bad, and now you face the consequences of those acts as kunai once told you. And if you survive this ordeal, as you have the others placed in your path you will learn from the experience and be the stronger for it, the voice responded.

Maybe, if I can survive and still be myself, I thought privately.

Gathering the last of my strength to resist, I smiled and opened my lips inviting his next kiss. He rumbled a triumphant growl deep in his throat and pressed me tight against him, thrusting his tongue deep into my mouth.

<<A predator knows his prey, eh? Was this how your mother taught you to obey her and make you hate the human part of your heritage?>> I murmured into his mind, and then bit down hard on his tongue.

With a mighty roar he flung me away from him, my head slamming hard against the post to which I was tethered. Leaping to his feet with blood streaming out of his gaping mouth, he raised his hand, power swirling into a violet whirlwind on his palm. Directing its force straight at me, he snarled, "I'll kill you for this!"

"Kill me? Maybe you will, but at least I won't die your slave," I told him. A satisfied smile curved my lips as I braced for his furious reprisal. Then in the next moment I was reeling as the onslaught of pain his vengeance had invoked struck, and I thought I truly might die.

Shielding my wounded body as best I could, I suddenly heard Kuweya's words repeating themselves again in my mind. *<<Pray, my Puhani war brother! Remember the prophet's teachings and ask him to help you.>>*

Pray, yes, I would pray...forming an image of Iyantsha in my mind I begged him for his help. *<<An evil malicer has me and wants me to betray my world and all I love. He is too strong for me. Please help me!>>*

And then my spirit was whisked away from all pain and I was gone.

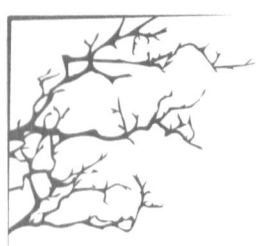

Chapter Nine

Within the Dream the power that had cloaked me in a luminous fog cleared away, leaving me standing knee-deep in the water of Saluuli Lake. It was early morning Sun beginning his journey for the day and burning through the pink mist on the eastern horizon. Far out on the water a few hungry geese were just finishing their meal before returning to the sky on their journey south for the winter. I could hear them calling to one another as they rose upward, their black silhouettes forming an arrowhead shape against the grey sky.

I took in a deep breath and savored the smells of wood smoke, roasting meat and rotting lake-weed submerged in the mud. Out in the reeds ducks were quacking out a danger call, warning all their little ones that a hunting fox was nearby.

Oh, how my heart longed to be there with them in my physical body and not just in spirit form within the Dream. I so missed being on the land living in harmony with the Earth Mother, away from the horrors of the live-away school and the chamuqwani who had brought so much destruction to our world.

Up the bank behind me I could hear singing and the rhythmic pounding of hand drums as the People gathered around the ceremonial fire to greet the day. It was late summer, a time when my relatives would come together to harvest cattail roots, cut reeds and hunt the birds heading south who stopped to rest on Lake's shore.

I listened...a lump forming in my throat. I had almost forgotten how comforting the sound of our healing songs could be for a wounded soul. They were beginning to dance, singing the five songs given to the Prophet on his vision quest, songs the Sky Beings imparted to him to help us heal this wounded world. Tears blurring my vision, I stripped off my filthy blood-stained clothes, sank to my knees and then swam out to immerse myself in Lake's healing green water.

<<Holy Beings of Earth Mother and Sky Father, I am so lost, and afraid, and maybe ashamed of what I've become, too... Help me find my way again. Ahaiya, Holy Ones please help me.>> I prayed.

When I raised my head the Prophet Iyantsha and two of his apprentices were waiting for me on the shore. He looked much as I remembered him. He was a dark squarely built man with a cloth band across his forehead, and his long grey braids were woven with brightly-colored yarn.

He studied me with both his clear brown eye and the one covered with a milky film through which he could see into the Dream. <<Wind whispered to me that you would come, young Puhani. We have been waiting for you.>> He motioned me out of the water.

As I stepped onto the bank his two apprentices came to me and brushed me with branches cut from one of the sacred desert trees. I felt their feathery touch brush down my body and breathed in their resinous fragrance. Tears formed in my eyes again as Tiwari, the one I remembered from before, prayed to the Spirits of the land to help me.

When they finished I felt more at peace. Taking me by the hand Iyantsha led me back to the circle. Around me the praying and dancing continued. Instructing me to stand he asked his helpers to paint me with white and red paints made from desert clays. Beginning with my forehead they painted sacred designs over my body, first on my back and then on my front.

When Tiwari got to my chest and saw the malicer's mark burned into my flesh he gasped, glancing at the Prophet for direction. <<Leave the brand alone for the moment,>> he instructed them. <<I will deal with that when it is time.>>

After the glyphs dried, Iyantsha motioned for me to lie down on a reed mat near the fire. Kneeling beside me he studied me again with his milky spirit eye. <<I can see that your crystal guardian is still with you, that is good, but I also know it cannot help you at this time. This malicer is very strong; he is a powerful enemy.>>

<<He is. And like me his lineage includes kindred from the Beyond. His mother's people the Crokno want to destroy our world. The malicer has been sent back to us to help accomplish that end.

<<I've made stupid mistakes and now he has imprisoned me. He wants the crystal because it is still linked to my Benefactor. It is hiding because it is afraid—I am afraid; I think he is too strong for me.>>

My spirit body trembling I spat out the rest of it. <<I can't let him make me his slave and take the crystal. To protect this world and everyone I love I will have to kill myself if he presses me too hard.>>

Rising up on an elbow I looked into his eyes and pleaded. <<Older brother, can you help me? I know that I'm responsible for this trouble; I didn't listen when I was warned. And now I am so confused and afraid.>>

Pushing me down flat on the matt again, he calmed me by laying a hand on the top of my head.<<Your ancestors and the Earth Mother have laid on you a heavy Burdon to carry. But be at peace, younger brother. The Holy Ones have also gifted you with powerful allies to aid you.>>

<<So, does that mean that you will help me fight my... our enemy?>>

Iyantsha chuckled and told Tiwari to bring the helper who had come for the ceremony. <<I think, younger brother that you were only listening to part of my teachings when you staid here before. Like many young men you were more interested in following Golannah and your adopted father into war than understanding the true meaning of my message.>>

He sadly shook his head then continued. <<I cannot help you in that way; you and your relatives from the Beyond must fight that battle if it comes to that. The power gifted to me is for healing, not fighting.>>

When he saw the dismay on my face he smiled and patted my shoulder. <<Now, now don't give up hope. I can't fight your battles for you, but I can heal, or change this,>> He tapped the brand on my chest. <<So this fearsome malicer's power over you will be lessened or gone completely. We shall see which, as I work.>>

Tiwari had returned and opened his blanket to reveal a rattlesnake twined around his middle. Uncoiling her he handed her into the Prophet's reaching hands. <<Ah, see, younger brother, here is an old friend come back to aid us.>>

Wrapping herself around the Prophet's arm Rattlesnake raised her head and looked at me, her forked tongue flicking out to savor my taste.

<<Ahaiya, Honored Spirit. Thank you for coming. I have missed you. I should have listened to your wise council. I am sorry.>>

In the Dream it is easy to lose track of time. As with other healing I had witnessed him accomplish with his spirit helpers, the rattlesnake bit into the Prophet's hand, her magical venom enhancing the power of his own Gift.

When he laid his hand upon the grand intercessor's mark I felt the healing power burning deep into my soul. I endured the suffering, because I could also feel it transforming Hoyt's malice into something more benign.

<<From within the Dream I cannot remove this brand from your physical body,>> he explained as he finished, <<but what I *can* do is change its shape so he can't use its puwa/power to harm you in future.>>

Later when I was able to see the scar burned into my chest I saw that the Prophet hadn't changed the brand's physical form, but when I looked with my Spirit Sight I could see that it had been transformed into a glyph of protection against evil.

Hoyt still had plenty of tricks he could use against me I was sure, but the glyph had lessened my fear of him and he could no longer control me by using it.

WHEN I CAME BACK TO my physical body I was once more alone in the dark of my cell. My body hurt—and hurt bad—just like after my first session with the malicer.I had no idea how long I had been "away," but it had been definitely long enough for me to be hungry and extremely thirsty. Groping about in the straw I found the water bottle the praiser had left me and to my joy there was still some liquid in its bottom.

Now that I was awake the ghost returned to sit on the moldy straw beside me. <<Baby and I missed you.>>

I groaned and turned my head to see her. <<Asiya, little one. I see you still haven't named baby yet, why?>>

She shrugged. <<Maybe his name is going to be baby, eh?>>

I chuckled, but even that hurt my throat. I was still thirsty. Hoping to distract myself from dwelling on my discomforts we talked for a while, me letting her prattle on about the happy life we would have once I helped her pass through the portal to the land of our ancestors.

Then suddenly I heard the cellar door flung open and two men cursing and dragging someone between them were coming down the stairs. Whoever their prisoner happened to be wasn't making it easy for them. He was fighting and cursing them all the way.

Then I smiled when I heard Matoqwa say, "Not fair. He started it. Why aren't you putting that lying dog turd of a head boy in the Perdition Box along with me?"

"Because there are only two cells down here," Doff growled, "and the other one is occupied with your friend the witch, that's why."

"And besides, you are always causing some kind of trouble anyway," the other man added. "So maybe you like being down here with the bugs."

As I heard them locking Matoqwa in the cell next to mine, I shouted, "Brother Doff, could I please have some water—and some mush? It's been so long since anyone has brought me anything to eat or drink, please."

They paused, but Doff didn't answer at first. "Better tell someone to feed him," the other man advised as they climbed the stairs. "I don't know what the grand intercessor plans to do with him, but he might take his anger out on us, if the boy dies in the meantime."

Doff thought about it for a moment then said to me, "All right, zaunk. Now that you are awake I will have the cook make up two meals to send down here this evening."

"Thank you, Brother Doff."

When they were gone and we were alone in the blackness Matoqwa said, "When that dog fart of a malicer came roaring out of the Box covered in blood, we thought you might be dead. Tas, how are you really? Are you all right?"

I snorted a laugh. "I've been better. And you were right to worry; he almost *did* kill me that last time. And what did you do to get tossed back in the Box again?"

He chuckled and then scooted closer to his door so we could hear each other better as we talked. "Not much. I just had a disagreement with piss drinker Ronalton and bloodied his nose for him, that's all. I probably will be out of here in the morning. Doff will need me to dig potatoes and carrots soon enough. I just started the fight with him so I could be sent down here to check on you and give you the news."

News… not sure I could handle bad news if that was what he had to offer, so I delayed his answer by asking a question of my own. "How long have I been down here?"

He thought about it for a moment then said, "Not sure exactly but I do know it's been three days since the malicer came running out of the cellar bleeding, and then locked himself in his room. What did you do to him?"

"I bit him." Matoqwa laughed, but I cut off his merriment by adding, "But he nearly killed me for it."

I had no wish to share anymore details of that session with him, so I changed the subject. "I hope you are right about getting out of here soon. I wish I could do that, too, even if it meant digging potatoes till my back broke," I said and heard the wistful tone come into my voice.

He made no comment to try and cheer me up, for which I was glad. then he continued, "Yeah about that, my real reason for getting tossed back into this stinking cell was to tell you that Kutima has managed to secretly get a letter mailed to our friend Collin, so don't give up yet."

I felt my mouth drop open and a spark of hopefulness kindle in my chest. The Prophet had promised I would have powerful allies…"That's good, but how did he do it; how did he know where to send a letter?"

"Don't know I guess there were some letters in Administrator Rizdale's office that gave him what he needed. He said he found letters hidden away that had been sent by our friend to you. Collin wanted to check on how we were doing."

"I never got any letters or even heard about them," I said indignantly.

"Yeah, I know. The dog humper of a director has been answering them for you."

"Figures," I grumped. "So how did Kutima get his letter out to Collin without the priests knowing and stopping him? They always read the letters boys send to their families first before mailing them."

Matoqwa chuckled. "Since the malicer showed up and has been poking around and examining records in the school office Rizdale has been hiding in his room as often as he can. He's been letting the breed and a couple other smart-assed boys work in the office doing the easy stuff without supervising them so closely.

"On the day the mail was due to be sent off, Rizdale got called to a last minute meeting, and since the breed was working in the office that morning the priest let him take the mail bag out to the cart without the usual supervision. Our brother was able to slip his unread letter in the bag with no one the wiser."

"I hope it found its way to someone who can help all of us."

Matoqwa grunted his agreement. "Don't know about the letter getting through, but there is definitely something going on. The director and the intercessors have been having lots of secret meetings. Everybody is nervous and it isn't only because the grand intercessor is still here."

"Tell Kutima to be careful—all of you be careful. All those priests are dangerous enemies. Anyone caught could be killed and buried in the fields with no one the wiser."

"I'll tell them, but you be careful yourself, siyatli dog turd."

I let out a long sigh. "I'll try, my brother, I'll try." He grunted, not sure he believed me.

Changing the subject, I asked, "Any word as to when the temple guard is arriving to escort me and the malicer back to the father emperor's big town?"

"No." Matoqwa let out another soft laugh. "And there may not be for a while yet. I didn't know Kutima had it in him to be so brave. He's been secretly tearing up the grand intercessor's letters before they could be mailed, so I don't think guards will be coming for a while, and by then…"

That was exciting news, but I didn't want to get my hopes up too high. Hoyt was going to figure things out soon enough—and be furious when he did. "Tell Ku-Keveneth to stop meddling, before he is discovered. Grand Intercessor Hoyt is a very dangerous and powerful enemy."

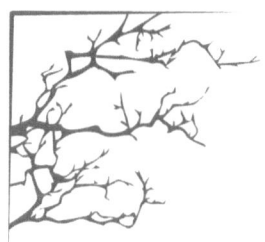

Chapter Ten

Matoqwa was right about him being let out of the "Box" next morning. I guess Doff did need him to dig potatoes. After he left there was no one to talk to for several days but the ghost. My boredom only broken by meals delivered to me by silent priests who barely looked at me.

Then one morning just after I had finished my mush the grand intercessor himself returned. I sensed the anger vibrating off his Spirit Fire before he opened my cell door and motioned for me to come out. Red flames of rage stuck out like porcupine quills from his aura. He was furious with someone, but I didn't think it was me.

My heart sank to the ground when I noticed he was dressed for a journey. In spite of Kutima's brave attempt to delay him, the guard from the temple must have come to escort us back to the city. To my surprise, however, I learned that he was going by himself.

His mouth thinning into a cruel line he surveyed me for a long moment, before speaking. "Affairs in the capital require my immediate attention so I am leaving this morning. It would be unwise of me to bring you with me at this time, so I have decided to leave you in your current accommodations here at the school for now.

"I have told the director to care for you well until I return," he said. "If anything were to happen to you in the meantime he will be imprisoned and be tried and burned as your accomplice, so he's not going to let that crazy old celibress—or anyone else bother you.

"When I return I will have a troop of temple guards at my back, and then you *will* be leaving with me, be sure of that, rebellious witch."

"I have no doubt of that, grand intercessor, but while I remain in my prison do you think you could also ask the director to have someone clean up my accommodations, as you put it? I wouldn't want to die of an infection or a terrible disease while I am waiting for your return."

He snorted. "Hmm...and a bath." He wrinkled up his nose in disgust. "I wouldn't want my guards and I to smell your stink all the way to the capital. Yes, for my own comfort I will tell him."

I relaxed, relieved to have him gone for a while even though still confined. Maybe in the meantime someone would come to rescue me, or I could use my Qwakaiva and somehow escape

Alas, that was only wishful thinking on my part. The malicer had one more surprise for me that would ensure my obedience. As I was turning to go back into my cell he swiftly stepped close and placed his hand over the brand on my chest.

"So, just to make sure you can't make trouble by telling anyone that might show up from the capital about our little 'talks' while I'm gone I will have to do this..."

But when he put his hand on my chest and tried to pour his Qwakaiva into the brand, the glyph Iyantsha had placed underneath sent his power shooting back to him in a stinging burst. With a curse he drew his hand back and glared at me, his face contorting into a terrible snarl. "Who has done this to you?" he demanded.

I shrugged. I wasn't going to betray the Prophet no matter what Hoyt did to me, I decided. "An Elder of my people has told me I have powerful allies," I said. "I guess he was right."

"Who, did, this, your father?"

I remained silent, refusing to look at him or answer.

I sensed his fury mounting, and then he relaxed. "All right, if my brand is of no use to me at the moment I will insure your obedience another way. I don't have time to bring you to heel with pain; my carriage will be here soon, so I will do this instead."

Gathering his power he touched my throat. Then I gasped, and began to choke, finding it hard to breathe.

"Calm yourself, boy. It will quickly pass; you aren't going to die. My conjure will be absorbed in a moment," he assured me.

Trembling and wide eyed I swallowed several times and finally was able to stammer, "W-what did you do to me?"

"I have merely silenced your ability to speak ill of me. Oh, you will be able to speak to your jailers and anyone else about mundane things, like bringing food or water, but the knot I have tied with my power won't let any information about me or our 'sessions' pass your lips—especially if you encounter the 'wrong' people," he explained. "If you try you will choke yourself until you stop.

"And to be sure no ally from the Dream can communicate or help you either I will also do this..." He formed another tiny whirlwind in his palm and then allowed it to disperse and encage me within a bubble of power that enveloped my spirit as well as my physical body.

As my Spirit Sight faded and my physical senses dulled as if I now floated underwater, he saw my horrified expression and gave me a mirthless smile. "This will keep you from running away into the Dream in future or calling upon your father and other allies to come to your rescue."

He chuckled as a new thought came to him. "Unfortunately my conjuring will mean that you can no longer amuse yourself by conversing with the ghost. You won't be able to see or hear her either. No dreams or nightmares will trouble your sleep, however, so enjoy your rest till I come back for you, my sweet little morsel."

Tears of loss and frustration blurring my vision he ushered me back into the stinking dark of my cell and locked me in. I sank down on the dirty straw and wrapped the blanket about my shoulders, the tears rolling uncontrollably down my cheeks.

THE MALICER'S PARTING words to me were that he hoped I would appreciate his company more when he returned. After a while being cooped up alone in total darkness with nothing to distract me from my misery I feared he had a point.

Ever since my birth I had been surrounded by family and friends or other-worldly companions in the Dream. Enclosed in his conjured prison, with only my fearful thoughts and the agonizing pain for company was devastating. I couldn't have imagined such a cruel torture before it happened to me.

At first I tried just to ignore my pain and sleep as much as I could manage, but that was difficult. Swallowed up by my own suffering, my days punctuated briefly by grim-faced priests who came to give me food and replace my piss jar I was forced to take a good look at myself and question the world as I had grown to accept it.

The Crokno malicer had forced me to view people and events in a way different from the one I had ingested with my mother's milk. He had shown me how Praiser Tom had been warped by his brutal childhood and that got me to wondering about boys like Ronalton and even the angry miners who had killed my family. What had happened to them to make them cruel and indifferent to the suffering of others?

I wasn't sure I was ready to forgive them or wholly regret how I had responded to their threat, but the insights I gained in my isolation did help me to understand my enemies at a deeper level than before—for which I was grateful later on in my life.

My memory is vague about how many days passed before a stomping and shouting commotion upstairs captured my attention and broke up my boring routine. Before I could puzzle it out, however, I heard the cellar door open and two sets of footsteps start down the stairs.

Was the grand intercessor back? No, I didn't think so. One set sounded like a man but the other was too light—a student—a woman? I trembled bracing myself for anything.

Then my door was flung open, and, what seemed to me to be a blinding light flooded the doorway. It was painful after being cooped up in blackness for so long. I cringed, shielding my eyes a fit of uncontrollable shaking enveloping me.

Someone cried out. "Oh Tas, what has that evil malicer done to you?" a shadow that sounded like Kutima cried.

In the next moment an unknown chamuqwani came in to my prison and gently carried me out and sat me down in Hoyt's chair. Getting more accustomed to the bright lantern light I blinked up at the man examining me. He was a pale-skinned chamuqwani with cropped brown hair and thick muscular shoulders dressed in the black jacket and trousers worn by men of high standing among them. He had strong features, though pleasant enough, and for some reason I couldn't detect the color of his eyes. His mouth was full-lipped, but devoid of the hard lines of cruelty I'd come to recognize in so many others of his kind.

Without turning to face his companion, he said in my Qwani'Ya language, "Thank you, young warrior, you did well to show me this."

Then in the same language I heard Kutima say, "He looks so..." Kutima broke off a sob catching in his throat.

I looked down at myself in the light. Dirt-crusted hair, bruised face and bloody clothes, I must have looked terrible and smell worse.

Still speaking my language the stranger asked, "Is there a doctor at this school?"

"Yes, but can't you just heal him?"

"I can 'help' him but the healing art isn't one of my Gifts, so for now we will use what the chamuqwani have available.

"But before you sneak out the back to get the school's doctor I want you to very quietly get Collin. If you remember, he is the dark-haired young man that came with Lord Bronworthy and the emperor's commissioners. He is sitting just inside the parlor door with a notebook on his lap. Tell him I need him, and show him where to come."

Kutima nodded, took one more horrified glance in my direction then hurried up the stairs. When he was gone the stranger came closer, his mouth hardening as he took note of every bite mark, scab and bruise. When I remained silent and just stared, he finally asked, "Tas, don't you know who I am?"

I shook my head and dropped my eyes, trembling. Without my Gift to aid me I had no idea who this chamuqwani stranger was, and I was afraid.

Then a buzzing noise echoed in the shadows of my mind, but I was unable to distinguish the sounds as words. I shook my head again, trying to clear it, but the more I tried to understand the buzzing only became worse.

He gave me a puzzled look and said, "Tas, what's the matter? I know I look different than I did at our earlier meetings. Use your Spirit Sight and then you will know me."

My whole body shaking with the effort I focused all my remaining Qwakaiva, trying to discover the identity of this unknown man, but I couldn't break out of the malicer's cage. Afraid and frustrated I swallowed several times before I could croak out, "C-can't—" Then my throat spasmed and I doubled over choking.

He studied me with narrowed eyes then pulled me into his arms and held me tight, murmuring soothing sounds next to my ear. "Ah, I understand now. Calm yourself, my poor boy."

I stiffened. I didn't want to be held—by anyone. After what the malicer did to me I was too afraid to trust in this unknown stranger's touch.

"It's all right, don't try to explain. Now I see the knot he placed to prevent you from speaking. Be easy, my son, I can fix that. I am here now and we will be leaving this place soon."

He'd called me his son, but neither Star Swimmer or Nachoga, my two fathers, looked like this man. As he laid a hand on my throat and the strangling pressure eased my confused mind took a moment, before I figured out that he was indeed my Seal father and that Star Swimmer had only shifted his form to walk unnoticed among the chamuqwani.

With a grateful sigh I relaxed into his embrace. Then as he held me Star Swimmer became aware of the other conjuring that had been done to me. Sitting me back on the chair he pulled open my ragged shirt to better examine my chest. When he detected the inflamed brand and understood its meaning rage mottled his features for just a moment before he mastered himself.

Then his mouth twitched when he recognized the Prophet's glyph hidden under Hoyt's brand. "That was very clever of you, my son. Kunai will be pleased when I tell him."

He frowned thinking, then said, "I can remove much of the Crokno's conjure now; the rest will have to wait till we have more time. I may be forced to leave you for a short while, but don't be afraid, I will be back for you—and take you away with me this time. We will leave this world so Kunai and other relatives can instruct you better.

"But first I must take back Kunai's token. The Crokno can't be allowed to have the crystal whatever may happen to either you or me."

Placing his hand over a spot a little to the left of Hoyt's brand Star Swimmer warned, "Brace yourself, my son. I'm sorry but this may hurt." Giving me no more warning than that, I suddenly felt a terrible ripping of my flesh as his spirit hand reached into my chest and pulled my hidden crystal guardian out.

Swallowing the tiny being himself Star Swimmer next eased the physical pain in my bleeding chest, but he couldn't fix the chasm of loss that he had just opened in my soul. I knew what he had just done was necessary, but the ache of the crystal beings loss was devastating.

He must have read the desolation on my face, because he repeated, "I'm sorry I needed to do that, Tas. I know you are hurting terribly right now, but don't give up hope. If we both survive this I'm sure you will regain Kunai's favor and a new ally will be gifted you."

Through the tears I could feel welling behind my eyes I began to stammer out a useless apology when the cellar door opened and Collin appeared in the doorway.

"Master Starwin, are you down here?" he called out softly as he took a couple hesitant steps into the gloom.

"Yes, scribe, I am here—and so is your young friend Tas," Star Swimmer said. "Please come down. You need to see all of this so you can report back to your patron and the emperor's commission."

Reassured, Collin climbed down to join us. He looked much as I remembered him from our past meetings. He was an intense young chamuqwani with long dark hair, full lips and thoughtful brown eyes. He wrinkled up his nose at the smell as he came completely into the cellar, and then, he noticed *me*. "Asiya, my friend," I murmured, and raised my face to the light so he could have a good look at me.

I saw the expression of shock come over his face as he saw the effects of the grand intercessor's torture for the first time. "Oh, Tas!" he breathed. "I never thought it would be like this—your letters."

I choked on a laugh. "I never saw your letters. Director Harriscot kept them and answered them for me."

Before he could ask more Star Swimmer interrupted us. "It is as we have told you, Collin Golbraith. Many of Djoven's faithful are being controlled by the Crokno, an alien race who wish to destroy your world," my father growled. "Right now, scribe I need you to be witness to these crimes and record for the Commission what we have discovered here."

Star Swimmer took down the lantern and handed it to him. "Look around you, scribe, observe and see what the children assigned to these foul priests have had to endure because of governmental negligence."

As Collin raised the lantern to have a good look, he said thoughtfully, "I wish Willum was here with his camera to document all this."

"We do the best we can with what is available," Star Swimmer said.

"Quite right," Collin agreed and did as my father suggested. He peered into each cell, noting the piles of rotting straw covered with ragged blankets stiff with dirt and dried blood, the stone walls behind decorated with streaks of mold, and the overflowing pee buckets in the far corner.

When he came back out from the second cell I said, "There's a ghost girl and her baby sharing my cell. She was molested, died in childbirth and then she was buried under the stone floor in there. The director and the administrator knew and did nothing to help her. Maybe someone could dig her up and give her and baby a proper burial."

Collin glanced back into the shadows as if hoping to see her. Star Swimmer laughed, "She is hiding at the moment, but Tas speaks true. I saw her and the bloody babe when I first opened his cell door."

"There are also children buried in unmarked graves in the orchard. A boy who killed himself because he was also repeatedly molested is there. Ask Matoqwa to show you."

Collin nodded. A distracted tone in his voice he asked me, "What is this place called?"

"The priests and the students named it, the 'Perdition Box.' When a child does something to displease one of the priest they are confined here—sometimes for days."

"Days? But these cells aren't suitable for even a rabid dog."

I gurgled a laugh, broken off quickly when I choked.

Star Swimmer put his hand on my throat again and the pain eased. "Collin, see if there is any water around here for Tas to drink."

Still choking I pointed back in my cell. Collin rooted around in the straw for a moment and returned with the bottle. He shook it and then handed it to me. There was a little; I'd been saving it, because sometimes my keepers forgot to bring more.

When I'd drained the last drop, he asked, "Tas, how long have you been confined here?"

I shrugged. "I have no idea, ever since Grand Intercessor Hoyt captured us, and brought us back to the school. How long that's been you would have to ask Matoqwa, or I'm sure Kutima would know."

"Kutima?"

I sighed. Why did he insist on using his chamuqwani name when he had a perfectly good Qwani'Ya one his mother gave him? "Keveneth, Kutima is his Qwani'Ya name. We grew up together back home."

Our talk was interrupted at that point by the school's doctor protesting with Kutima about entering the cellar. Star Swimmer motioned for Collin to go up and retrieve him.

When Collin had his back to us my father laid a hand on my shoulder, and murmured, "Have courage, my brave son, I have to leave you and return the crystal being to Kunai. I will be back for you I give you my word, and then I will take you away from this terrible place at last."

When Collin returned with the doctor, Star Swimmer was gone. Collin glanced around a puzzled expression on his face as he scanned the empty cellar. "He said he had an errand to do," I said to Collin, "but your friend also said not to worry; he will be back."

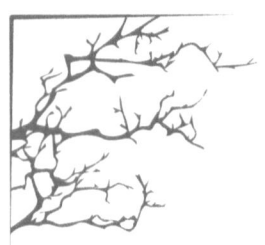

Chapter Eleven

Like everyone else who saw me within the Box that day Doc was outraged. Motioning to Collin to come closer, he asked, "Are you able to carry him up these stairs? I need to clean him up and examine him thoroughly in the infirmary not down in this cesspit."

Seeing the light flooding the hallway above I wanted more than anything to get out of this cellar—even if it meant imprisonment elsewhere.

"I-I think so—" Collin began.

Cutting him off I said, "I can walk, if Collin helps me, please let's just go. I have to get out of this dark. Lock me up somewhere else if you must."

Doc motioned to the stairs. "Take it as slow as you need to, boy. I will go ahead and get things ready." Grumbling to himself about superstitious fools still living in the dark time themselves, being worse idiots than the heathens they were supposed to be saving, he stomped up the stairs in front of us.

Unfortunately we were nearing the top, the light beckoning me like the Prophet's blessing when we were stopped by the director. "What, by the Mighty Thunderer are you doing, Scribe?" He roared.

So close, so very close, my heart nearly stopped within my chest and my knees shook so much I almost fell, but Collin was right behind me. murmuring encouraging words into my ear he helped me up the rest of the way and into the light. I leaned against him for a moment and breathed a sigh of relief. I whispered a small prayer of gratitude for even this little respite from the eternal gloom.

Hearing the director's angry voice in the hall Lord Bronworthy and the black-robed commissioners had come out of the parlor to investigate. Stepping back and wrinkling up his nose at my smell the director growled at Collin, "Who gave you permission to do this, young man?"

"Why, your own doctor is the one who told me to bring this poor boy to his infirmary, Director Harriscot," Collin answered.

"Impossible! He doesn't even know about—"

"As to what your doctor does, or doesn't know I couldn't say, director," Collin said, his voice even and not combative.

"All I do know is that he told me to bring his new patient to him, so he can be treated properly for his injuries."

Catching lord Bronworthy's eye Collin motioned him to come closer. "Yon, he is nearly impossible to recognize at the moment, but this is Tas. It is as our informants have told us these wicked priests have been keeping boys in filthy locked cells down that dark cellar and torturing them." He motioned to my many cuts and bruises.

Knowing we had an audience, Collin, enraged himself by that time, ignored my hand digging into his arm and continued, "He also tells me there is at least one body buried under the dirt down there, the body of a young girl and her newborn child. Isn't that right, Administrator Rizdale?"

Rizdale blanched then his face turned purple with outrage. "That's a filthy Lie. There's no bodies buried down there. That cellar is a place set aside to discipline unruly children—nothing more."

"Then you won't mind if we send for some men from the village to dig around and check to see if the lad is lying," the tallest of the three commissioners said, thoughtfully studying my battered condition.

"Quite right, Commissioner Orland," Lord Bronworthy said. Then ignoring the director's spluttered protests he motioned for Collin to continue helping me to the infirmary.

But once again the director stepped in front of us. "You aren't taking that boy anywhere. He is an accused witch. Grand Intercessor Hoyt himself has given me strict orders not to remove him from the perdition box." He pointed with a trembling hand down into the cellar from which I had just been rescued. "Take him back. If the doctor wants to see him he can administer to his needs down there! For the safety and well-being of all god-fearing people in this school and elsewhere the Temple has decreed that he be confined until his trial."

His voice quivering with both rage and fear, he pointed an accusing finger at me, and roared, "This foul creature has done terrible crimes. He must be made to suffer and burn for what he's done. That is temple law!"

"But it is not imperial law, director," the commissioner said. "The Empire has decreed that the barbaric torture and burning of people accused of witchcraft is no longer a suitable punishment for criminals convicted of any secular or religious crime.

"Even the High Divine of your temple has agreed to the Emperor's mandate. Surely you are aware of this? It was decreed more than a hundred years ago."

Harriscot sneered and waved a hand in dismissal of the notion. "Of course, I have heard of the law, but it was only a meaningless concession to the crown, agreed to by one of the High Divine's weak predecessors. The temple of today doesn't recognize its validity in certain circumstances... such as in this case."

Spittle spraying from his lips he pointed a shaking finger at me and accused, "You don't understand what we are dealing with here, gentlemen. You think he is just an ignorant, abused zaunk, but he isn't the innocent boy you believe him to be, I assure you. That evil child has used his powers to drive a priest to madness and terrify the rest of my staff and students."

"Nonetheless, it is the law of the land," another black robed commissioner argued. "And until your wild accusations are proven in an imperial court the young man in question must be treated in a humane fashion, director. That, too, is the law."

"And your racial slurs aren't appreciated by this commission, either, Director, please bare that in mind in the future," Commissioner Orland said.

Waving away the reprimand Harriscot repeated, "But the grand intercessor said—"

"Grand Intercessor Hoyt is facing his own difficulties back in the capital at the moment," Lord Bronworthy interrupted. "Might I suggest to you that you focus on saving your own skin and never mind the grand intercessor and his orders for now."

"There is still the question of money going missing, children starving and your books not being in order. Maybe you should concentrate on that and allow this poor young man to be cared for by the good doctor, hmm?" Commissioner Orland suggested.

"We have received a report from someone with temple connections that your books may show certain *irregularities. We also* have obtained a writ signed by the Divine Prelate himself to see the school's records..."

The commissioner said no more before the director blanched and then stepped aside to let us pass. Motioning for Collin to help me on my way we left the men arguing in the hallway.

I DON'T REMEMBER MUCH about the next few days while I recovered in Doc's infirmary. Grateful for his pain-killing medicines and a soft bed and clean sheets I slept as much as possible. When I woke Collin or another servant of the Emperor's commission was sitting by my bedside to see that I was fed decent food and not tormented.

I also had a few visitors, mostly other children curious to see the boy accused of being a witch. They would hide in the shadows when Doc or his helpers weren't around, their giggling and whispering giving them away. I ignored them as best I could and one of my protectors would shoo them away if they were too bold.

Claiming one of his terrible headaches had returned, Matoqwa got himself admitted to the infirmary after one of Doff's disciplines, but I doubted he was badly hurt. I think he was just there to make sure I was doing all right so he could report back to my war brothers.

I had always known Matoqwa to be a fearless young warrior when we ran free in the desert, so I wasn't surprised when I heard him bravely talking to Collin about the school when I woke from time to time.

Collin had also been assigned by Lord Bronworthy and Commissioner Orland to take down my statement as to what I had witnessed and endured while living at saint Yon's. So when he asked, I also suggested other boys and staff they might want to interview.

But I knew it would be a risk for anyone to speak out, because if they did they would be vulnerable to reprisals from the temple if the inquiry failed or was delayed. So I wasn't sure how much information the Commission might be able to gather to verify my accusations—and that worried me.

Collin especially remained my concern, because he continued to be very active in his condemnation of the temple and the grand intercessor in particular. So with that in mind, one evening when we were alone in the quiet ward and he had just finished telling me the story of how they had found the unmarked graves I'd mentioned, and an independently hired doctor had discovered evidence of malnutrition among most of the children, I reached for his hand to create an extra bond between us.

"Collin, I want you to be more careful about the accusations you are making about Djoven's temple and Grand Intercessor Hoyt to the commission."

He stared at me in astonishment, his mouth dropping open. "But why Tas, haven't you always claimed that it is my purpose to bring to light the injustices against your people?"

Yes I had. And in the greater plan that Kunai envisioned that was his purpose, true enough. I had seen it with my Gift. But because I *had* seen his future, I had also envisioned many dangers he might encounter if he chose to take up our cause—dangers that being only human he might not survive.

I took a deep breath, how to explain my concern for him without frightening him too much to carry on? "You know that I have certain Gifts?"

Giving me a puzzled expression, he nodded. "Yes I know that. Why are you bringing that up now?"

"Because maybe some of what the priests are claiming about me does have a seed of truth to it. I did have a hand in Praiser Tom's display of insanity, but not his attempt to kill himself. That was his own idea."

"I see." He hesitated, frowning as he considered the meaning of my words. For just a moment I saw fear come into his eyes, and just as quickly he suppressed it. At last he ventured, "If you did do some of what they claim, I'm sure you had a good reason."

"At the time I thought I did," I said. "The praiser like some others here, offer hungry children food if they will 'touch' them down there." I pointed to my crotch. "Praiser Tom was one such, Administrator Rizdale is another."

When I saw his eyebrows raise at that, I explained further, "Qwatola, one of my war brothers you met at our trial decided that death was the only way he had to escape the praiser's attentions."

Collin sat back in his chair, thinking. At last he said, "That's a very serious accusation, Tas. Are you sure?"

"About Rizdale I know only what the grand intercessor told me. About Praiser Tom I am sure, because he did the same to me after Qwatola was gone. To try and stop him from hurting another child is why I entered his dreams and showed him what he did to the innocent. His guilt is what drove him to despair; my meddling only made it happen sooner."

I sighed and dropped my eyes, not wanting him to see the discomfort I still felt after what I had caused. Then I took a deep breath and continued, "Left alone for so long in the dark I had plenty of time to think. Now I have come to believe that the praiser isn't an evil man, only a weak one who couldn't master the urges taught to him in his youth."

"But why didn't you tell the director or one of the other priests, instead of resorting to your other—Gifts—as you call them?"

"Because they already knew and did nothing about it. Take a look at Kutima's twisted finger and ask him about Administrator Rizdale—though he might be too frightened to tell you. It was the grand intercessor himself who told me about both Praiser Tom's childhood and Kutima's molestation, when he was having one of his 'sessions' with me."

"I see." His face contorted into an angry mask then he controlled his indignation and said as he rose, "I should tell Yon so he can relay this back to our colleagues in the Capital. There is a courier going—"

Still holding his hand I forced him to sit again. "Collin, there is more you alone should know, before you give the Commission some of the information I have shared with you. Grand Intercessor Hoyt isn't totally human. His mother is Crokno.

"As I think Master Starwin has told you, these beings wish to destroy our world and Hoyt has been sent back to further their plans. He is very powerful, ruthless, and much more experienced with his conjurings than I am. Please be more careful. He will destroy you and your friend Lord Bronworthy in—mind and body if he thinks you are a threat to him and his purpose."

Collin gave me a nervous laugh. "Not human." He patted my hand to assure me. "Undergoing the pain and tortures you suffered by the man I can understand why you might think so, but surely—"

"No, brother, I don't 'think' so I know," I said, my tone of voice stern. "I tell you true, because I have the Spirit Sight to see who he really is, so I am warning you to be careful."

He promised he would but I wasn't sure I believed him. When Collin left Matoqwa rose up on one elbow and called to me. Only a silhouette against the lantern light flooding in from the hallway he said, "I remember what you and the malicer were talking about down in the box. So it's true he's a sort of breed—like you, eh?"

I snorted a laugh then admitted, "Sort of. But he is also enemy—a very ruthless and powerful enemy so I hope my father comes back soon to free us."

Kuweya and Keveneth snuck in to visit just then which saved me having to answer more of the bear's questions.

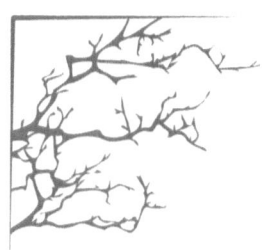

Chapter Twelve

Later, I couldn't explain what woke me, but as soon as my eyes opened I knew I was in great danger. It was late, the infirmary was quiet, only a dimmed lantern glowing at the far end of the room near Doc's office and examining room. From a bed further down the aisle I could hear Matoqwa's rumbling snore. All seemed quiet.

Beside my bed Collin slept in the visitor's chair his legs stretched out, his head slumped against one shoulder. He looked uncomfortable and would probably have a stiff neck in the morning if he remained much longer like that. I was just going to wake him and tell him to go rest in a proper bed when another sound caught my attention.

Holding a lantern he had removed from the hall grand intercessor Hoyt stepped into the infirmary. When he saw that I was already awake and watching him he smiled, showing lots of teeth. Noticing the other sleeping inhabitants of the room he waved a hand and a violet mist enveloped each of my sleeping protectors.

"Hello, little witch. Did you think you could escape me so easily, hmm?"

"No, but I could always hope."

He laughed softly and came over to my bed. I sat up and threw my legs over the side to face him. "My pets, as you call them, have been telling me stories of your willfulness."

Studying my neck with his Spirit Sight for a moment he growled a curse and said, "And I found it hard to believe, but now I can see that they spoke true. Someone has tampered with my throat knot, and the director confirmed it before I killed him." He shook his head in a mock reprimand. "Naughty boy, you have been talking to the 'wrong' people."

To distract both him and myself I asked, "The director is dead; why did you do that?"

"I could say I was doing my civic duty. When I surprised him he was burning the school's secret accounting books—the ones that would have sent him and Rizdale to the gallows maybe if the Emperor's commission discovered them, but that wasn't the real reason.

"No I killed him because I had warned him not to let you out of your cell. And, I am a man of my word.

"Of course when I take you away with me his death by magic will be just another crime to add to your long list of evil. Even your self-righteous lord and the Emperor's useless Commission might doubt your innocence before I'm done, hmm?"

Could that possibly happen? I prayed he was only toying with me again, hoping to destroy my confidence. I had heard no commotion earlier to announce his arrival, so I suspected no one knew he was here. I feared I was on my own—again. "If you are going to take me with you this time, then where are your guards?"

"My guards? Why in the Capital—guarding my suite—where I am supposed to be sleeping at the moment. I *do* plan to take you with me this time, but I have no need of an escort. We will return by the same means that I came here tonight."

He must mean by use of his power. I couldn't help the trembling I could feel forming a knot in my gut and radiating outwards to my hands. I hastily concealed them under my blanket, but it was too late. He noticed my fear and his mouth quirked. "H-how?" I stammered.

"Why through the Dream, of course. That is how we will go with no one the wiser about my visit." He chuckled. 'Once again these superstitious fools will believe you disappeared by using your evil magic."

I wasn't so sure about that. Though frozen and unable to move Collin's eyes were open, and he was staring at us. If the malicer didn't kill him before he left with me, at least someone could tell my father what had happened here.

Then what he had just revealed struck me, and I couldn't help showing my surprise. "Travel physically within the Dream? I had already sensed that you are here in body, not just in spirit. But how is that possible?" I blurted, ignoring my peril for the moment.

Hoyt clicked his tongue and shook his head in mocked disapproval. "Oh my sweet little morsel, your mentors and your father have sadly neglected your education. It is very possible with your unique heritage. And when you swear your allegiance to me and my kin I may teach you—but only if you please me."

Once again my feelings of self-pity and frustration for being only half-trained rose up to taunt me. How many terrible events in my life could I have prevented if I had been properly instructed...

Stepping closer he reached out a hand to me. "Come. It grows late and I will be expected to attend morning prayers soon, and before that I need to have you safely tucked away in your new accommodations."

Taking hold of my hand he pulled me roughly to my feet, then sensing the other change in my being he tore open my night shirt and glared at the healing wound just to the left of his brand.

Hoyt swore and gripped me by both shoulders his fingers, like iron claws, digging into my flesh. Holding me at arm's length he shook me and demanded, "What have you done, stupid boy? I can sense the change in you. Where is the token the dragon gifted you?"

In spite of the pain he was inflicting I managed to let out a mocking laugh. "It's gone, back to my mentor—a place where you can never obtain it, no matter what you do to me, Malicer."

I smirked, defying his growing fury. "Will your Crokno mother be cross with you for your failure? Wil she put you in her own version of the Box? Will her punishment hurt? I hope so." I laughed again.

Rage, loss, despair and fear, the play of emotions crossing his face in the next few moments before he regained control of himself terrified me. I knew I was playing a dangerous game baiting him to do further violence, but I didn't care. I feared he would kill me and I wanted to wound him as best I could before he ended my life.

His anger mastered for the moment he shook his head sadly and said, "What have you done, stupid siyatli? As you once told me—we are much alike—half-breeds of a sort. Both of us caught in-between two warring forces."

Releasing a hand he caressed my cheek, his voice sad with regret as he said, "Too bad, we could have done great things together, but now..." He took a deep breath and his grip firmed upon my shoulders again. "Without the surrender of Kunai's token you are of no use to me or my Crokno kin, so I will have to kill you, too, before I leave tonight."

His expression suddenly brightened as a new idea came to him. "Ah, but by killing you and blaming the director's death upon you, and maybe some others, if I have time—like the meddling old celibress and Lord Bronworthy, maybe I can at least salvage something from this debacle."

I could see the violet power gathering on his palm when a cool voice from the doorway of Doc's office said, "If you try to hurt him further, Hoyt, then it will be my great pleasure to end your life at last. Will Sabisa miss you, I wonder, or will she blame your countless debacles on your flawed paternal bloodline?

"She always blames someone else for her failures, you know. It's perpetually the fault of her mates when her warped children don't measure up to her expectations for them. Alas, she is never been one for self-examination."

No longer disguised in his chamuqwani form the Qwa'Nayhi Seal Man I knew as my father stepped all the way into the infirmary to face our enemy. Long brindle hair braided down his back, muscular arms and chest bare save for gleaming strands of power he was surrounded by a faintly glowing aura of blue light.

Concealing what he was conjuring in his closed hand Hoyt let go of me, and turned to face his new adversary. "Ah, Star Swimmer, we meet again. I hoped you might be the brat's sire. I suspected you would show yourself to try and retrieve the siyatli if I hurt him badly enough. And just as I planned you did come.

"But don't worry about my reception at home. When I give my mother your braid of hair attached to your bloody scalp she will be pleased. You and the rest of Co'yeh's clan have been a constant irritant for us for quite some time. One less of your kind will bring her much pleasure." Then without warning Hoyt threw the power he concealed into my father's face.

His attack had momentarily startled Star Swimmer, but the shield of Qwakaiva he had surrounded himself before entering absorbed most of Hoyt's first blow.

Before he could ready another attack, I did what Matoqwa had advised me to do when we were still in the Box. I drew back my fist and punched him as hard as I could in the jaw. Hoyt reeled backwards nearly falling onto my bed. His next magical arrow dispersed into a harmless mist while he regained his balance.

Before he could turn on me I grabbed Collin off the chair and rolled with him under my bed to be out of the way of my father's next attack.

The malicer now distracted I sensed his control of the conjure paralyzing my friend was waning.

I helped it fade then whispered next to his ear, "You need to get out of here. Keep crawling under the beds until you have reached the hallway then run."

"But what about you?" he murmured.

'I am staying to help my father if I can. Go!"

"Your father?"

"Yes, my father. He introduced himself to you as Master Starwin in his shape-shifted chamuqwani form, but they are one and the same." I motioned impatiently for him to keep moving.

"Shape-shifting... Then what you said about the grand intercessor applies to you as well." I could see the fear in his eyes blossom anew, but I had no time to coddle him and explain further. "Collin, you must go—now!"

He swallowed hard and then bravely said, "No. If you are staying then I will stay and help, too."

"You can't help us," I snapped. "You have no training or Qwakaiva for this battle. And if Hoyt captures you he will only use you as a hostage against us, or kill you. Go—now!" I gave him a shove to emphasize my words and he reluctantly began crawling through the dust and the shadows towards the door.

I would have liked to give Matoqwa the same advice, but he was too far away for me to do that safely. And when I snuck a peek over the edge of my bed I could see that he was no longer resting atop his own. I had no idea where he had gone; I could only hope that he had escaped as well.

And then I had no more time to worry about my human companions. The malicer had summoned his demon pets and my father was hard pressed to withstand so many attacks coming at him all at once. I wasn't strong enough to take on Hoyt, but I could do something about his annoying pets.

Though not visible to human eyes I had been aware in the back of my mind of the hissing flashes of blue and violet spirit light crisscrossing the infirmary as my father and the malicer battled. Outside I thought I could hear shouting and smell smoke but I banished that fact out of my mind. It wasn't important to our current situation. Helping my father here and now was what I needed to concentrate upon.

While I had been getting my friend to safety the two adversaries had battled back and forth across the long room leaving a shamble of scorched bedding and broken beds in their wake. Father was forcing Hoyt towards the inner room where Doc kept his tools and medicines and away from an easy escape into the hallway where innocents might be killed.

When his demons saw me heading in that direction they left off harassing Star Swimmer and swarmed me. I was still weak from my ordeal in the Box, so I had a whole new set of bites and scratches to display by the time we finished, but I managed to keep them occupied and fend off most of their attacks, while the adversaries from the Beyond battled with spears of power.

When I finally banished the little pests I became aware for the first time of the grey smoke gathering in the hallway. I heard the sounds of people shouting and frightened children screaming. The school really was on fire—we had to get out!

Hoyt had said the director was burning important papers when he found him. I guess he hadn't bothered to put out the flames after he killed him—and now...

When I glanced back into the infirmary to warn my father I saw that Hoyt had driven him to his knees and had created a knife out of spirit fire to finish off his enemy. Star Swimmer wasn't making it easy for him, grasping his outstretched arm and holding it in place. I could see the muscles bulging on both their arms as they battled with the Qwakaiva of Spirit and their physical strength to determine the victory.

I had to help my father if I could. Hoyt was a man full of tricks, I knew from bitter experience. *My mother is a bitch, but she taught me well*, I heard the malicer's words echo in my mind as I hurried towards them.

Before I could reach them and add my dwindling Qwakaiva to my father's power, Matoqwa surprised everyone when he stepped out of the shadows of Doc's office and plunged a knife hilt-deep into the unsuspecting malicer's back.

Hoyt roared, tried to reach behind him and pull out the blade, but it was beyond his reach. Taking advantage of the situation Star Swimmer leapt to his feet and slashed open the malicer's neck with a blade forged of Spirit Fire as he toppled to the floor.

As the malicer slumped dying Star Swimmer wiped a streak of blood from his face and grinned at Matoqwa. "Thank you, Young Warrior. That was bravely done. The Crokno have always underestimated our human relatives."

Matoqwa reached down and yanked the knife from Hoyt's unresisting flesh. He grinned back. "May Qwa'osi the otter forgive me, I never thought there would come a day when I would be helping one of Co'yeh's kin."

Star Swimmer laughed and patted his shoulder. "I'm sure my rival will get over it, should you make it back north to tell him."

Just then Keveneth and Kuweya rushed into the infirmary calling my name. They stopped with eyes wide when they saw the destruction created during the battle. "We came to tell you about the fire and see if you needed help—" Kuweya broke off when he noticed the body on the floor.

"We will be leaving shortly, young warriors, never fear," Star Swimmer said. Returning his attention to the corpse Star Swimmer knelt and reached his spirit-hand into the body, pulling out a small crystal, its facets radiating an angry violet light.

Putting it inside a glowing pouch around his neck he saw my surprised expression and explained, "Just as you had a token given to you by Kunai, so did the Crokno have a token given to him from his mother. If we make it out of here alive today, Kunai will be pleased with our work."

Standing, he put an arm around my shoulder and then ushered the three of us out into the hall. Star Swimmer cleared away the smoke as he forged a path for us from the building. Coughing and choking, we stumbled along in his wake, out the door and into the night.

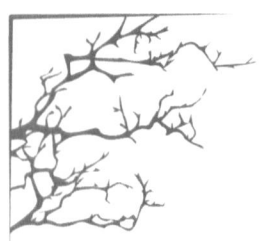

Chapter Thirteen

Once outside I could see that the fire had already engulfed much of the old wooden buildings that made up the school and the staff house. Light was paling the eastern sky, but the night around me was filled with the stink of charring flesh and screaming. Over by the barn I could hear Doff and a few of the older boys trying to lead the frightened animals to safety down by the river.

Children still dressed in their night clothes who had made it out before the upper stories were swallowed in flames huddled together in frightened groups, staring wide eyed at the destruction. Only Praiser Liucas and Celibress Dinana, who must have been on duty were present and trying to herd the students to safety closer to the river.

Then just as in my foretelling years ago I saw Inishkim and Jamiya carrying two coughing younger children out the front door as the hallway collapsed in flames behind them.

Where are the rest of the priests, I wondered as I scanned the chaos for anyone needing my help. Did their absence mean they were dead in the fire? Possibly, it would have been late, most of the senior staff asleep, when Fire began eating his way up the stairs from the director's office.

Glancing towards the priests' house I saw it was completely enveloped in a tower of flames. Matoqwa standing beside me growled a curse. "I can't believe it's gone."

"Yeah, it's really gone. And nobody can put you in the Box anymore when you misbehave, eh?" Kuweya joked.

Matoqwa punched him on the arm. "Damned right, I hope they all burn in the fiery abyss the dog humpers keep preaching about."

Just then Collin rushed over and threw his arms around me, Praiser Liucas, Keveneth and the rest of my warband trailing in his wake. Tears streaming down his face, he cried, "Oh, Tas, I thought—never mind what I thought—you are safe and that's all that matters." He hugged me again and held me at arms' length to examine me. Noticing my new set of demon bites he gasped. "You are bleeding. What happened?"

"The wounds are nothing, don't worry about me. I'll be all right."

Interrupting our reunion, Praiser Liucas said to Collin, "Master Scribe, I need you to help me get the survivors down by the river in case the fire spreads further. I'm sure they've seen the smoke and flames by now, but it's going to take a while for help to arrive from the village."

Star Swimmer put a heavy hand on my shoulder, urging me away from them. <<We need to go, before Sabisa and the others discover that their child is dead. We won't survive if we are here when they arrive.>>

Ignoring the priest for the moment Collin stared wide eyed at Star Swimmer once more disguised as a chamuqwani. "M-master Starwin?" he stammered. "Are you all right?"

Still with his arm around my shoulder he turned and gave Collin and the priest a toothy smile. "Quite well, Scribe."

Collin glanced back at the burning school. "But what about the grand intercessor? Where is he? Will he—"

His smile widening my father said, "Have no fear there, my friend. The malicer won't be troubling you or your lord in future. Unfortunately my son and I must leave you now. We have business elsewhere."

"You are leaving—now, and taking Tas? But I thought—"

"We will be in touch, Collin, never fear. You have done well tonight," Star Swimmer assured him. Then switching to the mind speech, he said, <<Help these people as best you can, but I must get my son to safety before the enemy comes searching for us.>>

Leaving, I was truly leaving? I had wished for this nearly all my life, but now that the time had come I felt my fear and sadness twist a knot in my heart. Looking up at my seal father with pleading eyes, my lips quivering, I begged, "Father, please give me a moment to say good bye to my brothers before we have to leave. I may never see them again."

He glared for a moment, then his expression softened. <<All right, but not for too long. I sense a disturbance forming from within the Dream.>>

Turning to Collin and my war brothers, Star Swimmer said, "Walk with us down to the river if you wish to say good bye to us."

As we headed to the river Praiser Liucas with Inishkim and Jamiya by his side called to us, "Please, we need help. Don' go."

"One moment, Praiser Liucas, I'm not abandoning you." Collin looked torn unsure what to do.

"Stay and help all you can, Collin." I slipped out of my father's grasp and took his hand. "Thank you, Collin for believing in and trusting me. This time I don't know if our paths will meet but I am grateful for your friendship and for what you have taught me about your people."

The tears coming back to his eyes he choked out, "But what about the string you gave me at your trial? It's at my home. I was hoping—"

I squeezed his hand tears pooling in my own eyes. "Keep it for me. I will be back for it someday," I said as I felt a foretelling envelope me.

Leaving the praiser's side when he saw us heading away Inishkim hurried over to grasp my hand. "Take care of yourself, Puhani, and come back to us when you can."

Sending a bit of my Qwakaiva into our clasped hands as a blessing, I said, "Stay with Praiser Liucas and get your education, then return to the Preserve. My Gift tells me you will be a great leader among the People in the dangerous times to come."

Turning to Kuweya, and Matoqwa as he left me, I took their hands, too, and said, "Thank you for all your service to the People and to me. You were my strength when I thought I couldn't go on. I will forever be grateful."

"Damned right, Siyatli Dog Turd," Matoqwa growled and surprised us both by hugging me. "Try to stay out of trouble wherever that damned seal man is taking you."

I choked on a laugh. "I'll try, my old bear, and you do the same." I released myself and said to Kuweya, "See that he does stay out of trouble for me—at least for a while, eh?

Kuweya nodded, gave me a sign of respect and took my hand. "May the ancestors and the Prophet's blessings go with you, Puhani wherever you travel."

I nodded. "Thank you for reminding me once again, brother. When the malicer was torturing me your reminder of the Prophet's teachings saved me. I am very grateful for your words."

"I am glad. I will pray for you."

The gift of prophesy still upon me I said to them, "You will go back to the Preserve. And when you do, take care of my sister Kitahtla and our other relatives if I am not able to. And Matoqwa, I foresee Xyilaha is looking for you. She will need you. Take care of her for me, too—if she will let you."

Then to my surprise Star Swimmer came forward and handed each of them a pouch containing chamuqwani coin. "I am in debt to you, warriors. With this coin you can buy horses to help you in your travels through life." Glancing at Collin, he added, "Perhaps the scribe and his lord can help you find your true destiny."

To Collin he said, "For these young warriors there is still the problem of their sentence under the Emperor's law. As a favor to me and my son let it be known that they died in the fire if possible. Give them different names and take them with you and help them return to their people if you can."

Returning my attention to Collin I said, "My brother Kutima—uh—Keveneth is a good student, and very smart. I would ask that you become his mentor and take him with you tonight—and keep him with you in the years to come. You will need a good scribe to help you with your work and my brother has both the knowledge of our traditions and the intelligence to be of great use to you in the future."

Collin studied the young man and smiled. "I will do that, Tas, if Keveneth himself is agreeable, of course."

"Of course," I agreed.

When I reached for Kutima's hand he shyly dropped his eyes, then said, "I will go with Collin if you wish it, Tas, but can't I go with you?"

Star Swimmer returning to my side after having private words with Matoqwa and Kuweya put an arm around my shoulder and shook his head. "I'm sorry, young warrior, that would not be possible. I can only bring Taswith me to the Beyond Place, because he shares my bloodline. A mere human would not survive where we must go."

Kutima sighed and nodded. "I understand; I thought it might be something like that, but I hoped—"

Tears blurring my vision I felt the foretelling again come over me and I took his hand. "Don't be sad. You will see me again, before you pass into the realm of our ancestors, my brother, I promise."

Turning away from them at last and sensing my father's urgency, I followed him to the river. By the reeds on the muddy shore we stepped into the water and waded out into the current.

With his help I changed my physical body into the seal form I often took within the Dream. Together we dived to the bottom where Star Swimmer created a portal and we swam into the beyond.

Just before we slipped under the brown water I happened to glance back at the shore and saw Kutima Collin, and my two war brothers had followed us down to the riverbank. I wished them well. And then we passed through the portal and we were gone.

The End

RUSHTON ARCHIVES: CONCLUSION of fourth interview with Indigenous Zacatik subject 297

Tasimu's story is continued in book five: *Reawakening Memory*

Additional Information for the books telling Tasimu's Story
Words in the Qwani'Ya Language:

Qwani'Ya Tsa'adi, or Fish People, what the Indigenous people living by Big Ice Lake call themselves

Qwa'osi the Otter Warrior, a guardian spirit protector of the Qwani'Ya

Co'yeh the Lake Seal, the Otter's rival, a spirit with both light and dark aspects

Siyatli, a child born to a human woman whose father is a lake Seal

Qwakaiva, a difficult word to translate in its full meaning, similar to what we might refer to as magic, chi, life force or shamanic medicine

Qwakaihi, someone gifted with great power who uses their gift for the good of others

Aseutl, a snake-like dragon figure some say lives at the bottom of Big Ice Lake

Kunai, a shape-shifting magical being of great power, and benefactor of Tasimu

Qwa'Nayhi a shape-shifting being able to travel between many realms of existence, like the Qwa'Nayhi Seal man who is Tasimu's father

Amima, mother in the Qwani'ya language

Appi, father

Ami grandmother

Ati, grandfather

Coshelah cousin, a person's patrilineal cousin. The Qwani'Ya claim their descent from their mothers, so the father's kin aren't as close and referred to differently

Chamuqwani, a term the Indigenous people use to refer to the Imperial invaders of their land

Asiya, a greeting like hello

Crokno, the name given the enemy from another dimension who Tas and his father battle, because they wish to destroy Tas's world

Unfamiliar Terms in the Chamuqwani Language

Zaunk, a degrading term used by soldiers and settlers from the empire to express their contempt for all Indigenous peoples they discovered during their conquest

Bucki, a derogatory term for an Indigenous man or boy

Cloocha or Cloocha-whore a demeaning term for an Indigenous woman or girl

Words in the Kukiya Language

Kukiya, what the Indigenous people living in the desert and mountain country out of which the Empire created their Tribal Preserve call themselves

Puhani, a person with magical powers, the same as a Qwakaihi in Tas's people's language

Puwa, the magical power, like Qwakaiva, that a Puhani can use

Akiyazi, the magical beings that have power over the rain and the water in lakes and creeks

Don't miss out!

Visit the website below and you can sign up to receive emails whenever Celu Amberstone publishes a new book. There's no charge and no obligation.

https://books2read.com/r/B-A-YGQM-THMQD

BOOKS 2 READ

Connecting independent readers to independent writers.

Did you love *Bitter Echo of Memory*? Then you should read *Refugees and Other Stories*[1] by Celu Amberstone!

[2]

Shape-shifting beings and magical powers move in the natural world, and curious humans find unexpected roles to play in these stories from a celebrated author. Selkies and dragons have their tales to tell here. Ghosts and aliens with their own agendas and a troll interact with humans in stories that reference myths in new ways. Here, the reader will find reverence and reflection as well as adventure, and even humour.

Refugees And Other Stories is a collection of stories by author Celu Amberstone. Previously available only in anthologies and magazines, these stories are gathered together here for the first time. Drawing on her Indigenous and Celtic heritage, Amberstone writes powerful fiction subtly different from the usual science fiction or fantasy adventures. The introduction to her fine collection of stories is written by author and professor Dr Allan Weiss, whose specialization is in Canadian Literature.

1. https://books2read.com/u/mvoAlj

2. https://books2read.com/u/mvoAlj

Amberstone integrates her Celtic and Indigenous heritage into these stories. Her characters (whether human, alien, or mythic beings) are strangers in a strange land, at the intersection of the real world and words of magic – and if that makes you think of Heinlein and LeGuin, you are on the right track.

Amberstone's seductive and enthralling stories employ fantastic elements to balance the joy of kinship with the devastating effects of colonialism. A must-read collection! - Dr Joy Sanchez-Taylor, author of *Diverse Futures*, and professor of English at LaGuardia (CUNY)

"Refugees," by Celu Amberstone, throws readers on an emotional roller-coaster ride within a refugee culture that has been rescued, transplanted, and controlled by ambiguous benefactors from a post-apocalyptic Earth. - Quill and Quire

Amberstone's tales reflect real-world challenges and what it takes to overcome them. - Dr Allan Weiss, author and associate professor of English and Humanities, York University.

Also very strong is Vancouver Island writer Celu Amberstone's tale of human refugees living on an alien planet under the supervision of alien Benefactors ("Refugees"). Amberstone does a nice job of painting the shades of gray in her paternalistic society. Humans who have lived on Tallav'Wahir for centuries lead peaceful and happy lives, but they are utterly dependent on aliens to make all the decisions about what is in their best interests. And when a new shipment of refugees arrives from a dying Earth, their assumptions and their security are badly shaken. - Donna McMahon for *SF Site*

The benevolence of an alien race that helped them come to this place, and requires their obedience to rules, is questioned over the course of the story, as is whether harsh decisions aimed at ensuring humanity's survival are an acceptable price to pay. - James McGrath, reviewing "Refugees" for *Journal of Postcolonial Theory and Theology*

Also by Celu Amberstone

Refugees and Other Stories

About the Author

Celu is of mixed Cherokee and Scots-Irish ancestry. Celu Amberstone was one of the few young people in her family to take an interest in learning Traditional Native crafts and medicine ways. This interest made several of the older members of her family very happy while annoying others.

Legally blind since birth, she has defied her limitations and spent much of her life avoiding cities. Moving to Canada after falling in love with a Métis-Cree man from Manitoba, she has lived in the rain forests of the west coast, a tepee in the desert and a small village in Canada's arctic. Along the way she also managed to acquire a BA in cultural anthropology and an MA in health education. Celu loves telling stories and reading. She lives in Victoria British Columbia near her grown children and grandchildren.

About the Publisher

Kashallan Press is an independent publisher releasing books by author Celu Amberstone. Among her books are critically-acclaimed works now re-released by Kashallan Press, and new works showcasing her talents in writing both fiction and non-fiction.